# Different Spaces
## ~ N ~
# Different Places

*Four novellas*

Eugene Rookwood

Dexcel Publishing * Indianapolis, Indiana

Different Spaces ~ N ~ Different Places

*Four novellas*

Copyright © 2013 by Daniel E. Perkins

ISBN   978-0-9704015-6-4

Printed in the United States of America

# CONTENTS

# Forward

## *Four novellas*

*I sincerely hope the joy and delight I experienced while writing these Novellas will be shared by you as you read them. I must confess that I only create characters...then listen to their conversations and write what they say. Sometimes I approve of what they are doing and sometimes I don't, but I never make any attempt to change or control those that can only run free in my mind. So settle in, buckle up and turn the page...*

**Eugene Rookwood**

*Ned*

*A slave…*
*that was never a slave*

# Chapter one

*I*t *was a sight the likes* of which we never seen before...nor since. More than a hundred grown people, black and white, men and women all crying like babies in true anguish and sorrow while four big black men slowly lowered the old slave into his grave. Till now nobody ever paid much attention to a slave burial, except for a few slaves and maybe an overseer or owner. And slaves were always buried in the backwoods or scruff land, but this old slave was being buried in the Graham family plot, right out behind the Wilson Creek Baptist Church.

Standing closest to the grave was Spencer Graham, the owner of Rolling Hills Plantation and of the slave being buried. Spencer cried and shook uncontrollably; he was nearing 70 years of age and had never known life without this slave named Ned. Ned was six years older than Spencer and was his playmate while growing up. When Spencer went to school, Ned was sent along to carry his books, drive the horse and look after his young Massa. When Spencer grew older and was sent away to preparatory school, Ned was again sent along to look after the needs of Massa Spence. He slept on a pallet in Spencer's room, listened through the open classroom windows and secretly studied his Massa's books when left alone.

During the summer's back on the plantation, Ned taught Spencer to hunt, fish, skip rocks across the pond, swim, ride a horse and during his fourteenth year, Ned took him to the old shack, way out near the end of the back lane where a slave girl named Dottie was waiting to take his virginity. After that encounter Ned and Spencer tried to screw every slave girl on the plantation. Several girls became pregnant during that summer and even more in the summers that followed. While Spencer's father, Asa Graham did not approve of white people lowering themselves to race mixing, he seemed to appreciate what he called a noticeable increase in productivity among his wenches.

Spencer gasped and wailed in despair at the grave site, it was Ned who was with him during his twenty-first year when he was abruptly called home from college. His father had suddenly passed away, the victim of a heart attack and Spencer was now the new master of Rolling Hills Plantation. Spencer had three sisters, all much older than he and two of them had husbands with designs on Rolling Hills. They had laid much of the groundwork for their takeover prior to Spencer's return home and it was only because Spencer had Ned to counsel him that he retained control of Rolling Hills.

As soon as he learned that Asa Graham had passed away, Avery Campbell, the husband of Penelope

Graham-Campbell, began pressuring the widow, Miss Priscilla to place all the affairs of Rolling Hills into his hands. He made repeated, pointed and direct reference to the fact that Spencer was an ill-equipped college lad while he was a successful plantation owner. The truth of course was that Avery and Penelope put on a good show but enjoyed nothing close to the success of which they bragged. When Spencer arrived at home and encountered his mother's doubt about his ability to run the plantation, he had a talk with Ned. Following that, another discussion with his mother revealed that her doubt about his ability was sewn by his brothers-in-law, Avery Campbell mostly and some by Joshua Ragsdale.

Upon hearing this Spencer had another long serious conversation with Ned then invited Avery Campbell out to Rolling Hills for a talk. When Avery entered the house and extended his hand to shake, Spencer leaned slightly backwards then delivered the most powerful right hook he possessed into the side of Avery's face. The punch smashed into his jaw, broke his nose and knocked two teeth loose. The older man collapsed like a bag of rags and Spencer pounced, grabbing Avery's shirt and twisting it, "Listen to me goddamnit" he snarled, his face glowing mad and only inches away from Avery's. "I, Spencer Graham am the rightful owner and master of Rolling Hills Plantation! I make the decisions, I call the shots and if you or anyone else takes a notion to second guess or undercut me…then goddamit you will answer to me and you will answer right away. My father was a man who didn't take your shit, well I am his son and I'm not taking your shit either! You are welcome to visit and be a brother-in-law…as long as you stay in your place and respect me as the master of this plantation. You go behind my back and start talking bad about me to my mother and I will drag your fat ass out to the whipping post, tie you up and whip you like a runaway slave! Do you fucking understand me Avery cause goddamnit I truly mean it!"

Avery nodded in agreement with wide frighten eyes. He quickly left the house in pain, properly chastised and deeply humiliated. Over the following years Avery rarely visited and never again criticized Spencer or made any attempt to seize Rolling Hills.

"Oh Ned...how do I carry on without you my friend," Spencer quietly sobbed. He remembered how Ned saved him from the greedy clutches of the charming and seductive Miss Catherine Devereaux. While he had been swept away by her beauty and sophistication, Ned was not impressed and very suspicious of the lady. With Spencer's approval Ned investigated Miss Devereaux using his network of many slaves on various plantations. He reported that Devereaux Acres was heavily mortgaged and behind on taxes. The entire Devereaux clan seemed to spend too much time cooking, drinking and having sex with their slaves to properly run their plantation. Of the six Devereaux daughters two had married into money that was now helping to keep Devereaux Acres afloat and the next one up, Miss Catherine, was actively shopping for yet another source of financial relief in the form of a well off husband. None of that seemed to make any impression on Spencer and he stayed enamored with the beautiful Catherine Devereaux until Ned's investigation revealed that while courting Spencer, Miss Devereaux was also being courted by three other gentlemen. For Spencer this news was completely unacceptable. He confronted then immediately ended his relationship with Miss Devereaux despite her falling to the floor and holding onto his leg while proclaiming her true love was only for him. When he pulled away and started to leave, Catherine Devereaux tore open her bodice and exposed her firm ripe young breast, "For you my love..." she whimpered. "These and all of me are yours. Come...take me...make me yours and only yours...I beg you...show me you are a man...MY man!"

"Go to hell!" Spencer growled. "You're a lying dustybutt! Go screw the other three peckers you got waiting in line." He stormed out the door, never looked back and never spoke to Catherine Devereaux again. He did note with some sadness that only a few months later Catherine married one of the other men she was courting. He was an older gentleman named Harvey Phillips who owned a small plantation nearby, and just as Ned predicted Harvey's plantation was soon sold off bit-by-bit in a desperate attempt to save Devereaux Acres. It proved to be too much for Harvey who first descended into alcoholism then finally took his own life.

Not long after his affair with Catherine Devereaux, Spencer followed Ned's advice and married his childhood sweetheart, Abigail Morgan. Abigail was a simple, sweet girl who had dearly loved Spencer most of her life. When they officially began courting, Spencer was somewhat surprised to discover the true depth of his affection for her. He had somehow always taken Abby for granted but not anymore. Their marriage was the best thing that ever happened to either of them. It was absolutely the happiest sixteen years of Spencer's life.

The newlyweds were delighted when their daughter Rosemary was born. But Abigail was a delicate lady and childbirth was unduly hard. It was almost seven years before Abigail again gave birth, this time to a boy the couple named Eli. Spencer's joy was tempered by his concern. As once again his wife had experienced a very difficult delivery and again the doctors warned against any future pregnancies. The final pregnancy came nine years later, it was unexpected and unsuccessful. Both Abigail and the newborn passed during delivery. Spencer was completely destroyed and it was only the strength of Ned that held him up. For several months following Abigail's death, Ned secretly ran Rolling Hills while Spencer quietly grieved his tremendous loss. Ned gave him time to shore up his fortitude, deal with his children and slowly regain his footing.

*Ned was my buffer*, Spencer thought, *always there with a good idea or solution. Showing the way then stepping aside, helping me to see and understand. Ned made me know that I cannot be truly effective until I truly understand a situation! He spelled things out, explained the consequences, even helped me understand my children and the good Lord knows that certainly took some doing.* Spencer glanced at his mother's nearby tombstone. He had been totally distraught when she passed and once again it was Ned who had provided comfort and direction. On the day before his mother's funeral Ned took Spencer to the old cabin at the end of the lane. "Do's yuh cryin heah in privates so's tuhmurrah youse'll be's strong in public," he advised then stood guard for more than five hours while Spencer cried and privately mourned the loss of his mother.

"I love you Ned, I have always loved you more than any creature on God's green earth and I always will…" Spencer cried out then removed the flower from his lapel. He kissed the flower then dropped it on top of the mahogany coffin now resting on the bottom of the grave. "Somewhere, somehow…we will meet again old friend…we will meet again," Spencer promised then turned and headed for his carriage. He could not bear to watch the dirt fill the grave, forever burying the only man he truly loved.

## Chapter two

*Rosemary Graham rarely showed emotion.* She had always been a little distant and mentally tough. Yet, like her father and many other sobbing mourners she stood at Ned's gravesite and openly cried without shame, her heart bleeding from the loss of this man she called her angel. Rosemary was a middle-aged spinster and very wealthy because she was the most respected and sought after dressmaker in this and several adjacent counties. She dabbed at her eyes with her handkerchief knowing that Ned and Ned alone was solely responsible for her success. She remembered that as a child she fell in love with Uncle Ned and still held a life long crush on him. He used to take her for long piggyback rides and sometimes held her way up high so she could pick the really good cherries or peaches or apples. Whenever he and her father went into town, Uncle Ned would always bring her a sweet or piece of candy. Rosemary was sixteen when her mother passed away and it was not her father but Uncle Ned that she clung to. She shuddered with the memory of how warm, safe and comforted she felt when he wrapped his strong arms around her. She clung tightly to Uncle Ned throughout the whole day of her mother's funeral and on that night and for several nights afterwards he came to her bedside to give her a big hug, tuck her in and stay close by until she fell asleep.

Over the following two years Rosemary fulfilled her deceased mother's role, being mistress of the plantation and looking after her father and little brother. She was becoming depressed and was very tired of the routine when Spencer sent Eli away to the same preparatory school he had attended. Soon after Eli left, Rosemary jumped at the chance to escape from Rolling Hills by accepting the marriage proposal of Will Truett. Will's father owned a saw mill in the next county and had a large family of eight children. Will fully expected to sire a large family of his own. During their courtship he frequently bragged in private that he was marrying Rosemary because everything about the way she was built suggested she was prime breeding stock. However, little more than four years following their elaborate wedding, despite his best and at times strenuous efforts, Will Truett and his wife Rosemary were still childless, and on their way to see some special doctors in New Orleans. Will had sired the off-spring of several slave wenches before and during his marriage so it was Rosemary who was in doubt.

Following an extensive examination and long conversation during which Rosemary recalled some serious childhood illness, the doctors declared her barren. Because of previous medical conditions, Rosemary was physically incapable of becoming pregnant. For Will Truett that news stung like a hard punch to the gut. He felt cheated and confused.

Rosemary was also stunned…but she done a poor job of pretending great disappointment. Inwardly she was absolutely delighted. Secretly Rosemary really did not like children and had never harbored any desire to become a mother. She assumed she would because she had no way to prevent it, but now hearing those doctors say she was physically incapable of bearing a child was the most glorious news she had ever heard. From the first day of married life she had lived in fear of pregnancy. The same fear that had always limited her relationships and the depth to which she could allow herself to be pleased. Now she was free, liberated and just that feeling alone made her hot and very aroused.

    Will was not aroused and the marriage quickly tumbled downhill. Shortly after they returned home from that New Orleans trip the arguments began. Will's disappointment hardened into bitterness and he soon declared that Rosemary was becoming too cozy and familiar with at least two male slaves. He accused her of adultery, kicked her off his plantation then sued for divorce. Rosemary fought back by dragging away as many of the couples possessions as she could. She also fought for and won a monetary settlement plus ownership of four slaves. When she returned to Rolling Hills, Spencer made her sell the slaves right back to Will Truett. He did not trust Truett or appreciate the way his daughter had been treated so he was not about to have their slaves on his plantation. In spite of fighting the divorce Rosemary was thrilled to be completely rid of Will Truett. With no one to answer to and no threat of pregnancy, life was poised to become very interesting.

Only a few short weeks following Rosemary's return to Rolling Hills, Spencer confided to Ned that he had spotted his daughter in a couple of suspicious situations with a young slave buck and he hoped nothing was really going on.

"I could not watch that! Even if she was having the time of her life I could not watch so I will not tolerate it! I will not allow any white woman especially my daughter to run around whoring on Rolling Hills!" Spencer declared. "And, it's not the sort of thing you want to talk to your daughter about either!"

Ned assured Spencer that what he saw was probably innocent and promised to have a talk with Rosemary just to make sure. Ned was a little amused by what he felt was nothing more than Spencer's fatherly suspicions until his conversation on the back porch with Rosemary. Their discussion began with small talk but soon turned to her new found freedom as a woman. Rosemary was more than full of herself and ready to bust loose in a wild sexual feeding frenzy. She agreed to heed Ned's advice and keep her activities discreet then told him that since pregnancy was no longer an issue for her, there was nothing stopping them from fulfilling her long time desire to share his bed and feel him enter her.

"Whut?" Ned snapped. "Gal, frum da top of yo head tuh da bottums of yo feets ah luvs youse lik muh own. And cause ah luvs youse, ah promise if'n youse ever sass me lik dat agin, ah'll snatch yuh cross muh lap and gives yuh ah whuppin yuh will not enjoy and yuh will not fogit!" He stormed off and it was probably the only time in her entire life that Rosemary could remember seeing Uncle Ned get mad...really mad.

Only a few days later Ned awoke to a house in turmoil. Spencer had caught not one but two young male slaves attempting to sneak out of Rosemary's bedroom. He intimidated them into telling him everything that happened under his roof, had them lashed for disrespecting his house then ordered Rosemary to pack her possessions.

After breakfast Spencer and Ned headed to town in search of a place for Rosemary to stay. Along the way Ned reasoned with Spencer on behalf of Rosemary. She was still his daughter and wasn't likely marriage material anymore so if he put her up in a boarding home he would have to pay the rent forever. Maybe there was a better answer to the question. When Spencer pressed for the better answer Ned admitted he didn't have one but pleaded for a few days to see what he could come up with. Spencer did not want to wait a few days to get Rosemary out of his house but he also did not like the idea of paying her rent forever either, so he grudgingly gave Ned three days to figure things out.

Ned spent most of that afternoon and the next day sitting under the big tree in the side yard sipping brandy. As the evening approached he sent for Rosemary who had spent the last two days hiding in her room. He said nothing as she slipped into the chair across from him while avoiding eye contact. For several long minutes Ned said nothing, he stared at Rosemary who squirmed and continued to avoid looking at him. Finally Ned poured a large shot of brandy into a separate glass and handed it to Rosemary. She drank most of it without stopping then finished off the rest in short order. Ned refilled her glass then topped off his own. "Didn't youse used tuh sew?" he asked.

"Sure. Used to sew a lot," Rosemary replied.

"If ah members right youse was pretty good at it...wusn't yuh?"

"I sure was. I made most of my own clothes and I made some gowns for a few of them fancy ladies in Hardin county too!"

"So how cums yuh stop sewin?"

"I haven't thought nothing about it since I been back here...and I don't have much sewing stuff or material."

"If'n youse got's all da sewin implements and materals yuh needs, den how long it takes fur youse tuh makes a fancy gown?"

"About five days if I have some help...why?"

"Never yo mind bouts why...gwine back tuh yuh room and ah'll has sum mo talk tuhmurrah maybe," Ned instructed.

Following the evening meal Ned advised Spencer of his scheme. Rosemary could earn her own keep and probably a whole lot more. It would only take a small gamble to find out and Spencer really had nothing to lose. First, to get Rosemary out of the house right away, Ned suggested quickly repairing the old cabin out at the end of the back lane and moving Rosemary into it. Second give her all the supplies, implements and help she needs to make an elegant ladies gown. Once the gown is made, take Rosemary and the gown into town to the general store. Pay the store owner to put the gown on display and schedule appointments for fittings. As soon as the appointment book start to fill, build a big sewing workroom right next to the cabin and give her more help so the orders can be filled without delay.

Spencer liked the idea of getting Rosemary out of sight quickly. He could not see the old cabin from the main house and knew it could easily be made very comfortable so he agreed to Ned's plan. He really didn't have much faith in Rosemary earning her own way but agreed to finance the gamble.

Rosemary was literally bouncing off the wall with total delight when Uncle Ned explained his plan for her future. She took the proposition seriously and jumped right in. She even actively participated in the renovation of the old cabin so she could move in only a day and a half later.

In just a little more than two months after the first gown was put on display, Rosemary had more orders and fittings than space. Spencer quickly realized her potential for success and authorized the building of a large workshop next to her cabin and soon the fittings were being made onsite.

After about a year Rosemary had streamlined her sewing processes and techniques and taught her staff of slave girls to routinely produce high quality products. She negotiated a separate display space in the general store and began spending two days a week in town taking orders and doing fittings. Her steady stream of customers continued to grow and for more than three years, Rosemary had all she could handle until the Tredwell sisters came along. Soon after her sister-in-law took over management of the workshop, Rosemary opened a dress salon in town then enlarged her workshop at Rolling Hills. She refined and trained four of the Tredwell sisters then used them to staff her salon in town and a second dress salon in Hardin County. In the midst of supervising her growing business, Rosemary bought a large fashionable house in town and a small building adjacent to it for use as her personal offices. While remaining single and somewhat aloof, over the years Rosemary has frequently hosted some of the town's most elegant social affairs and her reputation as one of the south's most celebrated dressmakers continues to grow as does her income; which at times has rivaled the income of Rolling Hills Plantation itself.

"Thank you Lord," Rosemary sobbed. "Thank you for giving me this powerful love...this precious angel." She softly touched Ned's coffin as it began its decent then collapsed into the strong arms of her black manservant and silently watched the coffin slip from view.

## Chapter three

*E*li *Graham was totally distraught* and in complete denial. He simply refused to accept the fact that his Uncle Ned was gone. Just the other day he, his father and Mica had supper, drank brandy and played cards with Uncle Ned. Supper at Uncle Ned's house was always a fun and relaxing event but the last time was special. Now Eli understood why Uncle Ned had given him a big hug right before he left the house. Normally he would feel privileged to get a good handshake but on this last visit Uncle Ned hugged him. Eli wailed aloud, blew his nose, stomped his feet in anguish then glanced at Lizzy and felt her pain.

Lizzy was Ned's bed wench and in her mind Ned was next to God. He was more than twice her age and she had only known and lived with him for just over eight years, but Lizzy loved Ned with a passion that even the Graham's found hard to match. She was born and grew up on Riverfront Plantation in Hardin County and had no idea who her father was. She was told that her mother was sold when Lizzy was very young. As soon as she was old enough to follow instructions she was put to work. All day, every day working in the fields, doing chores or washing clothes. As she became a young woman she noticed that many of the slave women around her where made into bed or pleasure or breeding wenches, but not Lizzy. Her owner was all but certain that Lizzy was fathered by one of his sons. He normally sold off all of his sons slave offspring, some as babies but most after they started to develop because of the higher price. Lizzy was tall and gangly and would not develop physically until much later in life. She never attracted enough of a price for sale so her master made sure she worked in the fields and was never used for sex. Inbred slaves had caused his daddy a lot of severe grief and consternation, nearly tearing the family apart back when he was a young man, so Lizzy's master tried real hard to make certain his sons were not pleasuring their own slave daughters. It was a rare occasion for Lizzy to lay with a man because of her suspect parentage and because her master tried to control all of the sex on his plantation just like he did everything else.

Riverfront Plantation was owned by C.T. Jennings, a tough minded, devoutly religious, heavy-handed cotton farmer that constantly drove his slaves in spite of allowing his children to be completely lazy and immoral. C.T. believed that slaves should toil from sun up to sun down, seven days a week, no matter what and no matter the weather. He would find useless things for them to do or rent them out during the slow time of the year just to keep them working. He believed that all slaves, mulattos included were only a step better than a mule. "Never let a slave rest!" was his motto and he delivered quick and severe punishment to those that dared to try and relax or break his rules. Like most of the slaves on Riverfront Plantation, Lizzy was overcome with joy when she heard the news that Massa CT's horse had thrown him. The Massa's head collided with a large rock and he died at the scene.

The joy among the slaves at Riverfront was soon overtaken by fear however as the family members squabbled and fought over C.T.'s estate. Because C.T.'s wife had died long before him, there was no widow and several contested wills. Willard Jennings and his brother C.T. Jr. fought for control and attempted to continue operating Riverfront Plantation with the same heavy hand that their father used until the whole mess landed in court. The judge threw out all of the various wills then ordered all of the assets of C.T. Jennings, including Riverfront Plantation, to be sold at auction and the proceeds equally divided among the heirs.

Spencer Graham heard of the auction and decided to attend and see if he could get some of the new fangled farm implements and tools that C.T. had frequently bragged about. Spencer and Ned arrived early, well before the auction was scheduled to begin and quickly settled on the items they wanted to purchase. Spencer was making a deal with the auctioneer when Ned casually glanced at the slaves in holding pen. Like all of the items in C.T.'s estate they too were going to be auctioned off. Ned sighed and started to turn away when he suddenly made eye contact with Lizzy. She was a tall mulatto with frizzy brown hair and a body well defined by hard labor. For an instant Ned was startled, as was Lizzy. They both felt a slight buzz, a "don't I know you" moment when their eyes first met and it was a very unsettling feeling. Ned stared at her and she smiled revealing a small gap between her front teeth. He stepped close to the holding pin and asked her name. When she responded he winked his eye and walked away.

Ned could and did have practically any woman on Rolling Hills Plantation whenever he wanted. He had sired several children over the years and until this moment never really wanted any woman to call his own. Ned motioned Spencer aside and asked him to add Lizzy to the items on his purchase list. Spencer was surprised. He studied Ned for a moment then smiled and added the slave girl to his list. He completed his deal with the auctioneer then supervised the loading of his new farm equipment onto his wagon. Ned made sure Lizzy found a comfortable spot to sit then headed the wagon to Rolling Hills as soon as his master climbed aboard.

Lizzy immediately fell in love with Rolling Hills Plantation. She shared Ned's room in the main house just off the back hallway. It was the first time Lizzy had ever slept in a real bed. She was accustomed to the sticks, hay and rags that was normal at Riverfront. For quite some time Lizzy was completely overwhelmed by everything around her, especially the people. Everybody at Rolling Hills was nice and friendly. People went about their labor but folks were not being stood over and beaten, and they didn't work like dogs from sun up to sun down...they didn't work on Saturday afternoon or Sunday either. She couldn't believe her eyes when she first saw slaves making music, dancing and drinking corn whiskey on a Saturday night. Lizzy couldn't stop smiling, her only real job at Rolling Hills was to be Ned's bed wench and help out here and there. From the moment they first made eye contact, Lizzy loved Ned and she really loved being loved for the first time in her life. Being Ned's bed wench was a job sent down from heaven. Lizzy also loved helping at whatever she was asked to do and frequently volunteered to help the cooks or laundry girls.

Only days after bringing Lizzy to Rolling Hills, Ned accepted Spencer's long standing offer to build his own house. In just over one month a sprawling one story house with a large front and back porch was built. Ned chose a spot just beyond the bend on the back lane. From his front porch Ned could see the main house and most of the shops and activity on the back lane. From his back porch he could see only pasture land and the woods far beyond, so he and Lizzy spent much of their private time on the back porch. The house was built to Ned and Lizzy's liking with a large formal circular foyer leading to a grand parlor on one side with a large dining room and kitchen area behind. On the other side of the foyer a short hallway led to an extra large bedroom and a small sitting room. Another short hallway in the middle of the foyer led past a storeroom on one side, a door to the kitchen on the other then on to the back porch. The house instantly became home, a real home and Lizzy was completely beyond thrilled with her new house, new love and new life.

She could not be exact because she didn't even remember her mother but Lizzy thought she was about thirty-two years old when Ned saved her from the auction and delivered her to a life she could never have even imagined. Her eight plus years on Rolling Hills had been a total joy. She felt proud and humble when Rosemary came to her house and offered her an important job in her dressmaking shop where Lizzy learned a real skill and became good at it. And, she was always delighted to accompany Ned to the main house or to Eli's house for a big family supper, but Lizzy was made most happy when the men of Rolling Hills came to her house for supper. There was always lots of food, lots of laughing and genuine happiness. After supper the men would go out onto the porch to smoke cigars, drink brandy and play cards. It had been just that kind of evening only a few nights ago, although as Lizzy now recalled, when the night ended it seemed a little unusual because Ned hugged everyone goodnight, even Mica. Lizzy swooned as she remembered the long passionate hug and kiss Ned gave her right before he told her he was going to his rest then went to bed. She didn't think much about what he said until she had tidied up the house a bit, put out the lights then went into the bedroom and discovered that Ned had taken off his clothes, gotten into bed and quietly passed away. Now he is being buried. Lizzy struggled with her grief but it tore at her and she comforted herself with the thought that she was very fortunate to have known and shared love with Ned…very fortunate indeed…and she would love him forever.

Eli Graham moaned, leaned his head back and looked to the heavens. *Lizzy woke up everyone on Rolling Hills that night trying to save Uncle Ned,* he thought. *It wasn't to be though, wasn't nothing old Doc Bateman could do by the time he arrived. He said Uncle Ned was old and just ran out of time, then offered to take Uncle Ned to town and open*

*him up to see if he could figure out why he died. His father
refused Doc's offer and ordered Uncle Ned's body be taken to
Horner's funeral parlor and treated like the most honored
member of the Graham family. There was a wake last
night at Rolling Hills and several folks including a surprising
number of overseers and plantation owners paid their last
respects.* Eli again glanced at Lizzy thinking, *she will be
okay because she's one of us. His father told both he and Lizzy
that as far as he was concerned she was Uncle Ned's widow
and entitled to stay in the house Ned built for her for the rest of
her life…and Rosemary offered her a suite of rooms in her place
if she wants to move to town. So yeah, she's a Graham…she
will be alright. But Uncle Ned?* Eli's lip began to violently
quiver and he could not control his crying, "It can't be! It
just can't be. We had a fancy funeral service and brought
him out here…now we are all gonna go home but Uncle
Ned will never leave this spot…it just can't be…no, no
can't be," he sobbed.

Mica put his arm around Eli and urged him to
leave but Eli refused. He was determined to stay with
Uncle Ned until the absolute end. Through his tears Eli
looked at the richly polished coffin recalling his first
memory of Uncle Ned. He had no idea how old he was
but remember being very young and Uncle Ned swung
him around and around until he was dizzy. He smiled
with the memory of being tickled repeatedly and
laughing so hard his sides hurt. Eli also remembered that
whenever he got into a real jam it was always Uncle Ned
that got him out. He could always count on his wise
counsel and always knew that their private conversations
were strictly confidential. Uncle Ned even achieved the
impossible and found a way for him to stay at Rolling

Hills, conquer his greatest challenge, be successful and...accepted by his father. At one point in his life he truly believed that would never happen.

## Chapter four

*E*ven *as a very young man,* Spencer Graham considered Ned to be the greatest and most precious gift he ever received from his father. He was determined to provide the same for his son and chose a young slave boy named Mica to accompany Eli to preparatory school. Mica was five years older than Eli and had been one of his early playmates. Spencer was confident with his decision because the two boys seemed to be best friends as was he and Ned.

Spencer was correct. Eli and Mica were best friends indeed. They were close from the beginning and only grew closer over the years. Mica accompanied his young Massa to the local school every day for just over four years, then for the next eight years Mica was sent along to look after Eli at Preparatory School. During their short stays back at home on Rolling Hills they kept mostly to themselves.

Eli was sixteen and idling away the summer on Rolling Hills when he was first challenged by his father to service some of the young slave wenches on the plantation. It was an awkward conversation that left

Spencer wondering if his son was all man. He expressed his concern to Ned and was reassured. Ned reminded Spencer that the two of them had been especially rambunctious, and the fact that Spencer's father did not approve made their sexual adventures even more challenging and fun. Ned was sure that Eli just needed more time.

Eli graduated from preparatory school but his grades did not qualify him for college so he returned to Rolling Hills without any stated plans or ambition. Everyone including his father was busy because the weather had been perfect all year and crop production was booming. At the same time Rosemary's dressmaking business was also booming so everybody except Eli was busy. Eli spent most of his time with Mica, fishing, riding horses, exploring or growing and tending to his experimental plants. Not long after his nineteenth birthday, Eli was again challenged to show some energy as a stud by his father and again it was an awkward conversation.

Spencer was visibly upset when he talked to Ned about Eli, "I tell you Ned it just ain't natural for a healthy young man not to have the slightest interest in gals. We got several dozen ripe young wenches here on Rolling Hills and I suspect he ain't touched a one of them," he fumed.

Ned was also becoming suspicious of Eli, "Well suh, da boy is startin tuh worry me sum too. Not cause he ain't coverin slave wenches doe, sum white folk lik yo daddy, jis doan wants tuh git dat close tuh slaves. Da boys aworryin me cause he ain't courtin naw showin no interest in white gals. Course hit possible he jis late cummin round...dat's happin befo...lots probably."

"Well...I'm not so sure," Spencer grumbled. "We were seasoned and experienced swordsmen at his age...do you remember the laundry gals we used to get every Tuesday and Thursday morning my last year in prep?"

"Ah sho do...Lena and Maggie Jo," Ned replied with a big grin. "Ah specially members dem cause dey liks tuh keep switchin up on us, den do us one at ah time. And ah members youse snuck out of class on dem days, den went back tuh class sum times smellin lik pussy."

"And you let me walk right back into class smelling like that and never said a word...why you old turd," Spencer chuckled.

"Hell...smellin lik pussy gots yuh sum respect," Ned grinned.

"What am I going to do here Ned," Spencer questioned after the two of them stopped laughing about their yesterdays. "How do I get some peace of mind about Eli?"

"Well suh, lets me take ah look at and maybe has ah talkin wit Mica. Ahs sho he knows Eli better'n any of us."

Spencer agreed and as always felt a lot better after talking out his problems with Ned. A few days later Ned reported that Mica had been unresponsive in conversation and because he had not pursued or covered any of them, the young slave wenches of Rolling Hills had long ago nicknamed Mica "pretty boy".

"I knew it! Goddamnit Ned, I knew in my gut that my son...MY son is a dandy boy...a goddamn fairy!" Spencer shrieked.

"Well...we doan knows dat jis yet," Ned advised. "We's too da place nah wheres ah gots tuh has ah real talkin wit mistah Mica and ah jis wants youse to knows dat dis gwine be sho nuff serious. Sumthin's gwine on cause Mica's pass twenty-foe yeahs and shoulda dun sired several suckers by nah. So we's gots sum serious talkin tuh do...course ah might has tuh git his tention furst...you unnerstand?"

Spencer understood very well and was anxious for Ned to find out the truth.

Due to many pressing responsibilities caused by the record crop production that was continuing into its second year, it was several days before Ned found time to seat himself under the big tree in the side yard and send for Mica.

"Whudda you want?" Mica demanded as he approached the tree.

"Sit down dere so we's can talk ah spell," Ned instructed.

"Ah don't wants to talk bout nuthin!" Mica declared.

"Ah didn't ask if'n yuh wants tuh talk, ah tolds youse tuh sit down so we's can talk and we's gwine tuh talk," Ned responded.

"Go tuh hell old man!" Mica snapped then strutted away toward the back lane. He advanced only a few yards before Amos and Big Levi snatched him off his feet and carried him towards the barn.

Amos and Big Levi worked in the blacksmith shop. They were the biggest and strongest slaves on Rolling Hills Plantation and used as the enforcers when needed. They were treated especially well by Massa Spence and enjoyed being called into action. With one on each side, they first carried Mica high in the air with his feet dangling at their knees. When he cursed them and demanded that they put him down, the two men grinned then slammed Mica to the ground and drug him the rest of the way to the barn. Inside they stripped away his clothes then tied a rope around his ankles. They threw the rope over a rafter then yanked Mica off his feet and tied off the rope leaving Mica hanging upside down, his fingers inches from the ground. Amos and Big Levi studied Mica for a few moments then left the barn laughing and congratulating each other on their fine work.

Several minutes later Ned casually strolled into the barn and briefly inspected Mica who said nothing but glared with anger. Ned picked up a long thick, flat wooden paddle and inspected it. The paddle had several holes in it designed to deliver maximum stinging and a deep burning sensation with even the lightest swat. Ned swung around without warning and slammed the paddle with all of his might across Mica's naked butt. For all of his twenty-four years of life, Mica had rarely been punished at all and until this very moment had never known real true pain. He screamed in anguish as excruciating red hot agony raced throughout his body. With force and purpose Ned again slammed the paddle across Mica's burning behind. He waited a few moments so that each lick could be fully appreciated then again gave Mica's butt all the paddle could deliver. Finally Ned stepped forward and leaned down until his face was only inches from Mica's, "Nah muh name is Ned...dats Mistuh Ned tuh youse and da longest day dat youse be's breathin air on dis heah earth, yuh ain't never gonna be old nough tuh calls me nuthin else...yuh unnerstands me boy?"

"Yassuh," Mica whimpered.

Ned again slammed the paddle across Mica's butt, "Yassuh whut? Whuts muh name damnit boy?"

"Waaaa...Mistuh Ned suh...Mistuh Ned!" Mica wailed.

"Aw right, nah dat we gots muh name unnerstood lets unnerstand sumthin else!" Again Ned slammed the paddle twice across Mica swollen and burning hot behind, adding yet another wide tender welt. "Nah dats fur sassin me boy! Ah ain't yo enemy and ah doan takes no sass, yuh unnerstand?"

"Yassuh Mistuh Ned yassuh! Ah's sho sorry suh...ah truly is. Please Mistuh Ned suh...ah truly sorry" Mica pleaded.

"Nah we's gwine ta talk and youse gwine tells me da truth," Ned explained.

After several minutes of intense questions that demanded explicit answers, Ned knew the intimate details of Eli and Mica's personal lives. He untied the rope and allowed Mica to crash head first to the floor, then stomped out of the barn angry and disgusted with what he had just learned.

For nearly an hour Mica did not move. Severe throbbing pain coursed throughout his whole body and he was in complete miserable agony. It was the most painful, humiliating and humbling experience of Mica's life. He found a new respect for Ned in that barn. From that point on he avoided him whenever possible and most certainly never even thought about disrespecting Ned again.

Having to tell Spencer Graham the truth about his son was the most difficult and painful conversation of Ned's life. He was extremely disappointed with Eli but had never seen Spencer so deeply hurt then completely and totally outraged. Ned was glad they had taken a long walk and was no where near the house. Spencer swore he was going to throw Eli and Mica out in the middle of the road and shoot either one of them if they tried to come back. For almost two hours he stormed around the plantation in search of the boys. Ned knew that Eli and Mica were hiding in the loft of the barn but he allowed Spencer to burn off his highly charged energy searching in vain.

For the remainder of that evening and throughout the next day Spencer paced around the house and said nothing to anyone. Late in the afternoon on the following day he was still doing a slow burn when Ned got a bottle of brandy then joined him under the big tree in the side yard. Ned poured two large shots, handed one to Spencer then sat down and drank his shot straight down. In spite of himself Spencer chuckled then done the same with his. Three shots later Spencer began to mellow into his old self.

"Have you seen either one of those little bastards," he asked Ned.

"Naw suh...deys layin pretty low," Ned responded knowing that he had not seen them because he didn't want to.

"Been thinking I might just send Eli off to military school and tell him he better make the most of it cause he is not welcome here," Spencer offered.

Ned did not think military school was a good idea. "Ah heahs life can be's awful tuff fur ah dandy boy specially round miltary folks."

"How the hell did this happen Ned? Was it my fault? Or did Mica make my son into a fairy?" Spencer questioned.

"Nah dats da thang, doan nobodies know," Ned explained. "If'n Mica taught Eli den who taught Mica. Ah ask after ah whupped em and he doan know. He claim he and Eli furst started messin wid each udder at school den found ah couple udder boys doin da same thang. So ah doan knows how hit happen! Ah doan knows if'n sumbodies can make youse ah fairy. Kinda seems yuh gotta wants dat. Ah knows hit sho ain't yo fault doe...yuh dun him right jis lik yo daddy dun youse right."

"My daughter's barren and my son is a goddamn dandy boy. Ned...that means I am never going to have a grandchild. Never going to have an heir for Rolling Hills...I got two goddamn children and well...hell both of them are barren."

"No hair fo Rollin Hills...dat doan seem right!" Ned declared.

"Ned, knowing that I will never have a grandchild, an heir for this plantation hurts even more than finding out that my son is a goddamn fairy,"

Spencer admitted. He was starting to tear up so he quickly downed another shot of brandy.

"Dat ain't right!" Ned repeated.

"No, sure isn't!" Spencer agreed.

"Let me thank on dis fur ah spell," Ned offered.

"Please do Ned, please do and if you can work this out there is nothing, including your own freedom, that you cannot have."

"Bein free in ah world dat doan cepts yo freedum ain't bein free. If'n ah works dis out, ah can finds several ways tuh enjoys yo gratstitudes widdoubt tryins tuh calls muh selfs free and havin tuh battles wid greedy and mean old white folks ever day."

For the first time in two days Spencer Graham truly enjoyed a good laugh. He and Ned were feeling no pain as they made their way to the dining room for the hearty supper they both now needed.

Ned sat on the back porch and drank coffee for most of the next morning. During the noon meal he advised Spencer that to clear out his mind he was going to find the boys then send Mica to work for Clem and he was going to lock Eli in his room. After that he could think properly and find a way to get an heir for Rolling Hills. Spencer was pleased. He liked that idea and his mood brightened considerably. He went back to work whistling while Ned went to his favorite seat under the big tree in the side yard. After a short while Ned sent for Clem Haskins, the overseer for Rolling Hills crop production and field slaves. He met Clem at the barn then went inside and ordered the boys down from the loft. Mica was turned over to Clem while Eli was escorted to his room by Amos and Big Levi. Ned locked the door to Eli's second story room then returned to his seat under the big tree.

About an hour later Ned went to the stable, saddled up a big gray mare and went for a long ride around the plantation. He did the same thing the next morning. Stopping at times to dismount and sit in various places for awhile and at other times riding the horse at top speed. By late afternoon Ned was back under his favorite tree sipping brandy and remained there until supper. After the evening meal Ned returned to the tree and the brandy. A short while later he was joined by Spencer who was weary from working on his accounting books and looking forward to relaxing under the tree for awhile. They talked at some length about the booming crop production and of Rosemary's growing operation before Ned revealed his plan to produce an heir for Rolling Hills Plantation.

"Well...furst off ah needs tuh no if'n da gal dat gives burth tuh yuh grandchilin gots tuh cums frum one of dem uppidy society families?" he asked.

"You know Ned there was a time when that would have meant something to me alright, but in view of the circumstances right now, I would be overjoyed to see Eli courting any white gal," Spencer sighed.

"Well long as yuh only quirements is dat da mudder of yuh grandchilin bes white, den ah thanks we's gots ah chance at getting youse ah hair fur Rollin Hills."

Spencer topped off both of their drinks. "I'm feeling better already let me hear it Ned."

"Well suh, durin muh talks wid Mica he cunfurmed dat Eli can raise his manhood and deliver seed. Nah dat bein so, den all we has tuh do is gits ah white gal heah tuh ceive da boys seed and makes youse ah hair. Nah dere's plenty po white folk round heah be glad fur dey daughter tuh stay at Rollin Hills fo ah yeah. Yuh mites has tuh hands dem ah few dollahs but heah da deal. If'n da gal catches Eli's seed and git's knocked, den pumps out youse a live healthy sucker, Eli will den has tuh marry da gal fur da chile tuh bes yuh hairs…yuh see whut ah talking bout?"

"I understand exactly what you are saying Ned but how do we get Eli to cooperate with your plan?"

"Yuh bribes him," Ned replied then began to chuckle. "Ah hads ah little talk wid mistuh Eli last nite and he do bout anythin tuh gits Mica back. So ahs suggest yuh tells em dat if'n he gits da gal knocked, yuh gives him Mica back and yuh'll gives him Mica's papers so's can't no bodies takes him away agin."

"Why you old devil!" Spencer grinned.

"Dat ain't all doe," Ned continued, "if'n da gal throws youse ah healthy sucker den tells Eli he doan has tuh lives wid da gal none atall, she stays heah in da big house. But if'n he marries her and makes da sucker yuh legal hair, den youse will lets him builds his own house way over on da udder side of Rollin Hills and youse will gives him da papers tuh one mo slave of his choosin."

"I like it Ned, I like it. But how do we find the gal?" Spencer questioned with great enthusiasm.

"Dat ain't no problem…yuh jis say da word and ah finds yuh one in a couple days boss," Ned responded with a big grin then drained his glass.

# Chapter five

*A*bner *Tredwell knocked the dirt off* his britches with his hat then smiled as he watched the well groomed mare briskly trot up the short lane to his shabby farmhouse. The mare pulled an expensive carriage in which Spencer Graham was riding with Ned driving. Abner was delighted. Only yesterday while delivering eggs to the feed store he heard that a wealthy plantation family was looking for a young white gal to live with them for a year. Even without knowing what they wanted the girl for Abner immediately volunteer his daughters. Abner Tredwell was a dirt poor chicken farmer with eleven children, eight of them girls. He barely scratched out a living on his two rocky acres of scruff land and was anxious to marry off his older daughters. Word got back to Rolling Hills that Abner wanted to talk, almost before Ned did that day.

To Abner's surprise Ned done the talking and got straight to the point. When he discovered that the Grahams wanted the girl to bear Eli's child it did not bother Abner in the slightest. He quickly offered his daughter Rebecca as being best suited to fulfill their request. "Now she ain't the best looker fer sure and she ain't my oldest but she's proven material," Abner declared. "You see bout two years back I had my sister's boy here helping me clear rocks. He was a young whippersnapper bout nineteen or twenty then. Hell Rebecca wasn't but seventeen and a virgin at the time, hell she musta been there twernt no boys round here no place. But I tell you my sister's boy was only here fer bout a week or so and yes sir bout two to three months after he left Rebecca was knocked and admitted my sister's boy was the daddy. She throwed that little youngin right over there with no trouble atall. So you can see she's proven material and it didn't take no time fer her to git knocked."

Less than ten minutes after Spencer and Ned arrived, Abner wrapped his eager hands around two hundred dollars with the understanding his daughter would be returned after one year if she was not expecting. If she succeeded in delivering a child she would then be married into the Graham family. A short while later, Rebecca Tredwell emerged from the house with a tiny bundle of clothes and climbed into the carriage. She was short, a little plump and a lot dowdy. She smiled and nodded a greeting when she got into the carriage but kept her head down all the way to Rolling Hills in an attempt to hide the growing grin that was spreading across her face.

When they arrived at Rolling Hills they all sat down for a meal. Then soon after Spencer Graham went upstairs to Eli's room to explain "the deal" to his son. Ned went out and sat under his favorite tree in the side yard and explained "the deal" to Rebecca. Ned was blunt and to the point. "We's brought yuh heah tuh gits knocked den burth ah healthy sucker fur Mistuh Eli. He da massa son and bout yo age but he ah dandy boy, mean he doan craves gals, he craves boys. But he still ah youn buck dat full of seed. Alls youse gots tuh do is catch enough of his seed tuh gits knocked...den burths a healthy sucker. When yuh duz, den Mistuh Eli will marrys yuh so's da sucker becums da hair of dis plantation and youse den becums da Misses of Rollin Hills and lives da rest of yo life heah...naw if'n yuh can't gits knocked in ah yeah den we takes yuh back home and maybe one of yo sisters will gits ah chance...yuh unnerstand?"

Rebecca was a little shocked by the knowledge that Eli craved boys but she was very impressed by what she had seen of Rolling Hills Plantation and chaffed at the thought that she could be replaced by one of her sisters. "Yes sir, and sir I really like what I done seen of this place so far so I'm gonna try real hard to make ya'll happy," she responded.

"Dere yuh go!" Ned complimented. "Keep dat spirit an yuh'll soon be's ah Graham! Nah youse'll be's asleepin in Mistuh Eli's room fur da furst two weeks. So yuh gits plenty chances tuh git knocked straight off. Den after da two weeks dun passed, Miss Rosemary, dats Mistuh Eli sistuh, she'll be's fittin yuh fur propur clothes and everthang and yuh gits ah room of yuh own down da hall. Den yuh can cum and gos as yuh pleases. Nah...yuh gots any question?"

Rebecca had no questions of any kind. She was absolutely certain that she had died and gone to heaven.

Rolling Hills Plantation was the finest place she had ever seen. She had walked on high priced rugs, tasted the best food she had ever eaten then wiped her mouth with fine linen. She found it hard to believe that she was being offered a wonderful life for doing nothing more than birthing a child. Rebecca was eager to get started on her mission and made even more so when she first saw Eli and was introduced.

Eli was also eager, but eager to get Mica back…forever. He was not impressed with Rebecca and did not look forward to what was expected of him. After several attempts at conversation, none of which succeeded, Rebecca started removing her clothes.

"What are you doing?" Eli questioned.

"Getting undressed," Rebecca responded. "They brung me here to have your baby and I can't get started with all these clothes on."

Eli was speechless and stared helplessly as Rebecca's clothes hit the floor. Once completely nude the young girl began removing Eli clothes while he stood frozen in place, somewhat overwhelmed by the sudden change in his life. He had been playing with his manhood at the very moment his father pounded on his bedroom door then marched in and explained "the deal", and now in spite of himself his manhood demanded attention. Rebecca quickly took advantage. She pulled Eli down on top of her, guided him into place and pumped her hips taking all of him into her. In short order Eli's seed exploded inside of Rebecca. She was thrilled but Eli was embarrassed and withdrawn.

Four days later during the late afternoon, Ned was seated in his favorite spot under the big tree in the side yard when Eli approached and asked to talk.

"Sho," Ned responded. "Pull up dat char dere."

"I can't do it Uncle Ned," Eli confided.

"Can't do whut?"

"I can't do it with that girl...I can't get it up Uncle Ned!"

"Eli...yuh gots ta covah dat gal...dat's da deal!"

"I know, I know...and I have tried...really tried, and so has Rebecca. I mean she has tried everything and I mean everything."

"How many times yuh dun poked her?"

"One."

"One? Foe days and youse ain't poked dat gal but one times?" Ned questioned in astonishment.

"I told you I can't do it, I can't get it up. I don't like girls, I never have!" Eli insisted.

"Well yuh gots tuh do sumthin!"

"I know Uncle Ned...but what?"

"Maybe youse outta close yo eyes den thanks bout yo boy Mica when youse tryin tuh covah da gal, dat outta do it."

"I tried that Uncle Ned and it worked until the moment she touched it then it fell over like a dead mule," Eli sighed.

"Wells youse gots finds sumthin dat'll wurk or yuh ain'ts libel tuh has no home...you no's dat doan cha?"

"That's why you gotta help me Uncle Ned."

"Whut da dickens yuh wants me tuh do?"

"If you could come to my room and let me see your pecker that would really get mine up...please say yes Uncle Ned."

"Youse dun lost whut little bit of mind yuh ever had boy!"

"No I haven't, I'm serious Uncle Ned...all I need to do is see it...I know it will work. Hell it's starting to work right now and all we're doing is talking about it. Please say yes Uncle Ned."

"Eli...boy...go way! Ah mites has ah talkin wid Miss Rebecca after supper...but ah doan knows."

"Please Uncle Ned please! Like you said my home, my life, hell my everything depends on this and I really, really need your help!"

"Eli...go way...ah talks at yuh later!" Ned poured a large shot of brandy, drank it quickly then poured another which he was sipping when Rebecca approached.

"Afternoon sir, Eli said you wanted to talk to me."

"Eli lied, ah said ah mites talk at yuh," Ned responded.

"He also said you are going to help us and I sure hope he wasn't lying about that too!"

Ned studied Rebecca for a few moments then told her to sit down and tell him what had been going on. She withheld no details and Ned was surprised by some of the things she had done trying in vain to get Eli erect. She told Ned that she knew Eli wanted him to come to their bedroom, and shocked him by saying she did not care what Ned's pecker done to or for Eli or where it went, as long as she received Eli's seed. Rebecca was clearly becoming desperate. She did not believe their one encounter was enough to become pregnant and was eager to secure her future on Rolling Hills. She pleaded with Ned to do whatever he had to. She reminded him of the prize at stake then suggested that if she failed, Ned's plan also failed.

In spite of himself, Ned was impressed by Rebecca and knew she was correct. He didn't care much for the idea that his plan could fail or drag out for years, especially if he could have saved it early. He drained his glass then took a hard look at Rebecca who stared back with pleading eyes. "Gwine back tuh yuh room...and tells Mistah Eli...dat ah'll pays ya'll ah visit foe ah goes ta bed...nah git!"

Just before going to bed that night, Ned sat on the front porch. He sipped brandy and smoked a cigar while waiting for Miss Ella to finish her chores. Miss Ella had been the chief housekeeper at Rolling Hills for many years. She ran a clean, orderly house and had her own small room behind the dining room. Once shut, her door was known to stay that way no matter what unless someone called Miss Ella's name.

Finally Ned went to his room and undressed. Then wearing only his long nightshirt, he made his way up the stairs, down the hall and into Eli's room. He was surprised to see both Eli and Rebecca lying on the bed completely naked. He stepped close to the bed without saying a word and began to unbutton his nightshirt. Eli stared at Ned's crotch while Rebecca smiled at him. Ned was not accustomed to seeing young white girls completely naked. The sight of Rebecca's tender young white body was way more appealing than Ned had expected. In spite of himself he felt his manhood began to rise when his shirt fell open and he really wanted to shove Eli out of the way. Eli stared at Ned's manhood and furiously masturbated for a few moments until he was fully erect. "Git on dat gal!" Ned demanded.

Eli climbed on top of Rebecca who guided him into her then gyrated her body in an effort to milk his seed. In very short order Eli snapped his head back and groaned in obvious orgasm. He then collapsed on top of Rebecca. When he turned his head to again admire Ned's manhood, Ned was gone. He quickly left Eli's room and hurried back to his own bedroom where he had a ripe young wench waiting.

Ned was satisfied with the results of his visit and reasoned with himself that his sacrifice was a small price to pay for the greater good. He knew it was going to be a lot harder to get Rebecca knocked once Eli was not being forced to sleep with her. They needed to get as much of Eli's seed as possible deposited into her during these first two weeks. He made four more trips to Eli's bedroom each time hoping that Eli would say he didn't need him. But, of course that didn't happen, instead on Ned's last visit he was standing close to the bed with his nightshirt hanging open. As before Eli had gotten erect and climbed on top of Rebecca who was hard at work beneath him. Eli stared at Ned's manhood as usual then suddenly grabbed it and licked the head. Ned jumped back then smacked Eli hard across his behind.

"Owe yeah," Eli moaned while Rebecca giggled.

Angry, Ned smacked Eli's butt again even harder and Eli cried out with pleasure then erupted in joyous climax. Ned stomped out of the room, he had enough, Eli was on his damn own.

By the end of the two weeks, Eli and Rebecca had successfully mated eight times and they were completely sick of each other. Eli was assigned to maintain stocks and make deliveries from and to the various storehouses and workshops on Rolling Hills. He hauled finished goods to town, brought raw materials back to the plantation workshops then helped out where needed. There was much to do and the days were long but Eli really didn't mind. He was preoccupied with the notion that he had done his best and fulfilled his part of "the deal". Eli did not want Rebecca back in his bed and was confident that she was knocked and any day now he would get Mica back...forever.

Rebecca was given Rosemary's old room and could not believe it was only for her. She had been astounded by Eli's room but hers was even nicer. She marveled at the two small rooms attached to hers. One was for clothes, nothing but clothes. Rebecca could not believe she had a whole little room for nothing but clothes. The second room held a wash basin, water pitcher, soft towels and a chamber pot. There was even a little door that allowed the servants to remove and clean the chamber pot from the hallway. Rebecca fell completely in love with her room. It was feminine, adorned with flocked wallpaper and lace doilies on the furniture. She admired the large white four poster bed with several big soft pillows nicely arranged on it. The bed had a full canopy with silk mosquito netting and the room contained several matching pieces of furniture. She inspected the floor to ceiling window that let in lots of light and the beautiful heavy satin drapes that framed it. Rebecca settled onto a large comfortable overstuffed chaise lounge and promised herself that she would never leave this place. She now had a fabulous room and a servant to clean it and make her bed. She looked around and thought of herself as a royal queen. She liked the feeling and prayerfully hoped she was pregnant.

When Rosemary came and took Rebecca for a fitting the women instantly liked each other and quickly became friends. Although Rebecca had learned to sew and make her own clothes by necessity, she was completely astonished at the machinery and efficiency of Rosemary's workshop. She was fascinated and wanted to learn how to operate the fancy sewing machines so she instantly accepted Rosemary's offer to become her apprentice.

Rebecca awoke each day in paradise with a big smile on her face. She had an even bigger smile several weeks later when she awoke with the telltale morning sickness. After Doc Bateman confirmed that Rebecca was with child, Rolling Hills erupted in wild joyous celebration.

# Chapter six

Ned *could not remember* seeing Spencer Graham happier. He briefly thought hard about the subject then decided this particular happy passed all others in memory. Work was ended early that day for everyone on the plantation, the chickens hit the skillets and the corn liquor flowed. Most folks on Rolling Hills didn't even know why they were celebrating but no one was happier than Eli. When he learned the news he jumped up and down with excitement then danced a jig with the reluctant but giggling Miss Ella. Ned was amused; he had never seen the strict Miss Ella have so much fun.

Following the evening meal, Ned and Spencer sat under the big tree in the side yard, lit cigars, drank brandy and congratulated each other for making the best of a bad situation. Now that they had a potential heir for Rolling Hills Plantation their attention turned to Eli.

"In keeping with the terms of "the deal", tomorrow I will turn Mica, complete with his papers over to Eli but I'm sure as hell not going to let Eli keep him in his room," Spencer insisted.

Ned admitted that he had been doing some thinking on that subject and suggested that since Eli lived in Spencer's house he must respect the rules. Mica would sleep on his old bunk in the kitchen house until Eli got a house of his own. Ned went on to recommend that Mica be given Eli's current job and Eli be sent to work as an apprentice overseer under Clem Haskins.

"Are you serious Ned? Eli? A dandy boy working as an overseer? I...don't know that I can quite see that one."

"Ah gots three reason why ah thanks dat way," Ned advised. "Furst da schools dun tol youse dat Eli ain't no cullage materal so dere ain't much else he can due of value. Den second, ah thanks Eli dun motured aright spec frum dis whole thang and's ready to moture alots mo. He'll benefeets frum da displin and sponsibility Clem dumands frum ever body outdere. Top of dat, Clem's cuntrac runs out in little over ah yeah and he dun bought him sum land and plannin tuh buys mo, dat doan feels lik he's lookin fur anudder cuntrac heah. So dens yuh be cravin ah new crop overseer, and if'n Eli all readys tuh go den youse gots an overseer youse can trust and one's dat doan needs no cuntracs...yuh sees whut ah talkin bout?"

"Yes, absolutely!" Spencer confirmed, "But do you really think a dandy boy will be respected as an overseer?

"Dat mites be's ah problem if'n Eli wus wurkin in town or sumthin whare sum folk mite trys to challenge him or sho's dispect, but Eli's a Graham and on Rollin Hills he da massa. Nah once he gots his own house and owns his own slaves, den dun been trained by Clem

Haskins ah thanks he'll be ready fo da job and ah doan specs he'll lets nobodies challenges him needder."

The following morning Spencer Graham set at his desk and signed the papers for the slave named Mica, transferring ownership to his son. He explained Ned's plan to Eli, then advised that he had already talked to Clem Haskins who was waiting to release his slave and he expected Eli to start work the first thing tomorrow morning. Spencer then added that he was pleased with Eli's performance with Rebecca and if he held his head high, learned his trade as an overseer and kept his personal life…personal, then he would again respect him as his son and as a man. He then told Eli he could have the rest of the day off to go collect his property.

Eli jumped to his feet, despite wearing a big grin, his bottom lip began to quiver and he started to choke up but quickly regained his composure, "My greatest pain is knowing that I hurt and disappointed you…and I can't tell you how happy I am that you are giving me a chance to prove myself. I've never told anyone, not even Mica, but even from the time I was little I have always wanted to be the chief overseer on Rolling Hills and I promise you Daddy, from this day forward you will be nothing but proud of me!" He accepted Mica's papers, his father's handshake, hurried from the house then climbed on his horse and took off across Rolling Hills at high speed in the direction of the overseer's field office.

Rebecca was somewhat overwhelmed by the attention and pampering that surrounded her throughout her pregnancy. Meals were prepared from her exact request and brought to her room when and if she desired. Miss Ella took her vitals every day and she even had a carriage and personal driver waiting if she wished to visit Rosemary's dress shop or go anywhere else, even if it was only a few steps down the back lane that carriage was always waiting. For nearly five months she continued her apprenticeship with Rosemary although Spencer limited her time spent working to four hours a day. She had no problems of any kind but for the remaining time of her pregnancy, Rebecca was mostly confined to the house and watched over by Miss Bessie, the most experienced midwife on Rolling Hills. Rebecca was also schooled by the exact and demanding Miss Ella on the ins and outs of running the large sprawling mansion. The old maid also drilled into Rebecca the rituals, manners and customs that were expected from the Misses of the Plantation. Miss Ella had always considered the Graham family to be among the most elegant in the state and she intended to work for no less. So with great patience and gentle firmness, Miss Ella slowly molded Rebecca into a Graham.

It was on a soft lazy summer evening when Miss Bessie put out the call for Doc Bateman. Then only a couple of hours before the sun came up the newest member of the Graham family loudly announced his arrival to the entire house. It was a rather quick, problem free delivery that Miss Bessie described to Spencer as being "as smooth as ah hen layin an egg!" Eight pounds two ounces of happy, healthy baby boy. The child was promptly named Eli Spencer Graham III, by the proud and happy master of Rolling Hills Plantation. Ned was way beyond amused to discover that Spencer and Eli shared the same name. While Spencer did not care for the name Eli for himself, he liked it for his son. Eli on the other hand did not care for the name Spencer but liked the name Eli. Spencer Graham did not understand why Ned found the whole thing so knee slapping funny.

"Well if'n youse is Spencer and dat is Eli, den youse outta names...whuts yuh gonna calls da sucker?" he asked while still laughing.

"Junior!" Spencer snapped causing Ned to drop to his knees and double over in laughter.

# Chapter seven

*T*he *wedding celebration* was grand and carefully planned. Thirty six days following the birth, two hogs had been slaughtered while a barrel each of rum, whisky, brandy and gin had been delivered and a large white tent was erected in the side yard of Rolling Hills.

The excitement that was building at Rolling Hills had also spread quickly throughout the Tredwell family because all of them had been invited to the wedding and to the grand party afterwards. Martha Tredwell was the bride's maid and the oldest of the sisters. She spent the night before the wedding at Rolling Hills to help Rebecca get dressed. The second oldest, Mildred, was completely unaware of the profound secret she would share before this special day was over.

On the morning of Rebecca's wedding, the Tredwell household was in complete turmoil. Six girls were fighting over clothes and desperately trying to look their absolute best…all at the same time. This was the biggest and finest event they had ever attended. In fact, except for a rare visit to town, this was the only event they had ever attended. And they attended in style. Mildred often reflected on how excited she was when the two big fancy carriages arrived at their shabby farmhouse and she settled into luxury for the first time in her life.

The weather was splendid and it was a long pleasant ride to the big Wilson Creek Baptist Church. Mildred felt elegant and important sitting among high class people in that fancy church. She watched with great interest as the reverend followed by the groom and his best man took their places. She thought Eli was handsome but wondered why his best man was a slave. She was thrilled by the music that suddenly filled the church then like the rest of her family was absolutely speechless moments later when her father escorted a radiant, polished, well groomed Rebecca down the aisle. Rebecca had always been the plump, dowdy frump that didn't even try to look her best. But on this day Rebecca had lost weight, her hair was styled, her skin was glowing, she was wearing a stunning soft yellow wedding gown and she was almost beautiful. Mildred stared at her and felt a powerful wave of jealousy.

Dressed in a well made suit with a morning coat, Eli played his role as if he really meant it and the service was touching and beautiful. A few minutes later another equally beautiful and touching service christened their son, Eli Spencer Graham III. None of the Tredwell family had ever witness a formal wedding or a christening

service and the beautiful ceremonies brought most of the
family to tears. Mildred received another shock when a
slave called Ned stood as the godfather for Rebecca's
child and Miss Rosemary Graham stood as godmother.
Mildred watched closely at the end of the service as Ned
tenderly carried the child from the altar to the waiting
carriage. He was dressed in a well fitting suit and seemed
too refined and well groomed to be a slave. In many
ways he was a very attractive male and Mildred's
curiosity was leading to admiration.

The carriage procession to Rolling Hills Plantation
was quite a sight. Reverend Wilkinson and the master of
Rolling Hills, Spencer Graham occupied the first carriage.
They were followed by the carriage carrying the bride,
groom, best man and bride's maid. Next came the
carriage carrying the godfather, godmother and the
newborn child. The Tredwell family followed in two
carriages and two more carriages carrying the friends
and servants of the Graham family brought up the rear.
The seven carriages moved down the road at high speed
while the excited and happy Tredwell family loudly
chatted and whooped it up until reaching Rolling Hills.

When the carriages turned onto the lane leading
into the plantation the Tredwell family fell silent in
complete awe of their surroundings. Bold columns across
the facade accented the large two-story mansion with
fully extended wings on each side that seemed to stretch
forever. The beautifully tended lawn and gardens were
truly a sight to behold and wonderful aromas filled the
air. The guest were seated at the longest table Mildred
had ever seen under the large white tent in the side yard,
then served from overflowing trays of the most delicious

food she had ever tasted. There was a liquor table and several side tables stocked with food, fruits and mouthwatering desserts.

Following the formal supper, Spencer Graham officially welcomed his in-laws to the family. He then announced that his brand new daughter-in-law Rebecca had told him that her father, Abner has been cravin a breeding sow for long as she could remember. So Rolling Hills was having a pregnant breeding sow delivered to Abner's farm within the next two days.

Next Rosemary hired Martha and Mildred Tredwell to work for her in-town operations. She made it clear that they would have to attend Miss Polly Garten's Finishing School to properly learn how to service and sell nice things to fancy ladies, but she would pay for the schooling in return for a contract to work when they finished. Rosemary wanted to move her operation out of the general store and open a dress shop in town but she did not want to do most of the work herself. And, to project an exclusive image she did not want to use slave women in the ornate front street shop she had planned for downtown. The Tredwell sisters were made to order. She had only to polish them.

Reverend Wilkinson concluded the speeches with a benediction then climbed aboard his carriage and headed back to town. As soon as the reverend's carriage turned onto the main road the party began in earnest. At the far end of the tent several comfortable chairs had been placed in a wide semi-circle, creating a dance floor or stage in the center. Music filled the air, liquor flowed and people danced. Mildred was jealous and amused as she watched Spencer Graham dance with his brand new daughter-in-law. They were both happy but it was the happiest day of Rebecca's life. She had done it...she was now a Graham and would never leave this wonderful place. Dancing with her new father-in-law was confirmation that her dream had come true and she cherished every moment.

The Tredwell family's experience with liquor had been limited to Abner's homemade wine and corn squeezings. Most of the family decided to sample each of the real liquors available at this party and the combination of gin, whisky, brandy and rum had the predictable effect. Soon most of the Tredwell family, Rebecca included, was completely drunk.

Out beyond the tent the slaves danced, at times leading their dance line into the semi-circle under the tent. Mildred was certain that the Graham's were mighty fine people because they had invited all their slaves to the party. They ate the same food and drank the same liquor; such a thing was unheard of to her knowledge. But the slaves made the party truly exciting. Their drums and provocative dancing aroused her. She had never witnessed such a display and truly enjoyed it. She also enjoyed an occasional admiring glance from Ned.

As darkness approached a large fire was built and cast flickering shadows across the bodies of the dancers. Mildred sipped from her glass. She had quickly decided she liked the taste of rum and stayed with it shunning the other liquors. She enjoyed the rum and the warm breezy feeling it produced. Mildred openly laughed at her drunken sisters attempts to dance then sat mesmerized when the slaves returned to the dance floor. Their glistening muscular bodies produced movement that seemed to become more erotic with each new dance and Mildred was completely captivated. Empowered by the liquor and feeling the heat of the evening she fixed her eyes on Ned.

Ned sat near the middle of the semi-circle next to Spencer Graham who was occasionally nodding off. Ned was quite happy and feeling no pain. It had been a perfect day and the complete fulfillment of his grand plan for Rolling Hills. He was truly enjoying the party and watched several slaves with great amusement. Ned knew that none of the slaves had tasted real liquor before this party and while many had drank themselves into a drunken stupor and lay on the grass grinning at the night sky; others were busy hiding small stashes of liquor in various places for future use. As the troop of slaves danced their way out of the tent Ned noticed Mildred starring at him. They starred at each other for a few long moments then looked away.

A short time later Ned stepped to the liquor table to refresh his drink and was quickly joined by Mildred.

"You craving me?" she quietly whispered.

Ned studied her for a brief moment, "Ah sho is!"

"Is there some place we can slip off to?" she whispered.

Ned took a long slow look around. Even for him this was a dangerous and risky proposition. Everyone of importance was incapacitated or occupied in some way which provided a rare opportunity. Mildred was a ripe, attractive young white woman that wanted him. She was the only thing that was denied him and it was the right time to collect this delicious piece of forbidden fruit.

Mildred closely followed Ned's instructions to wait a few minutes then slip out of the dark end of the tent. Go to the open porch all the way over on the far side of the big house. Go through the door at the end of the porch and down the hall to the first room on the left hand side. Go into that room, close the door and wait. Mildred was excited and her heart beat fast as she made her way to Ned's bedroom.

It was several minutes later before Ned entered. He lit a small lamp and noticed Mildred's clothes on a chair. Mildred was in his bed under the covers. Ned stood before her and removed his clothes revealing his hard manhood. He then reached down and pulled away the covers exposing Mildred's naked white body. Ned sucked in his breath. To him she was gorgeous. Her long auburn hair framed and highlighted her flawless ivory skin interrupted only by the pink nipples of her full succulent breast. Ned's eyes traveled down her body to the thin straight brown hairs that protected her most intimate flesh while Mildred reached out and stroked his manhood, amazed at its size and firmness. Mildred had very limited sexual experience and both of them were delirious with lust but Ned calmly used his considerable love making skills to help both of them get the absolute most from their short time together.

In just under forty-five minutes they were back at the party feeling happy and content. They had done it! Their experience was forbidden and crossed the line but was probably the most excitement or fun either of them ever had. Neither of them ever expected to have the other again, but Mildred went on to become the manager for Rosemary's Dress Emporium in Hardin County. And since Ned made infrequent deliveries of supplies and finished goods to the emporium, they found a way to please each other more than forty times over a span of about eight years.

By midnight on the day of the wedding, every soul on Rolling Hills Plantation whether slave or free was drunk, full of wonderful food or both. The party had slowed way down when the Chinese fireworks that were supposed to end the evening actually increased the excitement to a level of near frenzy. The eating, drinking and dancing began anew causing the party to last throughout the night and into the morning, before the Tredwells and a few friends of the Graham's flopped into their carriages and were driven home.

From the moment Rebecca's child was born, Eli had paraded around and put on a grand show. If you didn't know different, you would have thought he was the most in love young husband and the proudest young papa you would ever meet. It wasn't all an act however; Eli was thrilled by what it meant for him, his future and freedom. To show just how happy he was, as soon as the sun came up on the day his son was born, Eli went to town and bought a very large quantity of big cigars. He returned and gave every man, woman, boy and girl, slave or free on Rolling Hills Plantation a cigar. Spencer was often amused by the memory of that day and seeing nearly everyone on his plantation smoking or chewing on a big cigar.

When Eli presented his father with a cigar Spencer granted him permission to build his own house and Eli wasted no time. He already had the completed plans drawn by Jas. A. Hasbrook and Associates. Spencer was impressed. Eli had taken him seriously and planned for a real house. Hasbrook was top notch and the plans were first rate. They called for a large two-story brick residence with several fireplaces, a large formal parlor, dining room, library and a separate kitchen house. It was to be located on the far side of Rolling Hills Plantation near and fronting the Trestle Bridge Road. In fact, to get to Eli's house you had to go out the front lane from the main house and down Graham Road quite a ways then turn right on Trestle Bridge Road and travel nearly a mile or so to the lane leading to Eli's house or to "South End" as it would quickly be named for being on the south end of Rolling Hills Plantation. Because of excellent weather and the many seasoned and experienced hands brought to the task, the house was fully completed in a little more than three weeks. Eli and Mica camped at their home site every night during construction and moved in even before the job was completed. While the house faced the road and sported a long wide front porch, the two-story back porch overlooked the crop fields and provided a perfect vantage point for the overseer.

Both Spencer and Ned were very impressed with the house and with Eli's drive and determination to succeed Clem as overseer. They were surprised however by Eli's second choice of slave. With him living so far from the main house and main kitchen, they had fully expected Eli would select one of the cooks as his second slave. As they were considering with whom to replace the missing cook Eli announced that he had chosen to receive the papers for a young field slave named Buster. It seemed a perplexing choice to Spencer and Ned until Clem Haskins told Ned that although Buster was almost eighteen years, he wasn't much of a field hand and despite having probably the biggest manhood on Rolling Hills he hadn't showed no promise as a stud either. Clem seemed to think Buster would probably make a better house boy than field slave and, to Eli's credit, Clem gave no indication that he knew Eli was a dandy boy.

Once in his own house, Eli quickly grew into his own man. He completely and totally ignored his wife and son. When he was at the main house to turn in his daily report, Eli remained focus on the crops and slaves under his charge and never asked about nor visited with his son or wife. And, whatever happened within Eli's house remained there, without rumor or gossip. Both on and off of Rolling Hills Plantation Eli was quickly becoming known as a fair minded, tough and disciplined man. When Clem Haskins' contract expired it wasn't even a question, Eli became overseer for crop production and field slaves. A few years later he became Chief Overseer for Rolling Hills Plantation and no one was the slightest bit surprised or dared question Massa Eli about anything.

Eli never looked back. He took Clem's lessons to heart, made his own decisions, tried to be fair, stayed on the side of right and as time passed by, his efforts made significant contributions to the continuing success of Rolling Hills. More important than anything else however, Eli re-earned the respect of his father and of his Uncle Ned. That was and will always remain the one accomplishment of which he is most proud.

Eli blew his nose, wiped his eyes, snuggled close to Mica and watched as Mildred Tredwell Barnes and her husband Thad stepped away and headed in the direction of their carriage. He then looked at his sad, heartbroken bride of many years ago, standing next to their grown son on the other side of Ned's grave.

# Chapter eight

*T*ears *streamed down the face* of Rebecca Graham, even before she left the church and approached the grave site. If one were to have asked she likely would have described Ned as her favorite uncle. But he was much, much more. Secretly, Ned was the first man Rebecca ever deeply desired sexually. She had wanted him since that night in Eli's room when Ned first revealed himself and his eyes first fell upon her completely naked body. She truly wanted him and he truly wanted her. She knew it from the look in his eyes and the song in her heart. But it was never to be. Throughout their many years on Rolling Hills and despite almost daily opportunity, Ned went about his business as if the moment never happened. *Ned was so special,* Rebecca thought, *he showed his love by respecting you, showed you the path then got right out of your way and made you look smart. Life really wasn't worth living before Ned. I just didn't know it.*

She thought about the harsh and brutal years of her childhood. Being one of eight daughters and three sons born to a hardscrabble, poor luck chicken farmer. Sleeping three in a bed and wearing each others clothes. Growing up eating apples, pears and berries when they could find them. Squirrel, pone, pot likker and a few eggs plus a piece of chicken every so often, and seldom having more than one meal a day. She left all of that behind…because of Ned. She would never forget the day her father called all the girls into the house and announced that before the day was out one of the girls was likely going to be sent off to live with a wealthy family. He would not know which girl was going until he talked to the head man. Without knowing who would be sent or why, both of Rebecca's older sisters and the one just a year younger than she began primping and arguing over who was going to wear what clothes. Rebecca didn't bother; they were all much prettier than she and they knew it. Plus, Rebecca had a child and they didn't. She had a child because her cousin saw that she was vulnerable and took advantage after he had gotten turned down by both of her older sisters.

When the carriage arrived her father went out to greet the callers while everyone in the house peeked out the windows. Rebecca remembered how stunned she was to see a slave so well dressed and wearing such expensive leather riding boots. She was even more impressed by the fact that he seemed to be doing the talking. Rebecca was at first afraid, then moved to tears when Ned reached down and picked up her son, Rusty. Ned held the child high in the air, spun him around and around then tickled him before giving the overjoyed little boy a big piece of candy and watching him scamper away in total delight. Only Spencer was aware that Ned had just quickly inspected the child to be certain he was physically and mentally sound. Rebecca was still watching Rusty out of the window, but like her sisters and mother she was completely shocked and speechless when her father walked into the house and hollered for Rebecca to get her belongings and say her goodbyes. She could not stop smiling; she had never expected to be chosen but was the only one already proven and ready for the task at hand. When she settled into the luxurious carriage she wanted to scream out with joy and thumb her nose at her sisters...instead she kept her head down and done her best to fight back a joyous grin all the way to Rolling Hills.

Rebecca attempted to dry her tears while remembering that the whole scheme that brought her to Rolling Hills Plantation was cooked up by Ned. Soon after Rolling Hills became her home she quickly realized that Ned was the plantation mastermind. She also learned that it was not a good idea for people to lie to, disrespect, or try and trick or double-cross Ned. His retribution was always swift, just and very painful, sometimes in a variety of ways. Among a few Ned was feared. But among the many he was respected even more than the plantation master himself. He came to their rescue when she and Eli needed him most and was absolutely certain she would have never gotten pregnant if Ned had not stepped up. No one could possibly be more of a godfather to their son than Ned, and in many ways he was also the godfather of the Tredwell family. Rusty moved to Rolling Hills and attended the same preparatory schools and colleges that all the Grahams attended. Five of her sisters received education, training and wonderful very well paying jobs which they still hold and her father is now one of the county's major pork producers all because of godfather Ned. *Godfather Ned!* Rebecca smiled through her tears. She liked that term and was glad she had shared it with Spencer. He liked it immediately because he was quick to admit that Ned was the tower of strength that held Rolling Hills together.

Less than six months after the birth of Junior, Rebecca graduated from her apprenticeship under Rosemary and was named manager of the Rolling Hills workshop. Rosemary moved into town, putting complete trust in her sister-in-law who, as Rosemary quickly realized, was a much better production manager. Rebecca loved the challenge of producing very high quality goods in a short space of time. She loved teaching and encouraging, pushing then rewarding good solid effort. She loved her job from the first day she got it and loved it for nearly two years, until her one of her younger sisters was promoted to manager and Rebecca left the workshop forever.

The only problem Rebecca could ever remember having on Rolling Hills was with her personal life and Ned quickly solved that. Both Rebecca and her new son were healthy and happy. She had a dream life and a dream job but at times she was lonely. Not for her family but for the company of a man. She tried hard to fight it off by staying busy with her job and caring for her son. But quite unexpectedly Uncle Ned invited her for a chat under his favorite tree in the side yard. He offered her a glass of brandy then as usual got straight to the point.

"We's gots ah unnatuall sitasion heah on Rollin Hills and we's needs tuh deals wid it. Nah youse a youn wife who's husbum man didn't wants her in da furst place and he ain't likelys tuh starts cravin fur yuh in dis life, so dat leaves youse walkin round wid no man and cravin fur one. Nah at da same times we's gots massa Spence up dere sleepin in da big bed all bys his self. Ah no's da papers says da youse dun marries Eli…but ah thanks we both no's dat yuh really dun marries massa Spence and as da Misses of dis house, dat's who yuh outta be's covered by. Ah gunna has a talking wid da massa tuhmurrah and if'n he ask youse tuh jine him in resdence, den he be's askin fur youse tuh becums da true Misses of Rollin Hills and takes up ah regular place in da massa's bed. Yuh unnerstand?"

Rebecca was shocked; she nodded in agreement then drank the brandy straight down. She had trouble sleeping that night and all day at work she couldn't concentrate. Rebecca wasn't sure how she felt about getting into bed with Spencer Graham. She was lonely no doubt and was fairly certain she could not have Ned, so it seemed Spencer was her only choice, if in fact he even wanted her.

The next day Spencer allowed Ned to drag him away from his desk and go for a long walk in the middle of the day. He was surprised when Ned explained that he thought Spencer was just plain dumb for sleeping alone or using an occasional bed wench to satisfy his needs. He had a ripe, lonely young white girl right down the hall just waiting for his call. None of those names like daughter-in-law or son's wife meant anything in this situation. Rebecca gave birth to the heir of Rolling Hills,

she was the Misses of the Plantation and she was there
for the pleasure of the master. Because she was Eli's legal
wife he would get the credit should any additional
children just happen to come along. Ned insisted that
Spencer was a damn fool for not realizing that since Eli
clearly never wanted this ripe, eager young girl, and
since she is the mother of the plantation heir, that means
she is and always really was a bride for the master. And
because of Eli's complete lack of interest, Spencer owed
the young girl some attention! Unless he wanted another
Rosemary on his hands.

Finally Spencer got it. Until that moment he had
never even thought about courting or seeking another
wife. No woman could replace his precious Abigail but
Ned was right. Rebecca had delivered his heir but had no
one to hold her hand.  She had kept her part of the
bargain, was now family and deserved his attention.
Following supper that same evening Spencer asked
Rebecca to join him in residence.

Rebecca was nervous, flattered and somewhat
intimidated by Spencer's invitation. She nearly dropped
the wine glass she was holding then blushed hard before
responding with pleased acceptance. After taking the
master's arm and strolling up the winding stairs then
down the main hall, Rebecca was completely stunned by
the size, opulence and amenities of the master bedroom
suite. That served as a nice diversion for both of them.
For more than two hours they talked, relaxed with strong
drinks and became comfortable with each other before
getting into bed then mentally waking up.

Spencer was jarred awake by the sudden memory
of how wonderful and special it truly is to make love to
someone you really care about. It created very powerful

feelings he had not known since his beloved Abigail passed long ago and he made no attempt to fight them. Spencer was a seasoned, experienced lover and he utilized all of his many skills throughout that night. He was completely enraptured with the joy of young flesh and the long forgotten thrill of sharing real love.

Rebecca had lost her jitters and was relaxed and happy when she slid into Spencer's bed then awoke to a completely new world. She had experienced basic sex with two different boys but she had never made love with a man. Spencer took her to heights she didn't even know existed. He reached deep inside, unleashed her rawest desires then brought her to glorious climax after climax. After a brief while, following a whole lot of hugging, kissing and snuggling he did it all over again.

By morning neither of them had slept a wink but both were more than delighted with their night. Each knew in their heart that this romance was just beginning, was true and would last. They spent most of the next two days in the master's suite.

Rebecca was amazed at the size and grandeur of the Misses suite across the hall from the master. It even had an adjoining nursery and nanny chamber. After her personal items were moved from her old room she took her rightful place as the Misses of Rolling Hills Plantation. It was now her house and she was quickly accepted as the Misses by all, including Rosemary, Eli and especially the proud Miss Ella.

With all of her insecurities completely vanquished, Rebecca's pent up love and passion just simply exploded for Spencer, who remained energized and delighted to have a young wife he now adored. Over the next ten years Rebecca made Spencer the happiest man in the South by giving birth to four children of their own. Two boys and two girls, all happy, healthy and as Ned noted, normal.

Rebecca could have divorced Eli and married Spencer but none of them felt that any of that was necessary. The marriage was registered in the names of Eli Spencer Graham and Rebecca Tredwell, it would say the same if they went through the formalities and as long as they were happy, they didn't see that it was no one else's business. The Master and Misses of Rolling Hills Plantation are a slightly unusual couple that have remained unusually happy for a very long time and show no signs of changing.

Rebecca kissed her fingers then touched them to Ned's coffin. She paused for several moments after doing so then allowed her sons Rusty and Junior to escort her to their carriage. Eli watched them go. He leaned against Mica and watched everyone go. Slowly, one at a time, then in small groups the mourners melted away until only Eli and Mica remained. When the last shovel of dirt fell upon Ned's grave, Eli permitted Mica to lead him to his carriage so Buster could drive them to his father's house for the repast.

# *Epilogue*

$S$*pencer Graham* *made a brief stop* at his family's
burial plot behind Wilson Creek Baptist Church on his
way home from a routine trip to town, just as he now did
on every trip home from town since Ned died. As he
approached the plot Spencer noticed a scruffy middle-
aged white man tending the grounds. "Afternoon suh!"
the man called out. Spencer nodded then spent several
moments at Ned's grave.

On the way back to his carriage Spencer noticed
for the first time how well the grounds were being kept.
*The heavy sadness that always brings me here has never*
*allowed me to appreciate the beauty of this place or the fine way*
*it has always been maintained,* he thought, then took a long
look around and noticed the whole graveyard was just as
well cared for. He walked across the grave yard toward
the man that had spoken to him and was now vigorously
pulling weeds. "Pardon my good man but are you the
groundskeeper for the graveyard?" he asked.

"Yassuh ah sho is!" the man responded with a big
smile that revealed his missing front teeth. "Furst real job

ah ever had. Been digging graves and tendin dese grounds fer over thurty years now," he bragged.

"You keep this place beautiful and special and I want you to know that I sincerely appreciate that as I am certain do many others," Spencer responded.

"Why thanky suh, dat's real nice to heah. Ah enjoys muh work, course dere been a bit mo of it since dat grave you was visitin got put in."

"What do you mean?" Spencer questioned.

"Lots mo vistin since, lots of folk visit dat grave and steps on muh little flowers and plantlings. Dey tromps down my grass and ah gots keep seeding...but you know...ah really don't mind."

Spencer reached into his pocket and took out a twenty dollar gold piece then gave it to the groundskeeper, "This is for doing an outstanding job and for paying special attention to that very grave you just mentioned."

The groundkeeper first bit the gold piece then danced a jig, "Da only thang ah can say is thanky suh, thanky, thanky, thanky! Dis da most wunderful blessin ah done ever ceived in muh whole dadblame life. Doan you worry nun suh, ah'll sho pay real special tention to dat grave. Can ah asks you jis who's buried dere suh?"

Spencer smiled, "The man that is buried there is just exactly who that tombstone says he is," he advised.

"Can ah ask you whut dat stone say?" the groundskeeper asked.

Spencer paused for a moment; it suddenly occurred to him that throughout his entire life Ned had never asked him what anything said. Although Ned never admitted it, Spencer now realized that Ned could read…probably better than he could and it was just taken for granted. He chuckled then walked with the groundskeeper to Ned's grave, "That stone says "Here lies Ned Graham, born 1763, died 1838. Godfather of Rolling Hills."

# DESTINATION CHERBORG

*From a brick bungalow in Indianapolis…*
*to the shores of Normandy France*

# Chapter one

$I$t *was* 5 p.m., time to lower the flag. Tim Morgan stepped out his front door, breathed deep and smiled as he soaked up the sun. It had been an unusually windy day with a brief unexpected thunderstorm that gave way to a calm beautiful evening. After being drafted into the Army during World War II, Tim witnessed the raising and lowering of the flag nearly every day during his twenty years of service. Keeping that tradition he had flown his own flag in strict adherence with military protocol from the first day he retired. He stood and studied the flag for a few moments then suddenly snapped to attention and smartly saluted. Time and the weather had taken its toll. The right edge was badly frayed and ripped from snapping in the wind…it was time to retire the flag. Time to take it to the fire station for proper destruction and time to get another flag from the attic.

Timothy Joseph Morgan was a rural Kentucky farm boy when the Army came calling. He was sent to boot camp then on to join the Infantry fighting their way across Europe. The war ended two years later but Tim could not resist the sizeable re-enlistment bonus and signed up for four more years. While at home on leave during the last year of his re-enlistment, Tim concluded that the best life his hometown could offer did not begin to compare with the Army. At home he was called "Timmy Joe" in the Army he was called "Sergeant Morgan" or "TJ", that said it all as far as Tim was concerned. So with six years already served he re-enlisted again and made the Army his career.

Just after the Korean War was resolved Tim married his hometown sweetheart and shortly thereafter fathered two sons. Nine years later under pressure from his wife he retired from the Army with twenty years of service, a small pension and full retirement benefits. They bought a house on the north side of Indianapolis and moved away from the Army Post but Tim took a long time settling into civilian life. He worked a variety of jobs before finally finding a fit for himself as a production worker at an assembly plant. Over time Tim was promoted to line foreman on his shift then eventually to production foreman. He put in just over twenty-four years at the plant before he retired for the second time in his life.

Retirement was good for Tim and his wife, Louise. They were blessed with good health, had put both sons through college and paid for their house. They were free to travel, enjoy life and make frequent trips to visit their grandchildren. It was on one such trip that Tim got a painful shock which deeply hurt his feelings. He and Louise found themselves helping their daughter-in-law with her church rummage sale. While wandering among the items for sale in the church basement Tim came upon the model train sets. The very same trains he had purchased and given to his grandsons only a couple of years earlier. Tim grew annoyed as he carefully inspected the model train sets. Both were in like new condition, even the boxes. They were damned expensive model trains with lots of tracks and many accessories, which as far as Tim could determine, was neither played with nor appreciated. He had given the trains to the boys as a very special gift and had promised to buy more railcars, tracks and scenery once they put it all together. He grew angry at first then quietly purchased the trains when his daughter-in-law was out of the room and hurried them to the trunk of his car.

When Tim returned home he constructed a large platform in his basement using large sheets of thick plywood supported by and attached to several sawhorses. His plan was to create a model train display that would have his ungrateful grandsons and their parents eating their hearts out. But other things got in the way and Tim left the trains in their boxes on the platform for several years. He only started working on the trains after his wife passed away. They had been married almost forty-five years when her illness suddenly came out of nowhere then she was gone. Tim was at first completely lost without her. He started working on the trains as a way of getting his mind off his grief and slowly became addicted. At first he would wander into the basement just to admire the trains then notice something that needed assembly or fixing or rearranging and before he knew it several hours had passed.

Tim had been working on his train display today and planned to go back to it but getting a new flag out of the attic now took priority. After eating dinner and watching the evening news, he lowered the hatch and unfolded the stairs leading to the attic. He advanced far enough up the ladder to reach and pull the chain on the light socket. The light snapped on and Tim sighed; he had not been in the attic for more than two years. He had put most of his wife's personal belongings in the attic because he felt so much grief when he saw them. He could not part with them but could not spend much time looking at them either. After a deep breath Tim climbed the rest of the way up and looked about for the flag he knew was there. He searched for several minutes before remembering that he had two flags. One had been given to him at a World War II Commemoration and was kind of cheap but the other he had bought at the Post Exchange and it was first quality military issue. Both flags were in his footlocker which had several boxes stacked on top of it containing many of his wife's intimate possessions.

Tim gingerly moved the boxes one at a time. In doing so however, the bottom flaps of one box broke loose and the entire contents spilled onto the floor. Tim folded the flaps of the box then scooped the cards, photos and letters off the floor and put them back into the box. While doing so he glanced at an occasional photo or card and chuckled with the memory of how Louise had carefully saved every card, letter and photo she ever got. The material in this box was from early in their life but Tim was not interested in a trip down memory lane. He worked quickly but one letter in particular caught his attention so he looked closely at the envelope...the letter was from him. It was his handwriting and the return address began with Pvt. Tim Morgan. Tim stared at the envelope. It was addressed to Miss Louise Wainwright and the postmark was faded. He slid the letter out and read, "*Late August 1943 I think. From somewhere in hell aboard a Navy ship on my way to France I think. Hi Louise, this is the letter I promised to write. We don't have much to do aboard this ship so I got a moment to write and thank you and the others for that fine send off y'all gave me at the train station. It truly gave me a right fine feeling that I still have...and I thank you. Now y'all take care of each other and I'll be seeing you just as soon as this war is over...so long. Tim Morgan.*"

Tim blinked hard then sat down on a box. He didn't remember writing a letter to Louse in 1943. They did not start dating until well after the war had ended. Had to have been 1947 or 48. He thought for a moment then remembered that back when he first left for the Army, Louise Wainwright was a perky young preacher's daughter. She convinced most of her father's congregation and many others to show up at the train station to pray for the safe return and bid farewell to each departing soldier. It had been a warm memory for a brief while but quickly faded amid the horrors of war. Tim decided to examine the letter more closely so he put it into his pocket then placed the other material back into the box. After taking the best flag from the footlocker he put the boxes back on top, snapped out the light and climbed down the ladder.

Tim Morgan had always been possessed with a poor memory. For some reason things just escaped him but that fact didn't bother him much. He had completely depended on Louise to remind him of things or jog his memory. Detailed memories of his early days in the

Army and of the many events of World War II were very
limited at best. This letter caused him to remember his
send off at the train station and he was very curious
about what else it could help him remember.

Sitting at his desk Tim closely examined the
envelope. The postmark was faint even in good light. He
used his magnifying glass and discovered there were two
postmarks. One overlapped the other so Tim could only
make out a few letters. In the center of the postmark were
the letters APO which he recognized as being part of the
military postal system. The other letters around the top
of the postmark were spaced apart and spelled out C-h-e-
r-b-o-u-r-g. Tim looked hard but no other lettering was
visible. "Cherbourg...hum Cherbourg. I know I've heard
that name before," he mumbled. Tim read the letter
again. "Hum...aboard a Navy ship...headed to France.
Cherbourg, France...hey I did write that letter! I wrote a
bunch of letters aboard that ship and mailed them at
Allied Headquarters in Cherbourg. CHERBOURG!
THAT'S IT! THAT'S IT! Son-of-a-bitch...the money's in
Cherbourg...after all these years I finally remember!
CHERBOURG!"

Tim did not often drink liquor but he dug an old
bottle of brandy out of the pantry and poured a large
drink. After he settled into his recliner, sipped the brandy
then closed his eyes, the memories of Cherbourg flooded
back as though it all happened yesterday. Cherbourg was
on the Normandy coast and Tim was attached to the
Army's 9th Division and part of the follow-up force. They
came ashore at Cherbourg and followed the Marines into
Normandy then across France to the Siegfried Line and
into Germany. Tim remembered the fright he felt and the

smell of death in the air when they came ashore. Two days later he was loaned to another unit and sent on a search and destroy foot patrol along the road leading from Cherbourg to Valognes. He had not seen any action up to this point and was jumpy and scared.

Corporal Eddie Clayton had seen considerable action including the D-Day invasion and understood how Tim felt. He liked Tim and took him under his wing. Because they were on a foot patrol, from two to six soldiers went ahead of the main body. They were called the scouts and two or more soldiers followed some distance behind the main unit, they were called the rear guard. Corporal Clayton was a rear guard and he asked for and got Tim as his shotgun. Separated from the others with plenty of time to talk and get to know each other they quickly became buddies.

On the return leg of their mission Tim was more confident but still jumpy. Their unit had encountered only sporadic and limited resistance with just two real firefights. They suffered no casualties while eliminating sixteen German soldiers before the road was declared open and safe. It was only a small taste of what was to come but Tim was beginning to develop that numb shell which overcomes every soldier when he truly understands that his job is to kill people.

As they were approaching a sharp bend in the road, Tim and Eddie were tired and looking forward to getting back to camp then hitting the sack. They were moving quickly yet cautiously up each side of the road when an old man came down a path and begin stumbling up the road toward them. He was babbling in French, a language neither Tim nor Eddie understood, and carrying a big leather pouch. Both Tim and Eddie held their ground and leveled their weapons at the old man who continued toward them before he stumbled and fell to the ground. The two soldiers quickly advanced. Tim kept his weapon trained on the old man while Eddie first searched him for weapons then took his heavy pouch. The old man continued to babble in French while Eddie opened the pouch and discovered it was stuffed full of gold coins and U.S. greenbacks. It was a fortune! Simple as that...they were rich. They hurried away leaving the old man lying on the road and celebrated their good fortune by taking turns carrying the pouch. But because their fortune was too heavy to carry around and they couldn't ship it home, Eddie suggested they hide the money. It really wasn't of much use to them until the war was over and they were out of the Army, then they would live like kings. Tim agreed as long as they took at least one hundred dollars each before they hid it.

Along their way they found a discarded ammo box among some clutter by the side of the road. It was made of metal and had a handle on each end so Tim and Eddie put the pouch into the box so they could share the load.

A few miles up the road Corporal Clayton spotted a small cemetery. "Perfect place to make our deposit!" he announced.

"Why here?" Tim asked.

"Cause it could hide here forever," the corporal advised.

"What are we gonna do?" Tim questioned. "Find a fresh grave and bury the money with the body?"

"Ha-ha," Eddie chuckled. "No need to buddy…we'll just put it under a tombstone. Nobody ever disturbs a graveyard, look at it! Probably been here two hundred years already," he concluded then marched to the edge of the cemetery and stood facing in the direction of Cherbourg.

After a quick study Corporal Clayton designated the third tombstone in the third row as the place to hide the money but that tombstone was too short so the fourth tombstone in the third row became the hiding place. Tim was deeply impressed by Corporal Eddie Clayton and eagerly followed orders to dig a hole under the tombstone. He dug at an angle so the tombstone would not fall over and they soon pushed the ammo box into the hole, filled it with dirt then covered it over with grass and leaves. Satisfied their treasure was safe the two soldiers hurried to camp. Each had one hundred dollars in ten and twenty-dollar bills stuffed in their pocket and a knowing smile. Just after noon the following day Corporal Clayton's unit shipped out. Four days later Tim's unit shipped out in a different direction.

Tim sighed and sipped his brandy. He had carried a card in his wallet with Corporal Clayton's name, service number and unit then searched for him after the war ended. To his complete despair he discovered that Eddie Clayton had been killed in action in September 1943. Eddie was his key to finding the money. Tim had counted on him to lead them back to it and without him he was lost. In fact he could not even remember the name of the town where they buried the money. Tim had fought in many skirmishes and major battles, covered a lot of ground and been through countless villages and towns. War blurs things and without Eddie to lead them to the treasure Tim had very little to look forward to, so he re-enlisted in the Army and moved on. His life changed and many memories including that adventure in Cherbourg just slipped away. Yet without really focusing on it for more than 50 years now, Tim had longed to know just exactly where it was that he and Corporal Eddie Clayton hid a fortune. Now he knew…and he knew it was still there.

# Chapter two

*E*arly *the next morning* Tim went for his usual walk then returned to his trains. He would tell you that his display was nowhere near finished but it was quite impressive. Tim had expanded the platform to three levels with over a hundred feet of track. There were bridges, tunnels, mountains, open ranges with cattle and horses; a couple of little villages and a real waterfall was under construction. Although he purchased various display pieces, Tim had built most of the display himself starting with a simple plan that just kept growing. The more he did the more he found to do. He was currently installing the waterfall and spillways which was a big project. When finished, the water will cascade down three levels into a small lake. Then a pump hidden under the display sends the water back to the top through a clear plastic tube creating a smooth continuous waterfall.

On this morning Tim worked slowly, finding it difficult to concentrate. His mind kept drifting back to the treasure in Cherbourg. *What should he do about it? Could he claim it? How? He is the only person in the world that knows where the treasure is. Should he write down what he knows...or just go get his damn money?* Tim sat in the middle of the display and looked around then advanced the control lever to forward. Both sleek HO gauge Lionel trains sprang to life and smoothly moved across the tracks with six richly detailed cars behind each locomotive. It was quite a thrill to watch them climb and wind their way up through three levels then descend with a great rush of speed over a bridge through a tunnel and across the plains. Tim sighed as he noticed a couple of places in the track that needed minor repair. He shut down the trains, snapped off the lights then went and sat on his front porch.

Shortly after noon Tim had lunch then went to the Woodbury Bowling Lanes. His good friend Harvey Smith worked as a clerk at the Woodbury in the afternoon. It was a get-out-of-the-house job for Harvey who was also retired. The place was never busy in the afternoon and it was common for Tim to stop by for a chat or to practice for his Friday night league game. Harvey was on the same team and they often practiced together. Today however, Tim did not have bowling on his mind. "Harvey my friend," he called out, "how would you like to go to France?"

"You kidding? Karen would love it!"

"Did I say anything about Karen?" Tim sharply questioned.

"Well you don't think she's just gonna up and let me go off to Paris all by myself do you?" Harvey shot back.

"Did I say anything about Paris?"

"You know Karen and I had talked about a trip to Paris awhile back...we hadn't planned on taking you though...ha-ha," Harvey chuckled.

"Shut-up knucklehead and listen for a few minutes this is serious stuff!"

"Yes Sir Sergeant Morgan," Harvey teased.

Although Tim was a few years older, both men were from the same county in Kentucky and briefly served together during the Korean War. Harvey did not make the Army a career and only reached the rank of Private First Class during his tour. Tim being a career man and a retired Master Sergeant was forever his military superior. For Harvey this was both a comfort and a joke.

"Listen!" Tim demanded. "During WWII me and a buddy came across a huge stash of U.S. greenbacks and gold. We hid it where we knew it would keep then moved out. Well, as you know, war is hell and over time I just plain forgot about it. After the war I discovered that my buddy had been killed in action and I had no idea what town we hid the money in so I moved on. Yesterday I found an old letter I had written to Louise and get this; it was from the same town where I hid the money. Just seeing that old postmark brought it all back. I know exactly where the money is and I know it is still there," he concluded.

"Well I'll be damned!" Harvey responded. "How much you think is there?"

"Millions probably," Tim surmised.

"And you really think it is still there?"

"Absolutely! I know it is!"

"Just how did you come by this money?" Harvey asked.

"Never mind that! The way I got it figured all I gotta do is fly over there, get my money and fly home. What do you think?"

"I don't know...I guess you can do that! If it really is your money."

"Of course it's my money!" Tim insisted. "Nobody else even knows it exists."

"But it had to come from somewhere," Harvey reasoned.

"It was spoils of war damnit! That's both legal and fair!"

"Perhaps," Harvey agreed, "but don't you think the French government might take exception to you collecting fifty years later?"

"Who said the French government is going to know anything?"

"Well I'm rather certain you should notify the French government or American embassy or someone. Suppose there is some significance or historical value to that gold?"

"That's the very reason Karen is not being invited on this trip," Tim snapped, "and you are starting to sound just like her. Not thirty seconds after I get my hands on the gold you two are ready to hand it over to some French moustache!"

"You are really serious about this aren't you?"

"Never been more serious in my life! And I'll cut you in on a piece of the action if you are willing to be a man and go on this trip ALONE!"

After several minutes of conversation, the two men agreed on three things. First Tim should go get the money, second someone should go with him and third Harvey was not that someone.

"How about one of your kids?" Harvey asked.

"What? Hell they would get even more official than you or Karen. I don't need any goody-pants do-gooders; I need somebody interested in swelling the size of their own pockets."

"Well what about one of the guys on the bowling team?"

"Hum..." Tim pondered. "Let's see there's Sammy Sorwell."

"Naw," Harvey responded. "Gotta wife and kids plus he runs his own electrical contracting business, he's too busy. How about Marlin?" he questioned.

"Nope! I don't like Marlin all that much. What about Eric?"

"You kidding?" Harvey asked in amusement. "You're talking about the original company man. You would have to be on his calendar at least six months in advance and have a clear listing of every detail...need I say more? Why don't you go on one of those tours, then sneak off and get your money, sneak back in then come on home?"

"I'm not sneaking around with a bunch of old fogies! I got pride! I was a military man you know. I fought in two wars and I am entitled to the spoils I secured for myself. As long as I am alive they are mine to claim!"

"Damn right! Give 'em hell Sarge!" Harvey responded with a big grin.

By the end of the day Tim knew he was going to Cherbourg. He also knew he was not going alone but he did not know who was going with him. He went to bed humming a happy tune. The next morning he had a light breakfast then walked to the nearby library. Tim had not been to the library in years but decided to do a little research on Cherbourg.

Not many people were in the library during that time of the morning and the librarian was intrigued by Tim's request for information on Cherbourg, France. She walked him to various reference books then lingered over several pages pointing out answers to his inquiry. Tim was both pleased and made uncomfortable by the closeness of the librarian. Several times she brushed against him or nestled her head next to his. Tim was 74 years old and although it was now somewhat a rare occasion he was still very capable of becoming aroused. He was feeling uncomfortable because he wished the librarian would go away and he wanted her to stay at the same time. She was an attractive middle-aged lady with a pleasant alluring smell and sultry voice.

In spite of his mission Tim found himself concentrating more on the lady than the material. "I'm going there," he blurted out.

"Really!" the librarian gushed.

"Yep! Got a lot of money there to pick up," Tim bragged. "You want to go with me? I'll pay for everything."

"Sorry," the librarian blushed. "I don't think my husband would approve."

"I'm not inviting him anyway."

"Well thank you for inviting me, but no," the librarian replied with a big smile then left Tim to his reference materials.

Inside one of the reference books Tim found and closely scrutinized several photos of Cherbourg. It was amazingly familiar and brought back many memories. He remembered that this town had a square lighthouse and was pleased when he found a photo of it. Like the town, it had been there with little change for centuries. This was the old-world where some things never change. Not the United States where things change overnight. In that part of the world he was absolutely certain his fortune rested undisturbed. He asked the librarian to copy a few pages and a map from one of the reference books and tried once more to entice her into joining him on his trip. She again openly flirted with him while refusing the trip but suggested that if he was serious about a traveling companion, perhaps he should consider a college student.

"A college student?" Tim questioned.

"Sure!" the librarian responded. "There are hundreds of students dying for a free trip to France. All you have to do is put a notice on the bulletin board at the college and your phone will ring off the hook honey," she advised.

"Just like that huh?"

"Yes sir, just like that!"

"Hum...might give that a shot," Tim concluded.

"Well thanks for using our library and don't be a stranger. We are here to serve you and we are here every day," the librarian responded.

"I'll see you again," Tim offered as he headed out the door.

"You better!" the librarian teased.

During another lengthy conversation with Harvey, Tim decided a college student might just be the right traveling companion. They disagreed however on gender. Harvey thought Tim should take a male while Tim insisted his traveling companion should be female.

"A strong young gal can carry just as many bags as a boy," he offered. "And she's a whole lot nicer to have around, not to mention there is always a possibility she just might jump in my bed."

"And jump in your wallet!"

"Ha!" Tim snorted. "I'll show you a thing or two about handling females."

"You'll show me a thing or two about getting taken advantage of," Harvey insisted. "Even if it all goes as you hope, the sex…if you got any could kill you. Hey it has happened before. An old guy has sex with a young girl and hey she's just got too much energy and he's got too much appetite and boom before you know it his heart can't take it and he's dead."

"Oh yeah…well if I go in the arms of a pretty young girl I won't be complaining."

"Why don't you just leave that question open and conduct your interviews here at the bowling alley," Harvey suggested.

"Hey that's a good idea. You don't think Mitch will mind me conducting interviews here in his place do you?"

"Of course not, we are glad to have anybody at all in here in the middle of the afternoon."

"Okay!" Tim beamed. "I'll bait the hook and see what we reel in."

"Sounds like a plan Sarge. You got your itinerary and everything all worked out?

"Yeah, pretty much. I talked to a lady at the Vanguard Travel Agency up the street. She didn't see any problems...in fact she gave me some notes...hum." Tim searched his pockets while Harvey refreshed their coffee. "Ah here we are, the lady's name is Nikki Simpson and soon as I get a passport I can fly out to Cherbourg just about anytime I choose. She even recommended a hotel. According to her it is the best in town and she can book it at a discount."

"What's the name of the hotel?"

"Ah...the Mecure Cherbourg Plaisance."

"The what?" Harvey asked with amusement.

"You heard me!" Tim snapped.

"What's that mean?"

"It means damn nice hotel!" Tim declared. "But it really don't matter all that much, I'll only be using the place for a couple of days."

"A couple of days...that's all?"

"That's all I need...way I got it figured I'll fly over and settle in. The next day I'll go get my loot and the day after that I'll fly home."

"Fly over, get the money and fly home. That's a lousy trip!" Harvey put in.

"It's a business trip, not a frilly vacation!"

"It's not a trip at all...it's just a long plane ride," Harvey countered. "Doesn't sound like a lot of fun."

"Business trips aren't meant to be fun!" Tim snapped.

"Yeah but you're trying to talk someone into going with you, so what's in it for them?"

"Hell! It's free!" Tim declared.

"Not good enough," Harvey insisted, "but if you are just going to fly over and come right back what do need someone to go along for?"

"I need somebody to carry a heavy bag and keep their mouth shut!"

"Ha-ha...that brings up another point. Have you given any thought to getting all that gold through customs?"

"Matter of fact I have done some thinking on that," Tim replied. "Cherbourg is on the Normandy coast of France which sits right smack dab on the English Channel. There are a lot of ferries...going and coming every day from Cherbourg to various destinations on the English coast. Then just up the coast there's a tunnel under the channel, it runs from Calais, France to Folkestone England."

"You don't say!" Harvey exclaimed.

"Exactly! I figure to get my money and take the ferry or the tunnel to England. I'll check out the ferry first because I figure customs are pretty relaxed there. You see the Saint-Laurent Cemetery is really the American Cemetery and it's in a little town close by called Coleville. There's a hell of a lot of GI's buried there and lots of tourist. I just might stop by myself because while I was at the library I confirmed that Corporal Eddie Clayton is buried there. Anyway," Tim continued, "once I get to England I'll go to London and get everything converted to pounds. Then I'll wire it to my account here and fly home from London."

"I'm impressed ole buddy, I really am," Harvey responded. "But don't you suppose those English folks might ask a few questions about a fortune in gold?" he asked.

"I thought about that too! I may have to convert small sums at several different exchanges but that shouldn't take more than a day or two."

"So this is really more than just a round trip to France," Harvey declared.

"Yeah I guess so," Tim agreed. "Fact is once I get all my money wired back, I'll give my companion a hand full of cash and they can go anywhere or stay as long as they want."

"You plan on telling them the purpose of this trip?"

"Hell no! You nuts? No way!" Tim declared.

"How you going to explain the heavy bag?" Harvey questioned.

"Hum...keeping them in the dark is not going to be easy," Tim admitted. "But all I really need is for them to carry the bag from Cherbourg to England and I'll have my eye on it every minute. Once it's in my hotel room in London they can shove off."

"You know Sarge, this college student thing may not be such a good idea after all."

"Why not?"

"You don't want to go treasure hunting with someone you really don't know," Harvey advised. "People can freak out when a lot of money is at stake. I know you are trying to keep them in the dark but what happens if they find out?"

"I'll admit I'd feel more comfortable with someone I know," Tim agreed. "I really need a partner...someone who will tell his wife that this is a business trip and he'll see her in a few days, then they will both be a lot better off."

"Forget it!" Harvey responded. "I'm not smuggling or laundering your spoils of victory with or without Karen. I will advise however for a small percentage," he chuckled.

"Which puts me back to square one."

"Yeah...you know Sarge this whole idea has been a lot of fun...maybe you should just leave it at that."

"What are you saying?"

"Come on Sarge? Why should you fly off to some foreign country and risk your neck for some old money you don't even need?"

"What the hell do you mean I don't need it?" Tim sharply questioned.

"Tim Morgan you're doing okay and you know it!" Harvey shot back. "You're getting what...at least two pensions and probably three, right?"

"Pensions my ass...I need that money! It's a fortune and it's mine!"

"Like hell you really need the money," Harvey snorted. "What are you going to do with it, pay for your grandkids college education?"

"Pay for my grandkids schooling? Hell no! That's their parents job...you ninny. My job is to live it up!"

"Ha-ha...and just how are you going to live it up?"

"By spending at least half the year in Hawaii that's how!"

"Ah...ha-ha-haa...Hawaii? What the heck are you gonna do over there? Ha-ha..."

"Enjoy the weather, the hula girls and being king of the hill!" Tim declared with a big crooked grin then continued. "But first I gotta get what's mine and that means finding a partner or pack mule to go with me. Hey you know I could just pay a hooker to go with me."

"A hooker?" Harvey questioned in surprise. "Now you are really asking for trouble."

"Think about it. Hookers don't care what your business is all about as long as they get a piece of the action."

"And you think a hooker is going to drag a heavy ass bag across two countries? Ha-ha-ha."

"Well...we would have to work that out..." Tim reasoned. "Maybe get one of those baggage roller things, yeah that's it!"

"Forget about the hooker Sarge. Keep the baggage roller but lose the hooker."

"You got a better idea?"

"How about we run down the list of trusted people we know?"

"Humrph...that'll be a short list!" Tim snorted.

"Well let's see...your kids are out, the bowling team guys are out..." Harvey paused, "hum...you got any lodge or legion buddies?"

"I've been to a couple meetings but most of those guys got one foot in the grave and the other on a banana peel."

"Well then we need to sleep on it!" Harvey declared.

"Maybe I should go get laid then I would probably think better," Tim suggested.

"Ah…ha-ha-ha," Harvey roared. "Man you probably would too…ha-ha…you're just a complete horned toad."

"You still got a wife…I don't!" Tim snapped.

"Yeah but me and Karen grew bored with sex a long time ago," Harvey admitted.

"Well I never did!" Tim insisted as he left Harvey laughing then slowly drove home, fixed his dinner and watched television for the remainder of the evening.

## Chapter three

*A*fter breakfast the next morning Tim briefly read the first section of the paper then went to the barbershop. He had been getting his hair cut in the same shop for many years and Lenny, his regular barber, was an old friend. While sitting in the barber chair Tim casually mentioned having some unfinished business in France and needing an escort for a trip.

"My nephew would leap at the chance to go with you but I'm not sure where he is at the moment. He dropped out of college and the last I heard he was hiking in the Grand Canyon," Lenny sighed. "But let me think a moment here. Hum...do you need the escort for company or security?"

"What do you mean security?" Tim asked.

"You know protection, muscle, pull off a caper if necessary and protect your ass at all cost! That kind of security!" Lenny explained.

"Now you're talking," Tim replied, "that's exactly what I need."

"You know that kind of hired help can cost a good piece of change don't you?" Lenny warned.

"Money's no problem! Do they take orders and mind their own business?"

"Hey look old buddy...we're talking about soldiers-of-fortune here okay," Lenny advised. "You know the guys that separated from the military but can't stay away from the battle...any battle. These are knife edge ex-GI's just waiting for orders...they rent themselves out and they will fight or do undercover stuff for any person or country but they are gonna cost you."

"How much?"

"Last I heard it was around a thousand a day for one man but I think that was the rate for fighting in live conflict. I don't know what the rate would be for just an escort."

"How do you get in touch with these guys?" Tim asked.

"Well there's a couple of ways. The dumb way is to answer an ad in the Soldiers-of-Fortune magazine. The smart way is to just put out the word that you are interested."

"Well how do you put out the word?"

"You just did!" Lenny replied with a smile.

"Okay...so how do I contact these guys?"

"You don't! They contact you!"

"Well I don't know that I like that arrangement!" Tim groused.

"If you want to deal with a soldier-of-fortune it's the only choice you got."

"Well I need somebody right away so if they don't contact me soon I won't need them at all," Tim snorted.

He paid for the haircut then left the barbershop thinking Lenny was full of crap. All that soldier-of-fortune talk was just a hat full of bull, he was still in need of a companion for this trip.

Tim went straight home and took a shower then read the rest of the newspaper before heading out to the grocery store. He stopped along the way at a department store then at his favorite hobby shop and bought a new piece for his train display. As usual he spent more than two hours in the grocery store and by the time he got home he was more than ready to relax. But it took three trips from the car to get all the groceries in and one trip to the basement to install the new piece in the train display before Tim could get to his recliner and relax. He was feeling upbeat but suddenly froze at the entrance to his living room. A large, menacing, grungy looking man was sitting in his recliner.

"WHAT THE HELL ARE YOU DOING IN MY HOUSE!" Tim hollered his heart beating fast as he dashed to the bookcase and grabbed a ceremonial saber from its display.

"Now just chill out pops," the man replied, "word is you are looking for hired help and that's who I am."

Tim stared hard at the intruder. He was tall with big hard rippling muscles that strained his battle fatigues. His hair was slick and pulled back into a ponytail revealing a face that was pockmarked and scared. His nose had been broken and his eyes were tight slits of cold meanness. Tim was still shaken. "How did you get in here?" he demanded.

"Never mind that...let's talk money," the man replied.

"Money my ass...you got no right to just barge into my house. Get the hell out of here...right now!"

"Now look pops...I done took the time to answer your call brother...you know? That means you need to throw me out something even if you don't have a mission for me," the man explained, "you understand?"

"I understand that I'm gonna shove this saber up your ass if you don't get outta my house!" Tim bluffed hoping the man would leave.

"Look...I'll break it down for you pops, my services cost five hundred a day for non-combat missions and a thousand for combat. I only interview once and if you don't have a mission for me the interview cost you fifty bucks for my inconvenience...get it!"

"I'm calling the cops and I'm gonna shove this saber up your ass if you don't get the hell out of my house and I mean right now goddamnit!" Tim snapped.

"Gimme my fifty bucks and it's goodbye forever...peacefully! Don't and well..." the man replied as he stood and towered over Tim, "I don't think that rusty old saber is going to help you a whole lot old man. SO GIMME MY FUCKIN MONEY!" he roared.

Tim quickly dug into his wallet and grabbed three twenty-dollar bills then threw them on the coffee table in front of the man. "Take it and get out now!" he demanded while fighting hard to keep his voice from shaking and exposing his fear.

After the man picked up the money and put it into his pocket his eyes seem to widen and become almost friendly. "Thanks for the tip brother...maybe I'll see you at a fire-base soon."

"Git!" Tim demanded, greatly relieved that the soldier-of-fortune was finally moving towards the front door.

"Gimme a hundred and I'll tell you how I got in," the man offered as he paused at the door.

"I haven't got a hundred!"

"How much you got?"

Tim glared at the solider then searched his wallet. He had been confident that his home was secure and he needed to know how this jerk got in. "I got exactly fifty-eight bucks, take it or leave it...then get out!"

The man snatched the money from Tim's hand. "You left your back door open when you brought your groceries in," he explained with a grin. "I had already scouted your place and was waiting. You made several trips so I just stepped in while you were at your car, made myself comfortable and waited. Would have been nice if you had offered dinner or a snack or something," he suggested as if he half expected such might really happen. As soon as he cleared the door, Tim slammed it shut then hurriedly poured a big shot of brandy and drank most of it in one swallow.

Harvey was completely aghast and sat with his mouth hanging wide open while listening to Tim tell of his encounter with a solider-of-fortune. "I can't believe you would actually trust Lenny of all people to recommend someone!" he scolded. "You didn't tell him about the treasure did you?"

"Of course not. I know Lenny is kind of an operator but he was worth a shot."

"That soldier guy could have killed you! I hope this has made you come to your senses and forget about this trip."

"I can handle myself...that punk didn't scare me none and I am not about to forget about this trip. This morning I went looking for a baggage roller and found a suitcase with wheels on it. Matter-of-fact I got two, a big one and a small one."

"Oh my God..." Harvey moaned.

"With these babies I may not need someone to tag along after all!"

"Tim you can't do this! You can't go!"

"Give me one good reason why I shouldn't!"

"How about because you are over seventy years old?" Harvey declared.

"So what, I still feel as good as I ever did and I'll bet I can whip your ass!"

"You're impossible," Harvey sighed. "Look if you must go on this wild goose chase please don't go alone."

"I've just about had it with trying to find a traveling companion," Tim fumed. "Too bad Corporal Eddie Clayton isn't still around...we'd meet up and have one hell of a time."

"Oh well...what the hell," Harvey sighed. "I'll admit I've been thinking a little about a traveling companion for you and I think you should reconsider Marlin."

"MARLIN?"

"I know you don't care much for Marlin because he's a little slow and still lives with his mama even though he's well past thirty-five..."

"That's why he's slow!" Tim interrupted. "If he'd be a man and step out on his own I'll bet he'd snap too in a hurry."

"Well regardless he fills your bill completely. He's the perfect pack mule," Harvey suggested. "He's available, not too bright and will do what you tell him."

"Yeah…all I gotta do is put up with him."

"He's your best choice."

"You know that bum wouldn't even be on our bowling team if we could have found any other guy!" Tim complained.

"I know, but he's still your best choice."

"That's the crappy part. Right now he's my only choice."

"So you gonna offer him the job?"

"Hell no! Well I mean I gotta stew on it," Tim grumbled. "Let it soak in for a while, then if I still haven't come up with someone else…maybe I'll offer him the trip."

"You could just as easily forget the whole thing," Harvey suggested.

"In a pig's eye!" Tim shot back.

Late Friday afternoon Tim put the finishing touches on the waterfall in his train display. It worked perfectly and he smiled with satisfaction then leaned back and sighed. It was bowling night and he still had not found a suitable traveling companion. "Well…" Tim spoke aloud, "it pretty much comes down to Marlin or a stranger…humrph, some choice!" He considered putting the trip off for a couple of weeks and take more time to find someone. But…it would still probably come down to Marlin or a stranger and there was no point in putting off the trip. It would only take a few days to get his money and be rid of Marlin forever. "So Marlin it is...damnit!" Tim growled with resignation.

It was an easy night for Tim's bowling team. To a man they were on top of their game and soundly defeated the opposing team, while battling among themselves for the title of "Strike-King". Every Friday they bowled three league sanctioned games against their opponents and the strike-king is the bowler that scores the most strikes in a row during any one of those three games. It was a heated competition within the team because the strike-king collects one dollar for each strike from each teammate.

For two weeks Sammy Sorwell had been strike-king but tonight he was tied with Harvey at the end of the second game. Both had bowled three strikes in a row. During the third game Harvey again bowled three strikes but Tim beat him out with four and won the title. Tim was very pleased with his team's performance and absolutely delighted with winning strike-king. It had been several months since he had won the title and he saw it as a good omen. Following the games, the strike-king always bought a customary round of beers, after which Sammy and Eric usually said goodnight and left. Marlin always caught a ride with Eric but on this night Harvey offered Marlin a ride home after Tim offered to buy another round.

As far as Marlin was concerned the only thing better than beer was free beer, so he eagerly accepted Harvey's offer for a ride and Tim's offer to buy another round. Most of the league games had ended and the crowd had left or was on its way out, so the men moved from the bar and settled at a table in the far end of the bowling alley. Harvey was anxious; he knew when Tim asked Marlin to stay for another beer he intended to invite him on his trip. Harvey was now thinking that neither of them should go.

"Marlin!" Tim began, "I want to talk to you for a minute and I'll get straight to the point. You may or may not know that I was in the Army during World War II. I followed up the Normandy Invasion and I have always wanted to go back over there. There is an American Cemetery there where hundreds of American GI's are buried and it has long been my desire to just go back and walk among the graves to show my respect and put my soul to rest. You know what I mean?"

"Uh...yeah I guess so," Marlin responded while emptying his glass.

"You want another beer?"

"Heck-e-yeah!" Marlin grinned.

"Tim motioned at the bar then continued. "The reason I'm telling you all this Marlin is because I need someone to go along with me and I'm offering you the trip expense free."

"Trip?" Marlin questioned. "Trip to where?"

"Normandy!" Tim snapped. "Normandy, France."

"France? What you wanna go over there for?" Marlin whined. "I don't like them Frenchies all that much."

"What the hell you know about the French?"

"Well I know they don't speak English!"

"Some of them do, some don't," Tim advised. "But the Saint Laurent Cemetery is American soil and it's only a visit, I'm not asking you to move there!"

"Why don't you give him the complete itinerary?" Harvey suggested.

"What's a i-ten-ary?" Marlin asked.

"It's a schedule," Tim explained. "You understand?"

"Course I do!" Marlin responded.

"Okay…good now here's the layout. We'll fly from here to the Normandy coast of France and check in at our hotel. The next day I'll visit the cemetery among other places and then the following day we will take the ferry to England and…"

"ENG-LAND!" Marlin shouted. "I love Eng-land."

"Yes…hum…well good…yeah good," Tim responded. "Ah…it will be a short trip…ah…we'll just be in and out."

"I really love Eng-land…hell, I love everything about Eng-land…them folks speak English you know," Marlin advised.

"So I take it you are willing to accompany me on this trip?" Tim asked.

"It ain't gonna cost me nothing is it? Cause I ain't got no money cept what little I can squeeze outta ma."

"Won't cost you a dime! I'll pick you up Monday morning and we'll get our passports then probably leave on Wednesday or Thursday…that okay with you?"

"Heck-e-yeah!" Marlin grinned.

Harvey shook his head in disgust. "Are you guys sure you want to do this…seriously?"

"Heck-e-yeah," Tim responded with a chuckle while Marlin continued to grin.

## Chapter four

$M$*onday started badly*. In spite of telling him twice then calling Sunday night and reminding him, Tim spent nearly an hour waiting in his car while Marlin searched for his birth certificate. "I thought you said you would have your papers and be ready first thing this morning!" Tim snapped when Marlin got into the car.

"I'm sure sorry Mister Tim but heck I was ready. I just didn't know ma would be gone this early. I suspect she musta stayed over at Mister Walker's place last night cause I ain't seen neither one of them this morning, so I had to search around for my birth certificate."

"If you say you are going to be ready then you should be ready!" Tim grumbled as he started his car and drove to the Vanguard Travel Agency.

The same lady, Nikki Simpson, helped both Tim and Marlin complete their passport applications and tentative travel arrangements. Tim had hoped to get the passports right away and was surprised when Nikki told him he and Marlin would need to have passport photos taken then deliver the applications to the downtown post office or courthouse. He was deeply disappointed when she went on to deliver the really bad news that it would take at least two weeks and maybe longer for the actual passports to be issued.

Disgruntled, Tim headed to a photo shop then stopped at a fast food restaurant before going to the post office. As the day dragged on he became more and more aggravated and embarrassed. At each place they had to wait in line and Marlin acted like a complete moron. While he waited Tim read any available literature, studied the buildings architecture or otherwise tried his best to avoid hearing Marlin tell his family's personal business to complete strangers. He was relieved to finally reach the counter at the post office but the clerk nearly caused him to have a heart attack when she asked if Marlin was his son.

While driving Marlin home Tim pulled into the parking lot of a liquor store. "Marlin how would you like a whole case of beer?" he asked.

"Oh...heck-e-yeah! There ain't nothing I'd like better than a full case of beer," Marlin declared.

"Well if you will do one thing for me we will walk into that store and you can pick out any case you want. That one thing is keeping your mouth shut about this trip. We're not even sure when the trip will be right now and I'd just assume we keep it to ourselves. So do we have a deal?"

"You mean you don't want me telling nobody about it?" Marlin asked.

"That's exactly what I mean!"

"Well I done already told ma and Mister Walker about it."

"Who's Mister Walker?" Tim questioned.

"I done already told you! Mister Walker is ma's boyfriend and sometimes he stays through the night and I..."

"Never mind!" Tim interrupted. "Have you told anyone else?"

"Uh...naw...uh-uh...nope...I ain't told nobody but ma and Mister Walker."

"Okay...you can tell them but no one else and I do mean no one. Now do we have a deal?" Tim asked.

"Heck-e-yeah you got yourself a deal!" Marlin agreed with a big smile.

While in the liquor store Tim bought a fresh bottle of brandy and an expensive case of imported beer for Marlin. "He might be stupid but he sure knows the good beer..." Tim muttered as he paid for the liquor. After dropping Marlin at his house Tim quickly drove home. It had been a long trying day and he was glad to fix a drink then settle into his recliner.

Harvey was relieved to hear of the delay caused by waiting for passports and amused by Tim buying imported beer for Marlin. "That moron better keep his mouth shut too!" Tim snapped while Harvey doubled over with laughter. When Tim began talking about other things Harvey dared hope his friend would decide against this insane trip, especially now that he had some time to really think about it. Little did he know that Tim was restless inside but refused to let it show. There was nothing he could do but wait so he absorbed his disappointment and occupied his mind with other things. He made another trip to the library mostly to visit the librarian and again try to entice her into accompanying him on his trip. She was again flattered and openly flirted but turned him down while complimenting his persistence. Tim was not the slightest bit disheartened; he went home and prepared an elaborate dinner.

For most of the next week Tim worked on his trains then began to sketch a drawing on paper. He wanted a mural painted on the wall behind the train display and it would have to be really special. Tim did not plan to paint the mural himself but he knew what he wanted and he needed to be able to show what he wanted before someone loused up his basement wall.

During the Friday night bowling Tim was his usual self. He barely noticed Marlin or his normal annoying antics. The team bowled well and for the second straight week easily defeated their competition and Tim again won strike-king. After collecting his winnings and taking an IOU from Marlin, Tim bought the customary round of beers. As usual shortly afterwards Eric and Sammy said goodnight and Marlin caught a ride with Eric. Tim was grateful that Marlin honored the bargain and kept his mouth shut about the trip. He was not about to answer any questions about his business from Sammy, Eric or anyone else for that matter and as far as he was concerned the less said the better.

Over the next several days Tim finished his sketch for a wall mural then enlisted the help of Harvey to select an artist. Harvey didn't like the design, "Its just sky with a few hills and trees," he complained. "Why don't you put up an impressive big city skyline? Now that would show some class!"

"What are you...nuts? This is the wall behind a complete model train display. The layout has got its own towns and countryside. This mural is meant to compliment the display...not louse it up!"

"Yeah, but it's dull," Harvey insisted.

"Sure it's a little dull," Tim conceded but I'm nobody's artist. I'm sure a real artist can bring it to life and spice it up a bit."

"Hey you know just a few years back Karen painted a mural on her mother's basement wall. She done a hell of a good job too, it was great. She painted the wall a beautiful blue then painted a lot of fish and aquatic things on it. It looks like an aquarium especially in low light. You should see it...no better yet you should have Karen take a look at your wall."

"No thanks!" Tim groused.

"What do you mean no thanks...you haven't even seen what she can do!"

"And I don't want to! I know what I want."

"And I suppose this is it!" Harvey snickered while holding up Tim's drawing.

"Damn right that's it! There's lots of stuff in that drawing, waterfalls, mountains, cabins and other things you obviously cannot see. It's going to knock your socks off soon as I find a professional artist to put it on the wall."

"Ha-ha," Harvey chuckled, "this whole deal can become quite an expensive production you know."

"Nonsense!" Tim countered. "It's just painting a mural on a wall...artist do it all the time."

"Well I still think it's dull."

"We'll just see what you think once it's done," Tim chuckled as he bade his friend farewell, left the bowling alley then went home and prepared his dinner.

Following breakfast the next morning Tim studied his drawing for a few minutes. He thought about what Harvey had said then looked for ways to improve his sketch before deciding the sketch was great and Harvey didn't know what he was talking about. He put his drawing into a large envelope, walked to the library and explained to his favorite librarian that while he was waiting on his passport he was interested in having a mural painted on his basement wall. He swelled with pleasure when the librarian became excited by his drawing and suggested he paint the wall himself. He declined so she went on to suggest college students.

"It would be an incredible opportunity for a serious art student," she advised, "but it would go a lot faster if it was a group or class project. You could even have the tryouts submit a large rendering of their interpretation so you can get a good idea of what their finished work would look like. It's a great way to get first class work and it won't cost you a lot. In fact, the library would be happy to contact the local college and handle the details for you," she offered.

Tim was impressed and delighted. The librarian was his kind of gal and he eagerly promised to put her in charge of the project just as soon as he returned from France. Tim left the library with a spring in his step and whistled all the way home.

After a late lunch, he went to the basement and carefully measured the wall to be painted then decided to move the entire display away from the wall. He moved several pieces before the job proved to be more work than Tim felt like, so he went and sat on his front porch then read the newspaper.

The following morning he took right off where he had stopped, working slowly carefully moving the sizable display piece-by-piece. It was tiring work so Tim took several long breaks and was considering a nap when his doorbell rang. The postman looked tired and disinterested but Tim was beaming with happiness as he signed for the package. As soon as he closed the door he tore the package open and was greatly impressed with his new passport. After reading and admiring his new possession for a few moments Tim picked up the phone and called Marlin. "Has your mail arrived yet?" he asked when Marlin answered.

"You mean today?" Marlin questioned.

"Of course today!"

"Well...naw it ain't come yet today."

"Okay then be on the lookout for your mailman because my passport came in today's mail and... "

"I got mines yesterday!" Marlin happily exclaimed. "And it was so important looking and everything that ma and Mister Walker got all excited too...cause they done went and ordered them one right after we did."

"You got it yesterday?"

"Yup sure did!"

"And you didn't call to let me know?" Tim questioned.

"You didn't tell me to call or nothing."

"Hum...well so I didn't," Tim sighed. "But nevertheless we are all set to go now. Think you can be ready to leave in two days?"

"Uh...yeah I guess so...uh what should I bring?"

"Just a couple changes of clothes will do. I'll call you back when I have our final itinerary."

"Our what?" Marlin questioned.

"Our schedule! And make sure you keep that passport and your birth certificate where you can find them!" Tim ordered then hung up.

When Tim stepped out of the door of the Vanguard Travel Agency he had a big smile on his face and a confirmed itinerary in his hand. He and Marlin would fly to Heathrow Airport in London then take a commuter flight to Cherbourg. Nikki had confirmed the fact that he could easily book all local transportation on the spot and he had two open tickets for a return flight home from Heathrow. The open tickets meant he could book his return flight with only 24 hours notice.

He climbed into his car and drove away in the direction of the Woodbury Bowling Lanes. Along the way Tim began to rethink his decision to tell Harvey he was on his way. *He's just gonna whine and plead with me not to go,* Tim thought, *just like somebody's grandmother! I don't need that.* He turned left heading his car in the direction of home and thought about telling his sons about the trip but decided against that too. *I'll tell them all when I get back...yup, I don't need any nagging nellies worrying about every little thing and sowing their seeds of doubt,* he concluded.

Two days later Tim was surprised to find Marlin sitting on his porch waiting when he arrived to pick him up. "I got my passport, birth certificate, driver's license and two changes of clothes and one dress up outfit," Marlin proudly announced as soon as he climbed into the car.

"Way to go young man! Hell, I'm impressed!" Tim responded.

"I ain't never been on no airplane before," Marlin confessed.

"Nothing to worry about, you'll love it," Tim assured as he eased his car into traffic and headed for the airport.

"You really think so?" Marlin questioned.

"Absolutely!" Tim responded. "I remember the first time I flew it was quite a thrill."

"I sure hope you are right Mister Tim cause ma and everybody done flew somewheres but me. I ain't never had no place to go so I ain't never had cause to fly till now and I'm kinda excited but a little scared too…you know?" Marlin confided.

"Best thing you can do is calm down and relax! The way to do that is to shut your mouth and close your eyes then take several slow deep breaths and think of the fun you are going to have. The longer you do that the more calm you will become. In fact, don't say another word until I say something to you. You got that?" Tim questioned. "Well I asked if you got that?" he repeated.

"You said I wasn't supposed to say nothing!" Marlin declared.

"Um…yeah so I did. Well okay get on with it and remember breathe slow," Tim instructed while smiling inside because he had found a way to shut Marlin's mouth. He parked his car in the long-term lot and with Marlin in tow, took the shuttle bus to the terminal nearly two hours ahead of their flight departure. They checked in at the counter then headed straight for their departure gate. With time to kill Tim bought a copy of the New York Times, then after buying lunch for both he and Marlin, he settled down to read it.

Marlin meanwhile bounced around as much of the terminal as he had access to. He meddled with everything within reach and talked to anybody that would listen, telling them that he was going to Eng-land and then over to see some Frenchies. He would also explain that "he had never flew before because he didn't have no place to fly to, but Mister Tim needs him to go see the Frenchies and he didn't mind cause he lives with his ma and she's got a boyfriend named Mister Walker and sometimes he stays through the night and..." And so on until his audience found a way to escape. About twenty minutes before their flight was to begin boarding, Marlin found his way back to Tim. "There you are Mister Tim, I been looking all over for you. You was right you know, I'm having fun already!" he declared.

"Sit down Marlin," Tim ordered. "I'm glad you are having a good time and I'm sure you will have a good time on the plane. But we won't be sitting next to each other cause I made the reservation with short notice and we had to take the seats we could get. So we won't be sitting next to each other but we will be on the same plane and you make friends quickly. I'm sure you won't have any problem sitting next to a new friend will you?" Tim questioned while lying about the short notice booking. He had insisted they be assigned seats far away from each other.

"Well naw I guess I won't mind too much. That feller over there said they got movies and everything on the plane. He said they serve you dinner and beer too!" Marlin responded.

"You got any money on you?" Tim questioned.

"Bout ten dollars."

"Hurmph..." Tim snorted. "You have to pay for your pleasure," he advised. "Dinner is free but the beer is going to cost you. Here take this." Tim took fifty dollars from his wallet and offered it to Marlin.

"I can't take that money until I say what I gotta say," Marlin declared.

"Well just what have you got to say?" Tim questioned.

"Okay, the truth is I been thinking some on this thing and I don't think you and me are flying always to France just so you can walk around in some old cemetery. I think you going over there after something or the like, that's what I think!"

"And you have been doing all this thinking on your own? Tim asked.

"Well naw sir not exactly...but I done some thinking on my own about all this and I ain't gonna get on that airplane unless you tell me why we going."

"Well at this point it's a much easier secret to keep," Tim responded. "I wasn't gonna tell you until we got to France but the truth is Marlin we are going on a treasure hunt and I am the only person in the world that knows where the treasure is. Now since you are helping me, once I have the treasure I'll cut you in for a nice share and you just may come back home a rich man. But! You must do exactly as I say, do you understand?" he asked.

"Heck-e-yeah! What kind of treasure is it?"

"Never mind for now we'll talk more in France."

"Hell I'm just excited all over!" Marlin declared. "Can I have that beer money now?"

"Only if you agree to keep your mouth shut about the treasure. Not one word here, on the plane or in France."

"Hell you got yourself a deal," Marlin declared.

Several minutes later Tim settled into his seat aboard the airplane and chuckled, he could hear Marlin annoying the passengers several rows back. As the large airplane left the ground with a powerful thrust Tim relaxed and smiled. He was grateful to be on his way, grateful to have an assistant for the heavy work and grateful he did not have to sit next to that assistant.

# Chapter five

*After a long uneventful flight* the plane landed at London's Heathrow Airport and the passengers streamed off into the terminal. Tim was among the first to exit the plane and he waited for Marlin who was busy telling a woman passenger his personal reflection of the flight. "That's the most wild and scary thing I ever done...I mean this beats all!" he exclaimed to the woman who was desperately trying to distance herself. A middle-aged man nearby stared at Marlin with a look of anticipated violence. Tim chuckled with the thought that those poor folks must have been Marlin's seatmates. He stopped chuckling when Marlin spotted him.

"Hey there Mister Tim wasn't that a wild scary ride?" Marlin called out. "I liked it and everything but man that airplane blasted my ears shut and I had to keep swallering to open them up then they get blasted shut again...and I sure was scared when they landed that thing. I'd felt a lot better if that waitress lady had served me more beer...but she said there was a limit on how many I could have and she told me to keep my voice down and after a while she gave me a sleeping pill and it worked too and..."

"All right! All right, just settle down!" Tim demanded. He led Marlin through customs and on to their connecting flight.

"Are we in Eng-land?"

"At the moment yes! But not for long."

"Well imagine that...I'm in Eng-land," Marlin marveled.

The short commuter flight to Cherbourg was on a much smaller plane but Tim still managed to sit beside someone other than Marlin. He felt great and was pleased with his easy passage into England then into France. Because Cherbourg was a coastal town any currency was acceptable, especially US currency so Tim did not bother to exchange his money. An English speaking cab driver took them to the hotel and within minutes of landing they checked into the Mercure Cherbourg Plaisance Hotel. It was a comfortable upscale hotel with a full-service restaurant and bar. The staff was pleasant and the room was very comfortable with two beds and a full bath.

As much as Tim hated the thought he could not risk allowing Marlin to be on his own. So they were forced to share one room. Tim was pleased and surprised when Marlin wasted little time climbing into bed and going right to sleep. It had been a long flight and in spite of that unauthorized pill the stewardess had given him on the plane, Marlin was spent. Tim checked his notes and smiled, everything was working out right on schedule. He settled into bed and closed his eyes grateful that Marlin wasn't snoring.

Following breakfast Tim and Marlin settled into the same cab they had taken from the airport. Because the driver spoke English, Tim had given him a large tip and asked him to be available the next morning. The cab driver had never seen so large a tip and had been happily waiting for his "favorite Americans" for more than an hour when they stepped from the hotel. Tim ordered the driver to drive slowly and take the main road to Valognes and back. The cab driver was overjoyed, it was a beautiful day and he was going for a slow drive through the countryside with the meter running.

During breakfast Tim told Marlin that this was a study day. He needed to set everything up so that tomorrow they could go get the treasure. Today Marlin's job was to keep his mouth shut and not get in the way. Even without that instruction Marlin found little to say. He did not like France or French people. He sat upright and stared out the window at Cherbourg passing by and nothing he saw changed his opinion of France in the slightest.

Tim on the other hand looked with great interest and fascination. Some places looked vaguely familiar but most of the town was strange and new to him. Shortly after the cab had left the town of Cherbourg and was slowly cruising down the road toward Valognes, Tim spotted the cemetery. He looked long and hard and knew in his heart that was it. A satisfied smile crept across his face as he allowed the driver to drive all the way to Valognes where he bought coffee and pastries for himself, Marlin and the driver at a café. On the return trip Marlin remained quiet. He felt very uneasy in France and continued to sit on the edge of his seat and stare out the window. Tim chatted with the cab driver and admired the countryside then again took a long hard look when they passed the old cemetery. A short distance past the cemetery he noticed a café at the edge of Cherbourg. He wrote down the name of the café then instructed the driver to take them to the ferry port.

Again the cab driver was given a large tip and a time to pick them up following their round trip to England. Tim had done his homework and knew that the ferry to Poole, England was the shortest crossing. Still the ferry trip would take close to four and one half hours one way, but there was also a high-speed service available that made the same trip in just over two hours.

Since this was a scouting trip Tim had decided to take both. They would take the ferry to Poole, locate the train station, have dinner then take the high-speed service back to Cherbourg. He was most interested in the level of customs activity at both borders and brought along his small suitcase with the rollers to make this dry run authentic. They were right on schedule and boarded the ferry shortly after arriving at the dock.

Marlin was wide-eyed with awe while Tim was pleasantly surprised to find the ferry was far more than he expected. Her name was the "Barfleur" and she sported several bars, live entertainment, dancing, video cinema, casino game machines, several shops, children playrooms, sundeck, several restaurants and self service food salons, all while carrying a maximum 1212 passengers, 92 crewmembers and 590 automobiles.

After locating their seats Tim gave Marlin eighty dollars and told him to make it last. Marlin immediately headed for the bar and casino while Tim went to the sundeck, found a comfortable lounge chair and truly relaxed.

For Tim being aboard the Barfleur would be the high point of his entire trip. While enjoying the cruise across the calm and beautiful English Channel he met several ladies. Some very interested in him and he very interested in some of them. He had lunch with a very attractive lady in her sixties from his home state and afternoon tea with a very sexy and much younger lady from London. On a different trip he would have quickly altered his plans to accommodate a new relationship or two. But in spite of considering this a business trip, he still collected four names, addresses and phone numbers with the promise to be in touch.

Tim spent most of the trip on the sundeck and had all but forgotten about Marlin until he returned to his assigned seat as the ferry approached the harbor at Poole, England.

Marlin was sitting in his seat thumbing through a magazine. "There ain't many people on this boat that speaks English," he complained.

"Is that so?" Tim chuckled knowing that meant Marlin had been unable to capture an audience.

"I started talking to this one feller and he told me what I was saying was my personal business and he didn't want to hear my personal business. Then some woman told me to shut-up! She said, why don't you just shut-up! Right to my face and everything…can you beat that?"

"Well we will soon be in Poole, England…that ought to cheer you up!"

"It sure will! I love Eng-land!" Marlin beamed.

Once they cleared the port of entry, Tim took a long look around then hailed a taxi. He ordered the driver to go first to the train station then on a brief tour of the town. Poole was a small unattractive town and the train station was very near by. Tim took a brief look then motioned the driver on. He knew once he got to the train station he and the treasure was safe. From here it was only a three-hour train ride to London. Poole offered few places worth visiting and to make matters worse Marlin and the taxi driver each tried to out talk the other. After only a very short tour, Tim decided he had seen and heard enough so he ordered the driver to leave them at a restaurant near the port.

Following dinner Tim and Marlin strolled back to the dock then stepped aboard the high-speed ferry. This ferry was the total opposite of the fancy Barfleur. It was an all business no nonsense vessel. A true water coach that resembled the interior of a bus or airplane. There were none of the amenities of the Barfleur but it traveled at about twice the speed.

For the first time Tim found himself sitting next to Marlin, but Marlin was sullen. He didn't want to leave England and he really did not want to go back to France. "Why we gotta go back there?" he whined. "We just got here…just got to Eng-land…"

"France is where our business and belongings are at the moment," Tim reminded. "But in a couple days we will be back here and you can stay as long as you want."

Marlin remained sullen and said nothing as the ships engines surged to life and the vessel quickly and smoothly moved with increasing speed across the channel toward Cherbourg.

Tim was in high spirits and good humor. The dry run had been a great success with a nice bonus. The customs clearance had been nothing more than cursory looks at his passport in both England and France. Even Marlin cleared with little trouble and never did his suitcase attract the slightest inspection. He felt certain he could transport his gold with no interference and to put icing on the cake, he also had the names and numbers of four very delightful ladies. *I'm absolutely gonna keep in touch with all of them,* Tim thought. He was smiling when he looked over at Marlin who sat staring out the window with a gloomy look on his face. "How'd you do on the ship coming over?" he asked.

"You mean on them gambling machines?" Marlin questioned.

"Yeah. Did you make the money last?"

"Heck naw...I bought a few beers and played some games and stuff but I ran outta money."

"Well you gotta admit it was quite a ship!"

"It was all right..." Marlin conceded. "But I love Eng-land! I don't like them Frenchies!"

"What have you got against the French?" Tim questioned.

"I don't like them!"

"Why not?"

"Cause I don't like them...when I was just a little kid about twelve years old, a family from France moved in next door and everything. They didn't speak English very good and they had three boys and one girl. One of the boys was about my age but all the others were older than me. A few days after they moved in them boys...all three of them jumped on me. They held me down and whipped the tar outta me. Ma got real mad and went to their house and hollered at their ma. So after that they didn't hit me no more but they would hold me down and fart in my face or let their sister punch and kick on me much as she wanted to. I hated her...I hated all of them. I was in my junior year of high school when they finally moved away. The oldest one told me they was going back to France and if I ever came over there they was gonna hunt me down and beat the pulp out of my ass...and they meant it too! I don't like them Frenchies, I don't like them none at all...but I love Eng-land! I had a teacher Miss Hatcher, she was from Eng-land and she taught me about how Eng-land is the mother of the United States and everything. Heck we even got English from Eng-land and Miss Hatcher even said my folks probably came from Eng-land long time ago and I still probably got kinfolk's there..."

"Well after one more day and a couple nights in France you can explore England all you want," Tim interrupted. "How do you like this boat?" he questioned in hopes of changing the subject.

"I don't like it none, it goes too fast!"

"That's the whole point with a high-speed service."

"And they don't serve you no beer or nothing."

"Did you meet any girls on the trip over?" Tim asked again hoping to change the subject.

"Naw...women don't like me much...never have!"

"You got a regular gal back home don't you?"

"Naw! I done told you women don't like me much! I've knowed a few here and there but women can really get a feller in trouble...I know that...so I don't pay em no mind much."

Tim looked at his watch they were only about halfway through the trip. "Okay Marlin, it's been a long day so I'm gonna take a nap for a short while. You want this magazine?"

Marlin took the magazine and began thumbing through it while Tim closed his eyes and pretended to doze off. While relaxing Tim thought about the next day. The only thing that remained was to dig up his gold and check out of France. He could get it done as soon as they docked then leave France in the morning but he did not want to be in the cemetery after dark. The morning and afternoon was definitely out, but dinnertime drew folks home, so early evening was probably the best time to get in and out unnoticed. Then he would have time to examine the treasure in his room and with an early start the following morning he would be in London before sunset. With that settled he peeped at Marlin who was again staring gloomily out the window.

Having deposited his favorite Americans at their hotel upon their return from England, the same cab driver again picked them up late the following afternoon. Tim slept late that morning and allowed Marlin to sleep even later. He went for a long enjoyable walk around Cherbourg then returned and took a shower before having a very late breakfast with Marlin. They whiled away the afternoon and by the time the cab driver arrived both men were ready to get out of the hotel.

Tim first directed the driver to find a hardware or sporting goods store where he bought a small shovel with a collapsing handle. It was important that the shovel fit inside his little suitcase which he had brought along. His next stop was the little café he had spotted at the edge of town. After giving the driver a time to return, Tim treated Marlin to an early dinner and a beer.

Afterwards they walked down the road to Valognes for nearly twenty minutes before they reached the old cemetery. After seeing no one anywhere near the cemetery Tim's excitement began to grow and he was grateful that Marlin had been mostly quiet since they left the hotel.

Marlin moved cautiously, darting his head from side to side and staring all around as though he fully expected his former French tormentors were hiding behind the next tree. "I don't like graveyards!" he announced.

"Nobody in their right mind likes these places," Tim responded, "but this is where the treasure is. So let's get to it!" He stepped to the edge of the side at the corner facing in the direction of Cherbourg just as Corporal Eddie Clayton had done and quickly pinpointed the fourth tombstone in the third row but it just didn't look right. He walked over to the tombstone and after taking a close look knew it was not the right spot. "Something's wrong," he muttered to himself then walked back to the road and took a long look.

"What we waiting for?" Marlin questioned. "I don't like it here."

Tim ignored him and continued to study the cemetery. "Hum...I don't remember it being that close to the road." He carefully examined the road; clearly it had not been widened. "Maybe the cemetery has expanded," he reasoned. "Why of course it has!" he spoke aloud as he began walking across the cemetery along the top row of graves. "They were bound to need more space." As he walked he began to notice that the dates of death on the tombstones were after World War II, after he was there. About thirty yards across the cemetery the dates abruptly changed, the dates of death were before the war. Some long before. Tim identified the point were the dates changed then slowly walked down that grave line. On one side were deaths before 1943 and on the other side were deaths long after. He hurried back up to the first row then looked toward the road. "Yeah now this looks right," he assured himself. He stood facing in the direction of Cherbourg at the edge of the old part of the cemetery and quickly identified the fourth tombstone in the third row then marched straight to it.

Tim felt his heartbeat quicken as he closed in on the tombstone and knew it was the right one. "This is it…yes indeed! This is it! Ha-ha…come to papa," he sang out. Marlin stood at the edge of the road and watched until Tim called out to him. "Come over here and bring the suitcase."

"Has it gotta be way over there?" Marlin questioned. "I don't like it here."

"Just get over here!" Tim demanded.

Reluctantly Marlin slowly made his way across the cemetery trying his best not to step on any graves. He watched with wide eyes while Tim removed the shovel from the suitcase then marked out a section of ground behind the tombstone. "Okay now dig the dirt out of that area and we will get what we came for," Tim instructed.

"No sir! Not me…I ain't digging up no bodies!" Marlin exclaimed in near panic.

"We're not digging up bodies!" Tim snapped. "The body is over there, we are digging here…under the tombstone, cause that's where the treasure is…now get to digging and dig on an angle so the tombstone won't fall over," he demanded.

In mortal fear Marlin decided to get this job done as quickly as possible. He dug the shovel into the ground and tossed the dirt aside.

"Don't throw it all over the place, keep it in a pile close by…we gotta use that dirt to fill in the hole," Tim coached as Marlin dug faster. After a short while the shovel struck metal.

"I hit something!" Marlin shrieked.

"Good! Make the hole a little wider."

"You right sure I ain't digging up no casket?" Marlin nervously questioned.

"Hell no! That's an ammo box and the treasure is inside it so come on dig!"

Marlin quickly dug around the metal box and within only a few minutes he and Tim were able to drag the box out of its grave. Tim took the shovel and scraped the mud from the box then released the catches. His heart beat fast, he had a twinkle in his eye and felt like a kid on Christmas morning as he opened the lid of the ammo box. Inside lay the pouch, just as he and Eddy had left it. The badly decomposing pouch was covered with mold and rot.

"Gawd that stinks!" Marlin remarked. "Where's the treasure?"

Tim wrapped his hand in his handkerchief then picked up the pouch but it ripped apart and the contents spilled into the ammo box. Tim stared in disbelief, the cash had rotted, when touched it turned into mush or slime and the gold coins were no longer gold. Tim felt confused and disappointed but he quickly recovered and removed the rotting pouch, shaking all the coins from it then tossing all the pieces of the pouch into the hole. He ordered Marlin to help him dump the treasure out of the ammo box and into the suitcase. Once done they put the decaying box back into the hole then filled it in. They threw the shovel into the bushes then briskly walked back to the café.

Tim had a shot of brandy while Marlin had two beers as they waited for their driver. "What kind of treasure we got?" Marlin questioned.

"Well we had a lot of cash but it's all rotted…and we got a lot of coins which I believe are gold," Tim responded.

"Gold?" Marlin whispered in astonishment.

"Yep…I believe so, but I can't be sure until I have them checked out."

They hurried to the cab when it arrived and Tim was relieved to get through the lobby of the hotel with little notice. Once inside their hotel room, Tim carefully studied the treasure. None of the cash could be rescued so he concentrated on the coins. He distinctly remembered them being gold but he could not find a gold one in the whole lot. For the most part the treasure was a mess, the rotting money created a slime that coated and covered most of the coins. He washed a couple of them and lightly scraped at them with a nail file but still no gold showed through.

Excited by rescuing the treasure, Tim also felt disappointed because the treasure did not look like it did when they buried it. Regardless he decided to celebrate the successful mission; they had retrieved the treasure without any problem…that was worth celebrating. Tomorrow he would worry about what it was all worth in London. He closed up the suitcase, put it in the closet then invited Marlin to the hotel bar. To celebrate their success Tim had several drinks and got plenty tipsy while Marlin drank only two beers. About an hour later they called it a night and went back to their room. Tim was humming a little song but Marlin was quiet as each man settled into his bed.

# Chapter six

*It was late the following morning* when Tim awoke with a slight headache and feeling fuzzy. He sat upright and rubbed his head, cursing the drinking that caused his hangover. After sitting on the side of the bed for a few minutes he went to the bathroom and took a shower. Afterwards he felt considerably better and was ready for a hearty breakfast. He stepped from the bathroom drying his hair with a towel and called out to Marlin, "Let's go bud...time to get a move on." When Marlin didn't respond Tim stopped what he was doing and looked at Marlin's bed. Marlin was not in it. Tim looked all around the room then opened the door and looked up and down the hall but Marlin was nowhere to be found.

"Wonder where the hell that idiot went," Tim mumbled before suddenly his heart began to beat fast and he hurried to the closet then flung the door open. His small suitcase containing the treasure was gone. Marlin's suitcase was gone. Marlin was gone and quite clearly had ripped him off. "NO! NO HELL NO!" Tim roared. "That lousy lowlife moron sneaked off with my gold! Lousy little shit...I'll kill him! I'll hunt him down and break every bone in his face…one at a time. Now just where the hell would he go?" Tim questioned. He quickly dressed then hurried to the front desk. The shift had changed only a short while ago and no one currently on duty had seen Marlin leave. Tim took a cab to the ferry docks hoping he might find Marlin waiting to board the ferry. He knew it was a long shot but it was the only thing he could think to do.

Marlin's theft of the gold had come as a complete surprise. Tim never saw it coming and still could not imagine Marlin really done it on his own. But he was sure Marlin would not hang around France and the ferry would be his most likely way out. He hopped from the cab with a thousand questions on his mind and quickly searched the many places and faces on the dock. It was very late in the morning and he did not know how much lead-time Marlin had. If Marlin had slipped away before sunrise he could be anywhere by now. But if he was aboard the ferry to Poole that left a short time ago, Tim could take the high-speed service and be at the dock in Poole when Marlin arrived but that was a real long shot.

Tim was confident that Marlin went to England but a lot of ferries with many different destinations departed from Cherbourg. He thought about asking around the dock if anyone had seen Marlin boarding a ferry but realized that without a picture he really couldn't describe Marlin to a stranger, especially one that spoke only French.

For close to thirty minutes Tim walked around the docks or sat on a bench in anger studying faces before he stood and looked out over the calm English

Channel. "I can't believe it!" he whispered. "I've been beat by a moron! Naw...he had help. It cost money to take a cab and buy a ferry ticket. But...maybe he lied about spending the eighty bucks or maybe his mama pinned some just in case money to his underwear. Well no matter, it ain't over! No sir...not by a long shot. I know where the son-of-a-bitch lives and I swear I'm gonna hunt that moron down and when I get through with him what's left won't be pretty."

Tim took a cab back to the Mercure Cherbourg Plaisance and placed a call to Marlin's mother's house. He wasn't sure what he was going to say but maybe he could find out where Marlin went. No one answered after several rings so Tim hung up, called the airline and booked his return trip home. A seat was available on the next several flights out of Heathrow so Tim made a reservation then booked a commuter flight from Cherbourg Airport to Heathrow Airport in London. After a quick lunch while packing his bag Tim noticed a handful of the coins from the treasure lying on the dresser. He had been studying them the night before so he put them into his bag and checked out of the hotel.

Once he stepped outside Tim took a long look around for several minutes. For what it was worth his business in Cherbourg was finished, so he climbed into a cab and ordered the driver to the Cherbourg Airport.

On the long flight home Tim felt angry and cheated. He had been all the way to France and done everything right then got ripped off by a moron. *Well maybe I didn't do everything right,* Tim concluded to himself. *If I hadn't been sleeping off one drink too many I would have woke up before that bum left.* Tim decided to get his mind off Marlin and the treasure by reading a magazine but that didn't work, so he made detailed notes on each of the four ladies he had met. He was especially interested in the one that lived in his state and put her first on his list. When the evening slipped into night Tim reclined in his seat and drifted off to sleep. A few hours later as the plane began its descent Tim awoke with his mind back on Marlin. *He had help!* Tim assured himself; *somebody had to coach that moron.*

As the big jet touched down in his hometown, Tim became even more determined to get what was his or get even. The plane arrived late in the morning so Tim had breakfast at the airport then drove straight home. He called Marlin's mother's house again and again no answer. So Tim put the coins from the treasure into his pocket then drove downtown to a very exclusive rare coin dealer.

He had discovered the dealer in one of the slick upscale magazines he read while on board the airplane. The dealer explained that to properly identify rare and unusual coins, such as those Tim presented, would require considerable research that was only done during a complete appraisal. The appraisal was guaranteed and would require Tim to leave at least two of the coins for two business days and pay a sixty-five dollar appraisal fee. Tim was impressed with the store, the staff and even the receipt he was given. The receipt provided the weight and general description of Tim's coins and listed his appraisal appointment time at 4 p.m. two days later.

Tim strolled out of the coin shop with a smile on his face but as soon as he started his car the smile disappeared and he drove straight to Marlin's house. Upon arriving he was disappointed to see the door closed and no one in the yard. "Since you won't answer your phone let's see if you answer your door!" he growled while getting out of his car. He marched across the yard and the front porch then rang the doorbell twice. A few seconds later he rang the doorbell again and knocked. No one answered the door and he didn't hear a sound but he still rang the doorbell and knocked once again.

After waiting a few minutes Tim knew no one was going to open the door so he knocked hard one last time out of frustration. Just as he left the porch, Tim suddenly froze in his tracks when he heard an elderly voice call out, "They ain't home!" He struggled to locate the voice for a brief moment before seeing a little old lady standing amid the potted plants on her porch next door.

"Oh I see...why thank you ma'am," Tim smiled. "Would you happen to know where they are?"

"You kin folk or something?" the old lady quizzed.

"Yes ma'am," Tim beamed then whispered, "or something."

"Well I don't expect them back for a spell."

"When did they leave?"

"They come into a piece of money you know," the old lady explained. "The boy Marlin left first. Seems like he went to France...I believe it was. But he wasn't gone no time at all...just two or three days before Myrtle told me he done come into a real big piece of money and her and Walker Reynolds...that's her boyfriend you know... they left out of here yesterday morning. She said they was going to meet up with Marlin in England then go to somewheres in California for a spell. That's what she said anyhow."

"Did Myrtle say exactly where in England she was going?"

"No she did not," the old lady responded.

"Did she mention what town in California they planned to visit?"

"No, all she said was somewheres."

"Well thanks for talking to me. Matter of fact if I had known Myrtle had such an attractive neighbor I would have visited a lot more often," Tim lied then winked his eye and left the old lady blushing.

Again as soon as Tim started his car the smile disappeared. "I knew that idiot had help," he muttered while maneuvering his car through traffic in the direction of the Woodbury Bowling Lanes.

Harvey was in complete disbelief as Tim told his story. He repeatedly gasped or interrupted with, "I can't believe you done that!" By the time Tim finished Harvey was impressed, excited, jealous and angry. "Let me get this straight, you guys actually dug up a box in a French cemetery and it was full of gold and money?" he questioned in a high pitched voice.

"Well the money had rotted, been more than fifty years you know," Tim replied.

"And Marlin just got up and snuck off in the middle of the night with it?"

"Well that's the hell of it! That's the part I blame myself for. I had a few drinks that night to celebrate a successful mission and I shouldn't have. Matter-of-fact I was wondering why Marlin only had two beers. I figured it was because he was so spooked about being in France. Now I know it was because the rotten shit was planning to rob me."

"And you say his mother is in on it?" Harvey questioned with disbelief in his voice.

"Absolutely! The neighbor lady had all the details. She knew where Marlin went, when he left and when his mama and her boyfriend left for England. And she knew they are supposed to go on to California. Can you imagine that? Living it up on my money!"

"I would never have imagined Marlin's mother being involved. What did you say her beau's name was?"

"Uh...uh...Wallace Re...no Walker Reynolds."

"Hum...Walker Reynolds...never heard of him," Harvey mused. "Wonder what he does for a living?"

"I don't care what he does cause I'm going to take him out!" Tim snapped. "I'm going to take all of them out...and I mean it too, this ain't over by a long shot!"

"Whoa...what the hell are you talking about...taking someone out?"

"Just what I said!"

"You can't be serious?" Harvey insisted.

"Oh yes I am! Those bastards stole a fortune from me and I'm not just going to lay down and take it."

"What are you gonna do? I mean you can't exactly call the police."

"I don't need the police," Tim advised. "I'm going to see Lenny in the morning and put a couple of them solider-of-fortune fellahs on the thieves trail."

"Soldiers-of-fortune? Oh now that is a terrible idea!"

"No it's a great idea!" Tim countered. "The more I think about it the more I realize they set me up."

"What do you mean set you up?"

"The dummy's mother and her boyfriend must have figured I was going to France to pick up something valuable," Tim explained. "As I remember Marlin said they applied for passports shortly after he and I did. Then, Marlin was ready and waiting when I arrived to pick him up and just before we boarded the plane to leave he demanded I tell him the real reason we were going or he wouldn't get on the plane."

"What did you tell him?" Harvey interrupted.

"A limited version of the truth. Then...on top of that, he only had two beers the night before he robbed me so it all adds up. His mama and her boyfriend told him to steal whatever I came up with the first chance he got then run to England where they would meet up. They robbed me of a fortune so now it's time to put the soldiers-of-fortune on their ass."

"Tim, this is not a good idea! This could get ugly and very expensive. You know those guys don't work cheap."

"It's already ugly! And we are chasing a fortune in gold so I can afford expensive help."

"You sure it was real gold?"

"Of course it's gold! Here see for yourself."

Tim dug in his pocket while Harvey stared with wide eyes. "You got some of it?" he asked in astonishment.

"Yep a few coins, I took some out for a close looking at and left them on the dresser. They were still there after Marlin left so right now they are all I got from the whole trip. Go ahead and take a look," Tim offered laying two of the coins on the table.

"This doesn't look like gold!" Harvey responded after examining the coins. "In fact this doesn't look like much of anything but coarse metal."

"Well it has been buried for over fifty years but its real gold."

"Just how can you be so sure?" Harvey questioned.

"Cause I know what I buried! But just to confirm what I already know, I left a couple of the coins at a shop downtown for an appraisal."

"How many coins you got?" Harvey questioned.

"Eight."

"How many was in the suitcase?"

"Two…three hundred maybe."

"Wow…these coins are heavy. That could add up to a lot of money…if this stuff is really gold," Harvey declared.

"More than enough to track down and punish three thieves."

"You're not really gonna pursue that soldier-of-fortune idea are you?" Harvey asked.

"First thing in the morning!"

"Tim…not tomorrow…give yourself time to think about it. This could get real ugly. Give it a couple of days before you turn your dogs loose!"

"The trail starts growing cold while I'm waiting."

"Come on Tim…wait one day or two anyway! Wait until you get your coin appraisal at least. Then you will be in a stronger position and know your options."

"Now that's one of the few things you have said that makes any sense," Tim chuckled. "I'll spend tomorrow writing down all the important details of the trip then pick up my appraisal before I get down to real business."

"Well you had quite an adventure and you are alive to talk about it, plus you have some mementos so I would just leave it at that if it were me...I don't think those coins are real gold anyway," Harvey replied.

"Of course they are," Tim responded defensively. "You saw the receipt!"

"That receipt didn't say the coins were gold."

"Yeah...well they are gold all right...you'll see when I rub that certified appraisal in your nose," Tim chuckled as he bade Harvey farewell and headed for home.

Feeling somewhat weary, Tim unpacked his suitcase, had a light dinner, took a shower then climbed into his bed. *Nothing's better!* He thought to himself. *Neither fancy hotels nor treasures nor exotic places nor anything else is better than my bed...nothing.* He clicked off the light then quickly slipped into sound sleep. In addition to jet lag...travel is exhausting and Tim had some catching up to do on his rest.

Two days later Tim whiled away most of the morning and afternoon then headed downtown. With a lot of time to kill he stopped at the Vanguard Travel Agency on his way. He was concerned about being charged for Marlin's return airfare then was delighted when Nikki advised that he had purchased an open ticket and still had it. He could use it or exchange it for a ticket to another destination anytime he chose. Having settled that matter, Tim continued on his way and arrived at the coin shop several minutes early. He was immediately shown to a large semi-private booth, seated in a very comfortable wing back chair then offered his choice of refreshment. Tim requested coffee and settled back to wait while admiring the thick carpet, mahogany counters and expensive furnishings. He liked this shop, it had class and the staff made him feel important.

"Mister Morgan?" a slightly overweight and prematurely balding young man asked.

"Yes," Tim responded.

"It's my pleasure to meet you Mister Morgan my name is Justin Winters. I am a state certified rare coin and currency appraiser. I am also a member of the professional organizations listed on my card and displayed on the various plaques on this wall. I performed the appraisal on your coins and will be reviewing it with you." Justin placed a small velvet draped turntable on the desk then sat down. He placed Tim's coins on the turntable then took his notes from a folder. "Now I am certain you realize these are very unusual coins...correct?"

"Why yes, I was pretty sure they were," Tim agreed.

"Well they are not just unusual, they are unique. What makes them unique is the fact that while they look like unusual coins, they are not coins at all. They are tokens."

"Tokens?" Tim questioned.

"Exactly! To be more specific they are French ferryboat tokens," Justin advised. "You see coins are struck while tokens are stamped. Sometime shortly before the beginning of World War II these tokens were commissioned to celebrate the inauguration or anniversary of a ferry line. Commemorative tokens were in fashion then and this was one of the common varieties.

I know they are ferryboat tokens because of the nautical theme and French wording. I could identify the ferryboat company this token was stamped for but not the company that done the stamping. There is not a lot of information kept on tokens but I was able to date these to somewhere between 1936 to 1940. They are made of low grade nickel and lead and were plated with a very thin coating of imitation gold."

"Imitation gold?" Tim questioned.

"That's correct," Justin confirmed. "You can still see traces of it here and here. These tokens were not meant to pay for passage although I suppose they could have been. Their real purpose was to be given as mementos and for advertising. They were meant to be flashy but not to last. So that brings us to value...which I'm afraid is not very much."

"I guess not!" Tim groused. "Imitation gold tourist trinket how much can that be worth?"

"Well...if the gold plating was still in place they would be worth about two dollars each but in this condition about twenty to thirty cents each is their true value...and I honestly don't know where you could sell them," Justin responded.

"What if you had a whole bag of them...say three hundred, what would they be worth?" Tim questioned.

"Same thing. Three hundred of these tokens in this condition at top dollar would get you ninety to a hundred dollars...maybe."

"Would they pay more for these things in England or France?"

"No, in fact they would pay less because there are more of them around. Commemorative tokens have little value and are tough to sell," Justin explained. "I'm really sorry I didn't have better news for you…"

"Hey it's not your fault the stuff is junk! Hell I appreciate the truth," Tim responded.

"Well thank you Mister Morgan, I did enjoy researching your tokens and I stand behind my written appraisal which is right here in this envelope. It is guaranteed to be accurate and provides all the same information I have discussed with you today. Do you have any questions?" Justin asked with a smile.

"No…can't say that I have," Tim responded. "Thank you for getting to the bottom of it young man."

"Well that's what we are here for Mister Morgan, it was my pleasure to be of service to you," Justin concluded as Tim stood and made his way towards the door.

Feeling frustrated when he stepped from the coin shop Tim settled into his car and quietly studied the tokens for a few moments. Another shocking and bitter disappointment. First his treasure is stolen and now he is told the whole thing is completely worthless. "All this for nothing! Absolutely nothing!" he sighed. "Time for a drink…a real strong drink."

With his spirits sagging, Tim started his car and headed for home. A few blocks from his house however, he abruptly changed directions and drove to the library. The librarian was deeply impressed when Tim showed her the ferry tokens and requested her evaluation. She studied the appraisal then assured Tim that the appraiser was both certified and highly respected. His reputation was at stake with every appraisal so Tim could rest assured that his information was correct. She then took a scheduled break from her duties and showed Tim to the employee lounge because she wanted to hear the whole story of his trip to France. She had thought Tim was just talking about going to France all this time and never really expected he would actually do it. She sat close to him with sincere admiration shining from her eyes while he told her the complete story.

"I was thinking about hiring a couple of them soldier-of-fortune fellahs to go track them down," Tim confided as he finished his story.

"Soldiers-of-fortune? Aren't they hired killers?" the librarian questioned with wide eyes.

"Well...they do whatever is necessary to accomplish their mission."

"And you are going to hire them?"

"Well I was thinking about it. I'm not about to just let those crooks get away scott-free," Tim insisted.

"Yes, I know you must feel awful but that's a terrible idea," the librarian responded. "That kind of action can haunt you or have a devastating impact on the rest of your life."

"It sounds fair to me!" Tim replied.

"Maybe that is fair," the librarian agreed, "but it does not provide either of the conclusions that will satisfy you."

"And just what conclusions are those?"

"Vengeance or justice. Vengeance can be yours only if you inflict retribution by your own hand and if you think about it you already have justice."

"I do huh...well I fail to see how?" Tim admitted.

"You said you planned to smuggle the treasure out of France and into England then convert and wire it home in small amounts, right?" she asked.

"Yeah, that was the plan."

"Then I'm sure you will agree that you would have been on pins and needles that whole travel day," the librarian pointed out then continued. "Even after you got to London your stress would have continued because you would have to leave most of the treasure in your hotel room or hiding place while you tried to convert little pieces of it. The fact-of-the-matter is they saved you all that stress PLUS the whopping disappointment of being in a foreign country and hearing that the treasure is worthless. Then what would you do? Bring it home and have it appraised here or just accept what they say and throw it out. Now your crooks are the one's sitting in England with a bag full of worthless tokens...and unless they have some money in the bank or credit cards with a sufficient balance they may have a problem getting back home," she concluded.

"So you think they done me a favor?"

"Exactly...don't you?"

"Hum...guess you could say that...in a way."

"There's your justice," the librarian beamed. "So you don't have to do something horrible like hire professional killers."

"I'd still like to put some heat under them."

"Please don't," the librarian pleaded while leaning closer and putting her hand on Tim's, "for me."

"Well since this stuff isn't gold I guess there is no point in turning the dogs loose...all they could bring back would be flesh," Tim sighed with a chuckle.

"Oh that's terrible!" the librarian exclaimed with a twinkle in her eye. "You're a real devil aren't you?"

"I can be," Tim offered with a big smile.

"Well it's too bad I don't have time to find out just how much of a devil you really are because I have to get back to work," the librarian responded while returning the big smile.

They stood and without saying a word tightly hugged each other but went no further. The librarian had to return to her station and Tim needed to get home. It was time to lower the flag...

*Wilbert Robinson, Attorney at Law*

*The legal communities' favorite lawyer… to avoid*

# Chapter one

"*I'm telling you he sits in front* of his open window every morning with binoculars and watches me walk to the bus stop!" the woman shrieked.

"And that's it?" Wilbert questioned.

"Well that's enough isn't it?"

"Hell no that's not enough!" Wilbert shot back. "You can't sue nobody for that! How do you know he is actually looking only at you? And where's the harm?"

"Where's the harm? That pervert is staring at my behind every morning through binoculars no less and you ask where's the harm?"

"Everybody on the street can see your behind lady and you can't sue people for looking. You got nothing here."

"I thought you were supposed to be a lawyer!"

"I am a lawyer and you are wasting my time so get out of my office."

As soon as the lady left his office Wilbert punched his phone and buzzed his secretary. "Lucy...who gave that crazy woman an appointment?"

"She was a referral from Jennings and Sweeney."

"From Jennings and Sweeney?"

"Yes…remember you agreed to accept their sexual harassment cases."

"Well I meant cases between a client and a company not some wacko broad and her neighbor," Wilbert fumed.

"Well…gee…I dunno sexual harassment is sexual harassment I guess," Lucy offered.

"Well I know! I know I don't want anymore wacko's wasting my time. Call Jennings and Sweeney and tell them to keep their looney's to themselves."

"You'll probably lose their other referrals as well."

"Then find a nice way to tell them we don't want their looney's or prescreen their referrals or hell do something…just don't let every garden variety nut ball waste my time!"

"I'll get right on it boss."

Wilbert leaned back in his chair and looked out the window at the building next door. It was all he could see from his window because his office suite was in the lower rent part of the downtown business district. He sighed and shuffled through the various case files on his desk. "Small change," he muttered, "nothing but small change." Wilbert's impatience was growing. He desperately wanted the wealth and respect that seem to come without effort to most attorneys, yet despite his eight years of law practice he still struggled to get by. In fact, he struggled to become a lawyer in the first place. Wilbert studied the degrees on his wall. It had taken six years just to get his bachelors degree. Not because he could not handle the academics, it was the finances that got in the way forcing him to drop out occasionally and work full time so he could pay tuition fees.

Wilbert had grown up in a working class family the younger of two children. When he was fourteen years old his older sister ran away and married her high school sweetheart who had joined the Army. Two years later his mother left. She simply hopped on the back of some guy's motorcycle and rode off. After that Wilbert was alone most of the time. His father was a construction worker, a macho heavy equipment operator who drank a lot and did not think much of Wilbert's ambition of becoming a lawyer. He made no secret of the fact that he wanted an athletic stud of a son and was disappointed with Wilbert. In fact he considered him to be a wimp. His father's disaffection was not new to Wilbert and did not dissuade him from his goal; in fact it probably reinforced it. Wilbert was short, somewhat overweight and loud. He held his own in most encounters but was lousy at sports and at making friends.

Soon after his mother left, Wilbert started working a part-time job and began a paper route he would continue until he finally graduated from law school. He seldom saw his father and moved out of his father's house only days after he graduated from high school. Wilbert found a cheap, tiny one room apartment he could afford and worked two full-time jobs for just over a year to save money for college tuition and expenses. Then due to his above average high school grade point average and SAT scores, he easily gained admission to the local branch of Indiana University. It was a city college without dormitories or much of a campus. Students lived at home and many, like Wilbert, worked to support themselves while attending school.

Wilbert was eager, worked hard and made very good grades but dropped out occasionally to work and save. To his credit he kept his focus, maintained a high grade point average and completed his bachelor degree in a little less than six years. He was overjoyed when he gained admission to law school but the academics proved to be very tough, demanding many hours of research and study. The long interruptions in his education and the lack of any real support or social life had begun to take its toll. Weary from his long journey Wilbert was soon overwhelmed. For the first time in his life he struggled with the academics but still produced respectable grades his first year.

During his second year of law school, Wilbert survived a horrible marriage to a woman that never stopped being in love with or making love to her long time sweetheart. She saw Wilbert as a meal ticket and relentlessly pushed him to give up his struggle to finish law school and become a teacher. After many fights, the discovered infidelity ended the marriage and Wilbert moved back to his one room apartment more determined than ever to achieve his goal. He could not quit or give up. His goal of becoming a lawyer was all he had…it was all he had held onto since his mother left. It was his ticket to respectability and importance but law school proved to be a most grueling test of his resolve. His grades suffered badly in his second year and it took everything Wilbert could muster during his third year to bring his grade point average just marginally above the required minimum for graduation. But he did it! He reached his goal and qualified for the degree of Doctor of Jurisprudence.

No one was happier or more proud than Wilbert. Only his sister and her kids came to his graduation but to Wilbert that didn't matter, he walked on air across the stage to receive his law degree. He was very close to the bottom of his class but you would have thought Wilbert was in the top ten. It was the happiest day of his life and he partied and celebrated for several days afterwards.

When the euphoria wore off Wilbert, like all new law school graduates, faced the state bar examination. One could not practice law without a license issued by the State Bar Association.

Wilbert was determined to become a real lawyer. He did not struggle through law school to teach or become a law clerk, so he took the bar exam at his first opportunity. The exam was far tougher than Wilbert had expected. He failed badly and had to wait six months before he could take the exam again. The second time Wilbert again failed to pass the bar examination but he did considerably better than his first attempt. For his third attempt Wilbert was ready. He had immersed himself in study, forcing facts from precedent setting cases and various other assorted legal information into his head.

Two failed attempts to pass the bar had truly frightened Wilbert to his core; failure at the finish line was not an option. He went into the exam room for the third time thinking that he had not come this far to wind up on the sideline, he had to become a real lawyer. Wilbert left the exam room feeling confident and a short while later his confidence was validated. He passed the examination and was admitted to the State Bar Association. Wilbert Henry Robinson had done it; he was now officially a state licensed lawyer.

Wilbert knew exactly what he wanted to do. He quickly set up his own law practice as a civil attorney. During his year-long wait to pass the bar he had worked for a personal injury law firm and liked what he saw. The money was in settlements and billable minutes, not in installment payments from thugs or small paychecks from the prosecutor's office. So criminal law was out. Wilbert had no taste for jails or police station interview rooms or gory evidence or even courtrooms for that matter. He much preferred the comfortable boardroom and the negotiated settlement.

In spite of his optimism business trickled in very slowly for the first year and a half and it was only his willingness to take the small change or difficult referrals from other law firms that kept Wilbert afloat. After settling a few cases by becoming loud and demanding Wilbert found his niche. He discovered that by peppering his opposition with intense rapid fire questions, while making extreme accusations or demands through loud bombastic bullying, in most cases would lead to a quick favorable settlement. Wilbert truly enjoyed winning; he liked being the tough guy and soon developed the reputation of being a lawyer to avoid. He prided himself on quick settlements and over the years built a modestly successful law practice.

Occasionally Wilbert got a good paying case but never the really big one that would define his career. Now eight years later he was feeling somewhat frustrated. He had worked hard and wanted to own a

Jaguar and membership in a country club like so many of his undeserving peers. Those spoiled and pampered fraternity boys from fancy schools who marched right through the system to their law degree without interruption. He didn't respect those guys, they were not better lawyers, they simply had connections he did not. And, he was not willing to be a talking head and work for those sons-of-bitches at a big law firm. So he would muddle along…content to be his own man but restless…

"Buzzzzit!" The buzzer on his office phone interrupted Wilbert's thoughts. "Yes" he answered, surprised to learn that he needed a drink of water to clear his throat.

"Your three-thirty is here," Lucy advised.

"Right and that would be…"

"David Blakely, the file is on your desk. Property damaged by a delivery truck…"

"Oh yeah…right, right…got it right here. Send him in," Wilbert responded.

David Blakely was not impressed with the settlement Wilbert had negotiated. "That don't sound like much," he complained.

"You didn't lose much," Wilbert responded.

"I don't see why you didn't just call it a total loss," David declared.

"Cause you would lose out if we did. It cost more to repair your car than it is worth, so we settled for the repair value which is more than twice the salvage value and about equal to the replacement value. Plus you still own the car which you can drive as is or get repaired. If we totaled it out you would get less money and have to buy the car back."

"So $2290 is all I get?" David asked.

"That plus the rental car," Wilbert confirmed.

"How long do I get to keep the rental?"

"They will stop paying three days after you sign this settlement. If you need the car longer then the rental company will bill you direct."

"I don't know...$2290 still don't sound like much."

"Look Mister Blakely, the salvage value on a 1987 Mercury is only about 600 bucks okay, so this is the best deal you are going to get. In addition to repair cost, you are getting a thousand dollars in compensatory damages, attorney fees and a rental car. Now that's about all the juice we can squeeze from this lemon so I suggest you sign the settlement and move on."

"Couldn't we do better in court?"

"No!"

"How come I see all those ads on TV with people getting thousands of dollars from their accidents?"

"Because they were injured Mister Blakely! A delivery truck simply backed into your car while it was parked with no one inside."

"Couldn't we say I was sitting in the car when it was hit and now I got like a delayed back injury or something like that?"

"Sign the settlement Mister Blakely."

"But...I..."

"Sign the damn settlement or get yourself a new lawyer!"

Following David Blakely's departure from his office, Wilbert sighed deeply as he settled back into his chair and studied a framed photograph of himself lounging in a hot tub inside a hotel suite in Las Vegas. He was ready to call it a day. In fact he was ready for a short vacation. He loved Las Vegas and went there often. In Vegas he was a king. It didn't take a whole lot of money to get a first class hotel suite, a first class woman and first class entertainment. He wasn't a true high roller but he gambled big enough to qualify for several perks and the preferred treatment he so loved. Wilbert briefly studied his calendar then punched his phone. "Lucy compress next weeks schedule into the first three days then book me into Vegas, arriving Wednesday night leaving Sunday morning...okay?"

"Sure, I'll get right on it...but you might be on the red-eye Wednesday night," Lucy responded.

"I'll take it, I'll take it!"

"Okay boss."

"Do I have anyone else today?" Wilbert questioned.

"Just one, a Mister Carlson at five thirty," Lucy advised.

"Five thirty?"

"Yeah...this is the guy that is flying in, Nathan Carlson, Senior Vice President of Monroe Pharmaceuticals. He called two days ago for a late appointment."

"Oh yeah...wonder what this is all about?" Wilbert pondered aloud. "Monroe Pharmaceuticals is a big player."

"He refused to provide any particulars so I just booked the appointment," Lucy responded.

"Well we will find out soon enough. In the meantime I'm gonna step out for a minute..."

"Not so fast!" Lucy put in. "I've got several documents that need your signature and it will only take a few minutes."

"It's never just a few minutes but nonetheless lets get it done," Wilbert sighed.

After signing all the prepared documents, Wilbert washed up and changed into a fresh shirt while Lucy dusted the office, made fresh coffee and cleaned their best coffee mugs.

Nathan Carlson was born into a very privileged family. He had been educated in the top Ivy League schools, was smart, soft spoken and very used to getting his way. Now in his early fifties, he had an annual salary of 2.3 million dollars and his annual bonus usually averaged around 4 million. The corporate jet landed smoothly and rolled to a stop only a few feet away from the limousine that patiently waited for his arrival. Nathan was not a happy man. This was not a pleasure or business trip, this was personal, disgustingly so. He climbed into his limo and in less than thirty minutes stepped out, entered the building and went directly to Wilbert Robinson's law office.

Wilbert and Lucy were both at their desks looking their professional best when Nathan Carlson arrived. Lucy greeted Nathan warmly and truly enjoyed their brief and very cordial exchange of words as she escorted him into Wilbert's office.

"Mister Carlson...the pleasure is all mine, how may I help you sir?" Wilbert greeted with his hand extended.

"Thank you for staying late on my behalf Mister Robinson," Nathan Carlson replied. "I have invested significant time and travel for this meeting so I will get straight to the point."

"Fine sir," Wilbert responded. "Where would you be most comfortable?"

"How about the conference table?" Nathan suggested pointing in direction of a small round table in the corner of Wilbert's office.

"Fine sir, fine," Wilbert agreed.

"Would you care for fresh coffee or water or perhaps a soft drink?" Lucy interrupted.

"As a matter of fact a cup of fresh coffee would be wonderful," Nathan Carlson replied as he made himself comfortable at the table. He waited until Lucy served the coffee then took several sips and appeared pleased. "It is amazing how comforting a good cup of coffee can be...and this is very good indeed," Nathan remarked.

"Why thank you sir, that just makes my day," Lucy replied with a big smile as she left the room and closed the door.

Nathan took his time and savored his coffee before leaning slightly forward, looking Wilbert in the eye and spelling out the reason for this meeting. "Mister Robinson I have a difficult situation. I know it is difficult because I have talked with several attorneys and not one of them has offered the slightest hope. So to impress upon you my seriousness, I have a check made out to you for one hundred thousand dollars. This check is just your retainer if you accept the case. If you decide not to accept the case then I have another check for five thousand as payment for this late meeting. Do I have your attention Mister Robinson?"

"Unwavering and undivided!"

"Good! Because I have a problem child Mister Robinson. May I call you Will?"

"Please do...that's a nickname I've always loved," Wilbert lied.

"Okay thanks Will. As I was saying I have a problem child and I know you are not married and do not have any children so I do not expect you to understand a fathers heartbreak. But my first born has always been a rebel. He ran away from boarding school when he was twelve, then ran away from home when he was fourteen and again and again. Finally after he turned seventeen his mother and I told him we had set up a trust fund in his name from which he could draw one thousand dollars per month and we would not look for him if he ran away again. We had hoped that would take away any reason to run and maybe make him think a little but he was gone before sunrise. In the twelve years since we have only seen him on his rare visits home."

"Over time we slowly raised his monthly trust allowance to twenty five hundred. His only access to that account is with his debit card and that has allowed us to track his whereabouts. We know he has lived in this community for about three years and we think he has been hanging around with a motorcycle crowd. At any rate, now he has gotten himself into some serious trouble and that is where you come in Will. Research and intuition has brought me to your office because you appear to be the exact lawyer we need. I know you are not a criminal lawyer but you have a rare earned reputation as being the one lawyer everyone in this local legal environment prefers to avoid. You find a way to close cases, get things done and that is precisely what we need. You see my son, Brian Carlson, has been arrested and charged with murder. He swears he is innocent and I believe him. I know my son! I know he could not shoot someone in cold blood. I am not asking you to represent my son Will, I am asking you to free him. My son cannot...will not go to prison and there is even some talk of the death penalty. This cannot happen Will...it simply cannot happen. Free my son...free Brian and I will have another check for you in the amount of two hundred and fifty thousand dollars. That is my situation Will...that is how you can help. Take my son's case...return him to us a free man..." Nathan's voice trailed off as his eyes began to moisten.

"Well...as you already know Mister Carlson, I am not a criminal lawyer," Wilbert advised. "But because I am so moved by your passion and flattered by your faith in me, I accept your son as my client and promise to do everything in my power to free him sir and I sincerely mean that."

"Thank you Will and God bless. I know it is a difficult case and you are right, I do have great faith that you are the attorney that will find a way to settle this mess and free Brian. Here is your retainer. I have released his current attorney but here is a general information file on the case and my contact information. Please feel free to contact me at any time but only with pertinent information I really need to know. If I am not available you may feel free to speak with my personal assistant, Madeline, about any details of this case or if you incur any expenses. Is there anything else you will need?"

"No sir not at the moment," Wilbert assured. "I will make my initial assessment tomorrow, forward it to you and get moving from there."

"Very good. Thank you again Will for accepting the case without delay or first asking to review the file. That strengthens my faith and I look forward to handing you that check for a quarter of a million," Nathan Carlson concluded with a relieved look in his eyes and wearing a faint smile.

"And I absolutely look forward to accepting your check Mister Carlson," Wilbert replied as he and Nathan Carlson shook hands before Wilbert walked his rich and important client down to his waiting limousine.

# Chapter two

**W**ilbert Robinson *returned to his office* and stared at the check. It was a cashier's check made out to him for one hundred thousand dollars. Wilbert seldom got a retainer and never had his fees or share of settlements approached anything close to this. He had never seen a check this big made out solely to him and suddenly here it was…his…all his no matter what. After several euphoric moments he shared the good news with Lucy then treated both of them to dinner at one of the city's finest restaurants.

"Can you believe one hundred grand just walks in off the street and jumps right into my wallet?" Wilbert grinned over dinner.

"Have you looked at the file?" Lucy questioned.

"Hell no…that can wait until tomorrow. Tonight I'm enjoying my good fortune."

"Aren't you even a little curious about why you were chosen for a criminal case and what the case is all about?" Lucy inquired.

"Not in the slightest," Wilbert shrugged. "I got a hundred grand in my pocket plus I'm not a criminal lawyer and Carlson knew it but picked me anyway. So this case obviously has some angles. All I got to do is find an angle that springs the kid and there is an even bigger check waiting when I do! This is the big time baby...the one we been waiting for and there is no way I'm gonna blow it!"

"It's a criminal case you haven't even looked at!" Lucy protested. "How can you be so confident you will win?"

"Because I'm Wilbert Robinson, Attorney at Law and I really need the fucking money...that's how! As soon as I close this case I'm going right out and buy myself a brand new Jaguar. All of my adult life I've been drooling over a Jag...now I'm going to own a brand new one."

Lucy shook her head "I don't know about you sometimes...but I hope you are right. You know this is about the most tender and delicious steak I've ever eaten."

"Yeah it is good huh? Well enjoy, eat up and drink all the wine you want," Wilbert offered. "Tonight we party; tomorrow we work our asses off...oh and cancel my trip to Vegas."

Early the next morning Wilbert briefly examined Brian Carlson's case file then took it directly to the law firm of Fisher and Logan. He left the file and a check for fifteen hundred dollars as payment for an assessment and recommended course of action for the case. As soon as he returned to his office Lucy advised that Fisher and Logan had called and asked if he could return to their office for a very brief meeting regarding the Carlson file.

"What? Right now...man those guys are fast operators," Wilbert responded.

"I can't believe you took that file to Fisher and Logan," Lucy remarked. "They are close to if not the top criminal lawyers in the state and I know their rates are completely off the chart."

"We have a high profile client with deep pockets so we will spare no expense in getting our client exactly what he wants, so we can reach even deeper into his pocket, okay? That is why I took the file to Fisher and Logan and that is why I'm hustling my butt right back over there. Hold the calls and juggle the schedule, I'll be right back," Wilbert responded as he hurried out the door.

Jeffery Logan and Wilbert Robinson first met in a preparatory class for the state bar examination. It was Jeffery's first attempt and Wilbert's third. By default they were assigned as study partners and neither thought it was a good idea. They did not care much for each other and spent their study time peppering each other with legal questions. Their exchanges became somewhat heated at times but neither could really stump the other. After taking the bar exam both admitted that their aggressive back and forth had probably helped them so they shook hands and parted as friends.

Over the years they greeted each other on the rare occasions when their paths crossed, and a time or two they stopped and chatted for a while but the two attorneys lived in very different worlds. Jeffery was very aware of Wilbert's reputation in the legal world but he was glad to see him anyway.

"Wilbert it's good to see you, how have you been?"

"Good Jeffery, real good and you?" Wilbert responded.

"Great, just great, come on in and have a seat. Wish I had known it was the Carlson file you dropped off I could have saved you a trip."

"You mean you are familiar with the case?" Wilbert questioned.

"We are the law firm old man Carlson just dropped; in fact we prepared this very information file!"

"Well dip me in monkey shit!" Wilbert responded in stunned disbelief.

"Exactly!" Jeffery agreed. "We were just as surprised as you. Now I am even more surprised because our firm has been replaced by you! No offense Wilbert, but you don't even practice criminal law do you?"

"I do now!"

"Well you are up to your ass in alligators on this one," Jeffery warned.

"How bad can it be?" Wilbert questioned.

"How bad? Wilbert, your client Brian Carlson is charged with premeditated murder in the first degree. The prosecutor has the murder weapon which just happens to belong to Brian. They also have witnesses to Brian fighting with then promising to kill the victim. Brian however insists he is innocent and will not budge, not even for what I think was the best plea deal we have ever achieved. The Carlson's will only accept one result and we cannot promise that so now the ball is in your court."

"Give me a quick run down on the chronology so I can get a feel for the fight," Wilbert requested.

"I'll do you one better and give you the complete overview...your machine running?" Jeffery asked.

"Yep...sure is."

Jeffery leaned back in his chair, "Brian Carlson is an auto painter by trade. He finished Madison Tech a couple of years ago and his specialty is custom work. He is a freelancer but frequently worked for a body shop owner named Charles Grant. Now just for reference, Charles Grant stood about 6'4" and weighed well over 300 pounds. He had long unkempt hair and a big bushy beard, so it's no mystery that he was nicknamed and called "Bear" by nearly everyone. This whole thing revolves around a dispute between these two men, Brian and Bear."

"On the night of the murder Brian claims he was hanging out at the Lucky Seven Bar when Bear showed up. As he prepared to leave, around eleven o'clock, he approached Bear about some money he was owed. They had a serious disagreement which spilled over into a fight that got them kicked out of the bar. The fight continued outside with Bear getting the best of it then getting on his bike and riding off. Several minutes later an injured and badly beaten Brian got to his feet and returned to the bar thinking Bear had gone back in. Once back inside he loudly threatened to kill the Bear and demanded to know where he was hiding, so the bouncer threw him out for the second time."

"At 7:37 the following morning a 911 call was placed by an employee of the Newride Body Shop. The owner of the shop, Charles Grant aka the Bear, was found dead, lying on the floor with three bullet holes in his forehead. The police tracked the Bear's last movements back to the Lucky Seven Bar, learned of the fight then interviewed Brian. They searched his house and came up empty then searched his motorcycle and found his 9mm pistol in the saddlebags. The pistol proved to be the murder weapon so Brian was indicted and formally charged with premeditated murder. Brian claims he was in no shape to ride his bike after the fight and the bouncer at the bar threw him into a cab which took him home. Once there his neighbor helped him into his house, patched him up and then went down to the Lucky Seven and got his bike. Now get this, his neighbor was apparently a biker chick because she got killed in an accident about two weeks after his arrest."

"So there went his alibi," Wilbert interrupted.

"I don't think she would have done him much good anyway," Jeffery responded. "There has been a spike in murders and the mayor and prosecutor are anxious to show they are tough. Because the murder happened a considerable time after the fight, they are saying Brian thought about it then planned and committed the act. That is premeditated murder and they are seeking the death penalty. The first lawyers on this case were a bunch of corporate big shots recommended by Monroe Pharmaceuticals. They were in way over their heads on this one. The best they could do was a plea bargain of thirty to life. From their perspective, negotiating away the death penalty provided a successful conclusion to the case and of course they were promptly fired by old man Carlson."

"We came on board, put our best brains to work then took the position of self defense. First we dispensed with the robbery charges. It was believed that Bear was also robbed of drugs and money so in addition to murder, robbery charges were also filed against Brian. But there was no evidence to support robbery charges so they were dropped. Next, using self defense we backed down the prosecutor and negotiated a plea of twenty years flat for second degree. From the death penalty down to ten years with good time and Brian is home free. I was impressed with the deal; it was a great piece of legal work. When I phoned Mister Carlson and advised him of our successful negotiations, he asked me to overnight a general information file of the case and a copy of the plea bargain. The next day he phoned me to say that the plea was unacceptable, his son was innocent and they would accept nothing less than acquittal. I reminded him of the prosecutions strong case. They have motive, witnesses to the threat and the murder weapon. The prosecutor also has a real need for convictions in the face of rising crime and if we go to trial the death penalty will be on the table. Given that, we do not feel we can produce a better result under the circumstances. I was trying to coax him to our position but Carlson wasn't having any of it. He told me we were removed from the case and to submit my final bill to Madeline then just like that the line went dead. And that was that until you showed up with our information file."

"Did you guys look into the kids alibi? Track down the cab? That sort of thing?" Wilbert asked.

"Come on Wilbert, there wasn't much alibi to look into. Sure we could hunt down the cab if there was one but who is there to say he didn't just go for a ride. Or take another cab and come right back and get his bike? See what I mean? The prosecutor is not joking around. They need blood and going for the death penalty gets them much needed positive press and one hell of a lot of points if they win the case. Brian has no verifiable alibi and no plausible defense. If he didn't do it then who used his gun and promptly returned it? See what I mean Wilbert? When you stick to the cold hard facts your boy doesn't have a snowball's chance in hell of beating this in court."

"So you guys just threw in the towel on the kid huh?" Wilbert questioned.

"He is not a kid Wilbert. He is 30 years old and we absolutely gave him and his family our very best. But our best was not good enough for the Carlson family so now you are next on their chopping block. Good luck pal...and I sincerely mean that. You are going to need all the luck you can get," Jeffery concluded.

"Yeah, well thanks for the briefing Jeffery, but I'll tell you what, I'm going to win this case. One way or another I'm going to win this case and you are going to buy me a steak dinner at Elmo's when I do!"

"You win this case Wilbert and I will buy you a steak at Elmo's every night for a week," Jeffery chuckled as he and Wilbert shook hands.

"I'm going to win and I'm going to hold you to that," Wilbert promised as he made his exit from the plush office suite of Fisher and Logan.

Late that evening Wilbert sat at home and listened to the tape of Jeffery Logan for the second time. He wasn't even close to feeling satisfied that he had gotten the best legal advice for his client. It did not seem that either legal firm gave any consideration to the possibility of innocence. What were the red flags? He knew they were there but he could not see them so he went to bed anxious.

The next morning Wilbert made several phone calls before leaving home. He had a light breakfast then on his way to work he delivered a check for one thousand dollars and the Carlson case file to the home office of retired judge and noted defense lawyer, Sidney Wyckoff. By the time Wilbert arrived at his office he felt considerably better and worked hard trying to clear his desk. He made good progress over that day and throughout most of the next until Sidney Wyckoff's assistant called.

"Judge Wyckoff will be available to confer with you regarding the Carlson case file at 4:30 this afternoon or if that is not convenient the judge will also be available at 6:30 tomorrow morning," Lucy advised through the intercom.

"I'll take 4:30," Wilbert responded. "It's at least a twenty minute drive so make sure I'm out of here on time."

"Well with the schedule the way it is that's really pushing it!" Lucy complained.

"So push it and get me out of here on time!"

Wilbert arrived at Sidney Wyckoff's home and was again impressed. It was a beautiful estate located in the near suburbs. A winding tree lined drive lead to a stately Mediterranean style mansion surrounded by rolling green lawns and well tended gardens. *I'm going to have a spread like this real soon*, Wilbert promised himself as he parked his car and headed toward the office entrance at the side of the house. Before reaching the door Wilbert was pleasantly surprised to see Judge Wyckoff waving to him from the patio in back of the house. Wilbert felt privileged. It was a beautiful afternoon and he was about to join one of the state's most renowned legal minds on the patio of his magnificent home. "Judge Wyckoff the pleasure is all mine sir," Wilbert admitted as he approached the patio.

"And mine young man and mine...please come make yourself comfortable," the judge chuckled. "Jenny come see to our guest please."

A maid delivered a glass of water and asked if there was anything else Wilbert desired.

"No, no thank you the water is fine," Wilbert responded.

"How about a cigar or some wine or brandy?" the judge asked.

"Maybe some fresh pastries or lemonade?" the maid added.

"No...no I'm fine really. Thank you very much but I am fine," Wilbert assured with a big smile.

"Good...good now let's began," Judge Wyckoff suggested.

"Do you mind if I have my machine running?" Wilbert asked.

"Now Mister Robinson...I am certain you realize that I would be somewhat insulted if you did not," the judge chuckled. "Let me assure you that I have personally reviewed your case," he continued then briefly thumbed through the Carlson case file before launching into a long rambling lecture on the inner workings of the judicial system.

Exactly thirty-eight minutes later Judge Wyckoff turned his attention to the Carlson murder case. He lit a fresh cigar, blew a large plum of smoke in the air then tossed the Carlson case file to Wilbert. "That is a text book plea bargain case, pure and simple!" he declared then went on to lecture for another fourteen minutes on the pitfalls of death penalty cases. "First and foremost you had to protect your name and professional reputation. Nobody wants to be represented by a lawyer that allows his clients to be executed. Plea bargain at any cost. Never risk taking a death penalty case to trial. Be smart! Be a lawyer not a social worker. Represent your client but know that a lot more guilty people are charged with crimes than innocent ones. Don't sacrifice your career by leading an exhausting crusade trying to save a dedicated loser. Jury verdicts cannot be predicted, plea bargain…plea bargain…plea bargain or get removed from the case. Just don't let your name and reputation get dragged through the slime of execution," Judge Wyckoff continued to drone on until a very attractive young lady appeared and announced that it was time for the judge to take his medication and prepare for dinner.

Wilbert was greatly relieved by the young ladies interruption; he had given up hope that the judge would be of any help and had spaced out most of his lecture. Wilbert was now looking for a way out and this was it.

"But I have more yet to share with my client here," Judge Wyckoff protested to his granddaughter. "It is my legal duty to properly and completely answer his inquiry…"

"Oh but you have sir, oh but you have!" Wilbert put in, "And quite eloquently too sir. I have it all right here on tape. Thank you so much for being so generous with your time and allowing me this visit. I shall always remember it," he declared while rising to his feet.

"You are certain I have satisfied all of your concerns regarding the due process of this particular case?" Judge Wyckoff sternly questioned.

"Yes sir, absolutely," Wilbert responded.

"Well then..." the judge reluctantly concluded. "You do have many of my basic conclusions on tape and...I see you are a quick study. The foundations I have just given you together with your reputation as a legal bulldog will serve you well. It is my expectation that you will become very successful over the coming years. This has been a most enjoyable afternoon and I am very glad we had the pleasure of chatting young man."

"Likewise sir, likewise," Wilbert replied feeling relieved but disappointed as he shook hands with the judge, smiled at the young lady then quickly made his way to his car.

# Chapter three

**W**ilbert *intended to return* to his office following his meeting with Sidney Wyckoff but changed his mind and drove home. He was truly in a funk and felt let down. He had paid $2500 for top tier legal advice and was struggling to find some worth or value for his money. He did not often drink liquor but as soon as Wilbert arrived at his condo he poured himself a double shot of scotch and settled into his recliner. "Twenty five hundred to hear pad and protect!" he spoke aloud to the empty room. "Pad your wallet while you protect your ass…guess that's what criminal law is all about. The client comes second, your wallet and ass comes first." Wilbert got up and paced around the room then briefly re-played parts of Judge Wyckoff's lecture. None of it made real sense to him and he was starting to feel a little woozy from the scotch so he walked two blocks to a café and had dinner.

On his return walk home Wilbert's focus began to sharpen. Slowly he started to understand why those big shot lawyers where not willing to take risks. The fees from any one case, no matter how large was not worth their reputation. That is why Nathan Carlson turned to him. As a civil lawyer he had no criminal reputation to protect. He was known for doing what it takes to win cases and being willing to gamble, so Carlson figured that for enough money he would take the risk...and find a way to win the case. "And the son-of-bitch is dead right!" Wilbert concluded aloud as he stepped back inside his condo.

Wilbert returned to his recliner and unfinished drink with a completely different attitude. "Carlson is not paying me big bucks for a freaking plea bargain and he is not paying me to cop out!" Wilbert spoke aloud. "He is paying me to beat the rap and spring his son. Now...let's see what are the options? Hum...money won't work; those corporate lawyers would have bought this whole thing off long ago if that were the case. Same for contaminating or eliminating the evidence...hum. We could go to trial and maybe slide a few bucks to a juror. Hum...all that assumes the kid is guilty. I need to have a talk with Brian Carlson. Then I need to forget all that fancy top tier shit about pad and protect and get down and dirty...fight this case from the bottom up. Yeah, I need to put together a legal team of street fighters and go after it."

Wilbert's enthusiasm soared. He hopped up fixed another drink and spent several minutes wandering around his condo fantasying about the fabulous legal team he was going to put together, before realizing that he really had no idea of where to begin a criminal case. "Hum..." he pondered aloud, "think I better start with a co-counsel, yeah a criminal trial attorney. A tough street smart fighter...somebody like...hum like...well I don't know," Wilbert chuckled. "But, I'll know tomorrow," he promised as he put the liquor away and headed for his bed.

Bright and early the next morning Wilbert strode into his office with a noticeable spring in his step. He knew exactly who he needed as co-counsel. He had thought about it on the drive to work and it soon became obvious. Over the years he had referred all criminal cases that came his way to about five different attorneys. Three of those attorneys were not partners but shared clerical help, machines and supplies in a cooperative office arrangement. All three were very competent attorneys but one in particular stood out. She was a stout, no-nonsense, middle-aged woman named Sylvia Maples. She had won more than her share of criminal cases and a few years back won a high profile murder case. Yet in spite of her legal abilities she remained a lower tier defense lawyer and that Wilbert concluded should make her hungry enough to be his perfect co-counsel.

"Get Sylvia Maples on the phone and tell her we need to schedule an urgent meeting today! The earlier the better...I repeat the need to meet today is urgent!" he ordered as soon as Lucy stepped into the office.

"Yes sir, just let me make coffee first," Lucy responded.

"No, coffee second call first," Wilbert instructed.

"Yes sir," Lucy replied then sorted through her rolodex. After making the call, Lucy reported that Sylvia Maples had wanted to know the topic of the meeting and was not pleased when Lucy did not know. Attorney

Maples was due to be in court until late afternoon and had early evening commitments but promised to stop for a brief chat after leaving court.

Wilbert was anxious because now that he had decided on Sylvia as co-counsel he wanted her on the job right away. He thought about his offer and decided to raise it, then made a brief trip to the bank before trying to concentrate on business as usual while waiting.

Sylvia Maples arrived late in the afternoon. She was pleasant but in a hurry and grateful that Lucy showed her right in.

"Sylvia! Thank you for coming by on such short notice," Wilbert beamed.

"Wilbert, this had better be good!" Sylvia responded as she took a seat, ignoring Wilbert's outstretched hand.

"It's better than good, it is great," Wilbert promised. "Sylvia I have been retained to represent a very upscale defendant charged with murder..."

"You? Representing a murder suspect? Since when did you start practicing criminal law?" Sylvia questioned.

"Only very recently and while I really have not dug into the case I feel it is one that I can win..."

"Win? How are you going to win a criminal case, especially murder? And you don't have any trial experience Wilbert?"

"That's where you come in. I need to hire you as co-counsel for this case and..."

"Ha-ha-ha...have you lost your mind?" Sylvia roared. "Co-counsel to you on a murder case? I know you are not sitting there thinking that I have the time, interest or the slightest bit of desire to tutor you in criminal law while trying to win a…"

"The job pays twenty five thousand cash retainer plus fifty thousand cash if we win the case," Wilbert interrupted.

"Well then where is my desk and where is the case file?" Sylvia questioned.

"I'll take that as a yes then, right?" Wilbert asked.

"You did say twenty five thousand cash retainer?"

"Got a cashier's check right here with your name on it," Wilbert responded as he handed Sylvia the check.

"Now we are talking…and another fifty thousand when we win the case right?" Sylvia asked.

"Right…a fifty thousand dollar cashier's check. I got an agreement right here for us to sign…here look it over."

"All righty then and yes that is a yes," Sylvia beamed. "I always did like you Mister Little Man. Now let me see that agreement then the case file so we can get to work."

It only took about two minutes for Sylvia to discover that Wilbert knew nothing about the case and had taken none of the required action. She set up shop on his conference table then mapped out the required activity for her and Wilbert. Then the next day she filed the necessary briefs and motions establishing the Robinson Law Firm as the attorney of record for the defendant and arranged for the two of them to meet and interview their client. Later that day she huddled with Wilbert to review the evidence file and formal indictment then prepare questions for their client.

Wilbert was impressed with Sylvia but none to enthusiastic about the realities of criminal law. He read through the indictment and evidence file and began to wonder if his client was really innocent. The evidence against him was very compelling but Sylvia did not seem discouraged in the least. "That's what the state has to say," she declared. "Now we need to hear what our client has to say. I'll meet you at the main entrance of the jail tomorrow at 2:30," she advised then hurried off to tend to other business.

The next day Sylvia found it amusing that Wilbert tried to hide his discomfort with being in jail. He stuck close to her and looked around in amazement until they reached the interview room. They took their seats in a small cubicle like room with a desktop and two straight back chairs on one side. It had a low partition down the middle and one straight back chair on the other side.

After a few minutes Brian Carlson entered the room and took his seat on the opposite side of the desk.

"I am Wilbert Robinson and that is Sylvia Maples. We are your new defense attorneys," Wilbert advised.

"I'm not interested in no stinking plea bargains!" Brian snapped.

"Neither are we!" Wilbert shot back.

"I don't give a shit how sweet the deal is man cause I'm innocent...hey wait a minute! Did you say you weren't interested in a plea bargain?"

"That's exactly what I said," Wilbert confirmed. "We are not being paid to plea bargain, we are being paid to settle this mess and get your ass out of jail."

"Whoa! Are you serious man? I mean like who are you guys? Did my father hire you?" Brian questioned in disbelief.

"Yes we are serious and yes your father hired us to defend you, so we are going to need your help," Wilbert advised.

"Well yeah of course...I mean like this is so weird...you're not just trying to butter me up for a plea bargain down the road?" Brian asked.

"I promise you no plea bargain! There is no money for us in a plea bargain. We are getting paid to find a way to beat this rap and with your help that is exactly what we are going to do! Do you understand? No plea bargain, no prison, nothing less than your freedom is our goal! Now are you going to help us?" Wilbert demanded.

"Anything you want. Anything I can do just name it!" Brian responded.

"Okay I want you to tell us everything about the night that Bear was killed. Take your time and tell us everything, every detail you can remember..." Wilbert instructed.

"And don't get annoyed if we stop you with questions. It is very important that we clearly understand everything you tell us," Sylvia added.

"Okay gotcha," Brian confirmed then began. "Well...man this is starting to feel real good, like I finally got somebody really on my side you know? I've seen a bunch of lawyers man...and every one of them has been wearing a three thousand dollar suit and shoving a pen and stack of legal papers in my face trying to get me to sign their great plea bargain deal. Now here you guys come...real people...willing to actually believe to me...wow that feels pretty damn good man. What was your name again?" Brian asked.

"I'm Wilbert Robinson and that is Sylvia Maples," Wilbert responded.

"Both attorneys?" Brian questioned.

"Correct!" Wilbert confirmed.

"All right Attorneys Robinson and Maples, you are my people so I'll tell you everything I know straight out honest. Man this feels good, finally! Okay...the night Bear got hit I was hanging out at the Lucky Seven Bar...well first I should tell you I am a painter by trade..."

"What kind of painter?" Sylvia asked.

"A professional automotive painter," Brian responded, "went to school and got my papers and everything. I work on motorcycles and helmets mostly but occasionally I paint cars too. That's why Bear owed me money cause I had painted some cars for him. I worked off and on at a lot of shops painting cars or bikes and never had no problem getting paid by anyone until Bear started selling coke. I mean like he had been doing it all along, so doing it wasn't a problem but selling it was. He started selling to pay for his own habit and didn't want to pay me until he first made a buy then a profit. Hey that's bullshit man and I told him so. He got paid when his customers picked up their cars so he could pay me. Not buy coke with my pay then try to sell enough to get my money back before it is all snorted up."

"So what happen on the night of the murder?" Wilbert questioned.

"Like I said I was hanging out, shooting pool and drinking at the Lucky Seven when Bear came in. I had already asked him for my money two or three times and it was due several days ago so I waited for him to come over and say something about it. But he didn't and after he had a couple beers I heard him bragging to the bartender about becoming master of the key before the night was over…"

"What's master of the key?" Wilbert questioned.

"Means he was gonna buy a kilo of cocaine and was busy taking orders," Brian explained then continued. "I knew that meant he had a lot of cash on him including my eight hundred bucks so I waited until I was about ready to leave before I went over and asked when he planned to pay me my money. He got all belligerent and nasty…told me he would pay me whenever he fucking felt like it and I could get the hell outta his face. I know it wasn't a good idea now, but at the time I was a little drunk and a whole lot pissed off, so I hauled off and punched ole Bear right in his big fat mouth. He fought back and we both got booted out the back door of the bar. I figured that the fight was over you know, and started walking toward the front where my bike was parked when Bear totally blindsided me with a sucker punch and I went down. Soon as I hit the ground he started stomping and kicking me, messed me up pretty bad before he stopped and went around front. After a while I got to my feet and went around front then back into the bar. I was mad as hell and I wanted Bear to know he was dead and I meant it. His fucking ass was dead!"

"You threatened to kill him?" Sylvia asked.

"No I said he was dead, that means his ass is dead to me. Even if he did pay me my money and apologize I still would not work for him, bail his ass out when he or one of his guys has screwed up a paint job or even speak to him. His ass is dead to me and dead is forever!"

"Then what happened?" Wilbert prompted.

"The bouncer dude pushed me out of the bar. My ankle was really messed up and my side hurt like hell not to mention my broken jaw, so I was in no shape to stand my ground or ride my bike home. I wanted to...but the bouncer drug me down the street a short distance then through me into a cab."

"Did you say anything to the bouncer while he was dragging you down the street?" Sylvia inquired.

"Hell yes...I called him every name in the book and I did threaten to kill his ass!" Brian recalled.

"Do you know what company the cab was from? Like Yellow Cab or Checker?" Wilbert questioned.

"No man...I was drunk and hurting."

"How about the color? Do you remember the color of the cab?" Sylvia asked.

"Naw...all I remember is that it was a car and it had a meter."

"Okay then what happened?" Wilbert asked.

"Well when I got home Katie, uh that's my neighbor from across the street...well, least she was anyway. Uh...she came and helped me get in the house. Then she patched me up some and fixed me a couple of drinks. After a while she went down to the Lucky Seven and got my bike, then she gave me some sleeping pills and that's about all I remember. The next day the cops showed up and arrested me for murder," Brian concluded.

"Why did you have a gun in the saddlebag of your motorcycle?" Sylvia asked.

"Why? Well...uh a few years back I spent a lot of money on those saddlebags. They came from Italy and were special made. When I first got them I noticed a holster inside made to hold a pistol. Then a little while later I was at a gun show and found a 9mm Glock that I really liked so I bought it, put it inside the bag and it's been there ever since," Brian explained.

"Have you ever held a license for the gun?" Sylvia inquired.

"Naw, never messed with no license or nothing," Brian scoffed.

"Have you ever used the gun?"

"Sure but just target shooting out in the country sometimes."

"Does anyone know that you have a gun in your saddlebag?" she questioned.

"Well...yeah...a couple of people do," Brian confessed.

"You threatened to kill the bouncer while he was dragging you to the cab; did you threaten to kill him with your gun?" Sylvia quizzed.

"Uh...yeah I might have...I was mad as hell!"

"Do you have any idea who could have used your gun then put it back into your saddlebags," Sylvia pressed.

"I wish I did! I'd fuck em up...that's for sure!" Brian responded.

"Okay...let's talk about your neighbor friend, Katie McDougal," Sylvia suggested. "You said she helped you into your house, correct?"

"Yeah man, she lived across the street and told me she seen the cab and wondered what had happened cause I always ride my bike. So she helped me get inside the house and get patched up and everything."

"You said she went to the Lucky Seven and picked up your motorcycle...how did she get there? Did she take a cab or did someone give her a ride?" Sylvia asked.

"Uh...I really don't know man, she told me she was going to get my bike and left. I think she went back to her place."

"Was there someone at Katie's house that could have given her a ride?" Sylvia questioned.

"Well yeah...I mean like Katie lived with her aunt and she had a car but I don't think she would have gotten out of bed. That old broad didn't like to be bothered much."

"Do you remember about what time Katie left to go get your motorcycle and about what time she got back?" Sylvia quizzed.

"I don't know man, I was pretty fuzzy. I can't remember much about the time," Brian admitted.

"Okay...I noticed a medical release form in your file; did you receive any medical treatment after your arrest?" Sylvia inquired.

"Uh yeah man, the cops took me to the hospital jail before they put me in here," Brian advised.

"How are you doing now?" Sylvia asked.

"Oh hey I'm fine...but I could use a few more of them painkillers though," Brian replied with a grin.

"That's all I have for now," Sylvia advised Wilbert.

"Do you know if your neighbor gave a statement to the police?" Wilbert asked.

"Naw I don't," Brian responded.

"Was she around when you were arrested?" he quizzed.

"I don't think so but to be real honest I really don't know," Brian admitted.

"Okay Brian Attorney Maples and I have work to do but we will stay in touch with you and together we will beat this thing. If you remember anything else no matter how small or insignificant it seems send for us…okay?" Wilbert concluded.

Brian blinked hard, fighting back the tears that filled his eyes. "Far out man! Like I said, I'm starting to feel pretty good about this thing for the first time since I got arrested. Attorneys Robinson and Maples you are my people…on my side. You have let me taste a little bit of hope…thanks man…you guys are special."

Wilbert and Sylvia shook hands with Brian Carlson, watched him exit the cubicle then left the jail feeling a lot closer to their client.

*Chapter four*

*The following morning* Wilbert was reviewing his notes regarding Brian Carlson when Sylvia Maples arrived for their scheduled meeting. "I listened to our interview with Brian last night and you know what, I believe he is innocent. What do you think?" she asked.

"Hum...I really hadn't thought about it," Wilbert admitted.

"Ha-ha, of course not," Sylvia chuckled. "Regardless I think we have a real chance at this one."

"How so?"

"Our defense is our client's innocence and his alibi basically revolves around two people, his deceased neighbor and that bouncer at the Lucky Seven Bar. If we can verify Brian's alibi we are home free," Sylvia explained.

"That sounds like a tough hill to climb," Wilbert complained. "I haven't seen any statement from a bouncer. Do we even know his name? If we are going to prove our guy is innocent we..."

"We don't have to prove innocence Wilbert!" Sylvia interrupted.

"Of course...the burden of proof is on the prosecution," Wilbert agreed. "But how do we bust their chops?"

"By reasonable doubt that's how. Right now we have a client with an alibi that can be verified. The more we can verify, the more reasonable doubt. Since the burden of proof is on the prosecution the standard defense in this situation would be to go to court and attempt to pick the prosecutor's case apart. But I think we can blow the prosecution away if we present an aggressive defense based on reasonable doubt. Juries must find a defendant guilty beyond a reasonable doubt and therein lies our victory," Sylvia beamed.

"What do we need to do?" Wilbert asked with rising spirits.

"Investigate the key points of Brian's alibi. Find the cab, find the bouncer, find as much as possible," Sylvia instructed.

"Not a problem, not a problem at all. I got the perfect man for that job."

"And just whom would that be?"

"A very good private investigator that I have used before, he is intense, detailed and very reasonable, name's Bradley Breedlove," Wilbert advised.

"Bradley Breedlove!　Oh my dear lord...I am certainly earning my money on this case. No offense Wilbert, but Bradley is even more annoying than you are. You are just real annoying when trying to settle a case. Bradley is completely annoying all the time. But like you said he is a good investigator, probably annoys people into telling the truth. And you are the lead attorney so you call the shots. I'll just have to repair my wounded soul somewhere on a beach after we win this case. Otherwise time is of the essence. We will need to notify the prosecution if we have to re-visit discovery."

"Discovery? You mean advise the enemy?" Wilbert questioned.

"Exactly! If we uncover any new evidence we have to share it with the prosecutor somewhat in advance of the actual trial," Sylvia confirmed. "I'll make a list of the factors and key points I feel need investigated and get it to you before the day is over. Then I'll wait to hear from you."

"Excellent! I'll get Bradley started right away. How long before we go to trial?"

"Little less than three months right now unless we ask for more time."

"I don't want more time I'm all for moving quickly," Wilbert admitted. "The sooner Brian goes free the sooner we get the big bucks."

"I want what you want!" Sylvia agreed then bid Wilbert farewell and hurried off to catch up with her work day.

Lucy contacted Bradley Breedlove and scheduled a 5:15 appointment. She was grateful that her boss had requested the late after hour's appointment because she hoped to be long gone before Bradley Breedlove arrived. Later that day Lucy was not happy when Wilbert reminded her that she had promised an elderly client that she would stay a little late so the old lady could pick up her settlement check.

"Oh shoot!" Lucy fumed. "I forgot all about Misses Gaynor...I sure hopes she gets here before Bradley."

As five o'clock drew near Lucy was greatly relieved when the old lady stepped through the door. After exchanging pleasantries Lucy hurried into Wilbert's office to get Misses Gaynor's file and check. She became annoyed when Wilbert insisted on checking a small detail in the file and was pushing him to hurry when her blood pressure instantly shot up.

Bradley Breedlove's voice boomed through the open door. "Well how are you doing mother, I'm Bradley Breedlove, Private I and eye…just like it says on my card. See look right here; see Bradley Breedlove Private I and eye. That's a capital I for investigator and that human eye in the background there…you see it right there? That means I'm watching…Bradley's watching. Bradley Breedlove, Private I and eye that's me…uh-huh. You go ahead and keep that card mother, never know when you might need Bradley Breedlove…"

Lucy grabbed the file and check then rushed out of Wilbert's office, "Uh Mister Breedlove, Mister Ro…" she began.

"Well if it isn't the charming Miss Lucy, I'm Bradley Breedlove, Private I and eye. I remember you and I'll bet you remember me too. Bradley Breedlove Private I and eye…just like it says on my card here. Take a look; you see the capital I…"

"I know Bradley I know," Lucy interrupted. "Mister Robinson will see you now this way please."

"You looking mighty fine these days Miss Lucy, yes sir. You know Bradley Breedlove doesn't have a first lady right now…and the way you looking you could become a candidate. I know you weren't expecting that

kind of opportunity...but what do you think...huh?"
Bradley asked.

"I think you are keeping Mister Robinson waiting
Bradley this way please," Lucy responded.

"All right, all right, I know you are just playing
hard to get! I get it...Bradley Breedlove can play the
game...but don't you let a good thing get away. You got
wise counsel sitting right there at your desk...tell her
mother, talk some sense into her. You just met me but I'll
bet you know a prize catch when you see one. I got
official business to attend to now but you ladies have a
great evening and if you ever need to know the truth
about something...all you got to do is call Bradley
Breedlove. Stick around, after my appointment I'll buy
you dinner...and you can spend some quality time with
Bradley Breedlove," he added as he passed by Lucy on
his way into Wilbert's office,

"That man is living proof that some people should
not be allowed to reproduce," Misses Gaynor
commented.

"Oh my...you are so naughty..." Lucy chuckled,
"and I couldn't agree more. Hee-hee-hee, here darling
sign right here and here so we can both be long gone
before that meeting is over."

Wilbert Robinson was among the few people that
did not find Bradley Breedlove annoying. The two men
shared many things in common and over time Wilbert
had come to appreciate Bradley's insights and peculiar
ways of looking at things. He was genuinely glad to see
Bradley and scheduled a late meeting so they could have
as much uninterrupted time as necessary.

"Bradley, it is good to see you. How have you been?" he greeted as the private investigator entered his office.

"Wilbert! Man you are looking great...looking great!" Bradley exclaimed. "I been hitting them...been a little slow at times...but I been hitting them. I even took on a domestic case but that shit didn't work out. Was a mess is what it was...lady wanted to know if her husband was cheating. Hell you know the son-bitch was...didn't take much to put together the goods on his ass. I showed her the evidence and that crazy broad went all to pieces. Every time I contacted her or tried to collect the remainder of my fee she got all hysterical...a damn mess you know? So I tried to get paid off the other end. The woman her husband was cheating with was also married so I figured she might pay a little hush mouth money. Turns out all that chick had to offer was her worn out snatch. Hell I knew it was wore out cause I had watched it being worked on so I just gave up on all that domestic shit. I'm still with Statewide Insurance though tracking down the liars and cheaters. You would be real surprised Wilbert at just how much weight a son-bitch with a bad back can pick up. I'm talking kids, bags of fertilizer, lawn mowers. Hell I've seen them on ladders, playing sports, working on cars...you name it. I feel sorry for some of them cause once Bradley Breedlove is on the case their game is over, done...finished! So how have you been Wilbert? You looking prosperous and healthy...all successful like you know."

"I'm fine Bradley, just fine and I have called you in to work on the most important case I have handled. This case is so important that I am doubling your customary fee and asking you to put this matter ahead of all others," Wilbert advised.

"Done, already done! Double the fee and you get all of me! Everything is focused; go ahead boss Bradley Breedlove is yours...all yours!"

Over the following two hours Wilbert shared the evidence file, client interview tape and other pertinent information with Bradley. The two men discussed the case at length before agreeing on an investigation agenda. Bradley was assigned to; a) locate the cab that took Brian Carlson home, b) track down the bouncer at the Lucky Seven Bar on the night of the murder, and c) discover how Katie McDougal got from her house to the Lucky Seven Bar to pick up Brian's motorcycle.

"Anything else?" Wilbert questioned.

"Yeah something's bothering me," Bradley responded. "You said the police found the gun in the boy's saddlebag right?"

"Right, why?"

"Well what about fingerprints. If they done ballistics test to see if that gun was the murder weapon, did they also dust the gun for fingerprints?"

"Good point!" Wilbert agreed. "Damn good point. I'll get right on that one tomorrow."

"And I'm climbing all over the questions on my plate. Sticking like crazy glue, looking everywhere at everybody. Bradley Breedlove is on the case, at double the fee...the truth can't hide now...ah naw! I'll have answers...real answers, real soon boss, real soon."

"The sooner the better Bradley we are fighting for a man's life on this one," Wilbert advised as he walked Bradley out of the office.

"And we gonna win...take that to the bank! Bradley Breedlove won't let you down...cannot lose...will not lose and just might win the hand of your charming assistant in the process," Bradley suggested with a big smile.

"Well good luck with that one and be sure to call as soon as you turn anything. Goodnight Bradley," Wilbert concluded.

Exactly one week later Wilbert sat at his desk preparing for a meeting with his investigator and co-counsel. Wilbert had never felt better or more successful. Early in the week he had followed his instincts and listed the cost for his research, co-counsel and investigator as expenses then submitted that to Nathan Carlson's assistant, Madeline. Two days later he received a check and note. The note read, *"Congratulations on the establishment of the Brian Carlson Legal Defense Team. Keep up the good work! Nathan Carlson."* Wilbert was ecstatic; he did not have to pay the team from his retainer. He got back all the money he had paid out and also got some needed encouragement. Plus on that same morning Sylvia called with information to report and the next day Bradley did the same. Wilbert hummed a happy tune while he prepared for his meeting.

Lucy on the other hand was frantically dashing about the office, trying to complete all of her chores in hopes of leaving early and avoiding Bradley Breedlove. The meeting was scheduled afterhours and because of his cheerful mood, Wilbert allowed a grateful and relieved Lucy to end her workday nearly an hour early.

When the meeting started Wilbert got right to the point. "First both of you need to know that as of four days ago you were added to the Carlson family payroll as official members of the Brian Carlson Legal Defense Team. Mister Carlson is watching and sent his congratulations to me for adding each of you to the team."

"Means he had us checked out!" Bradley interrupted.

"It also means that as an official member of the legal team you will also receive a sizeable bonus when we win this case," Wilbert advised.

"Me? Bradley Breedlove?"

"Yes you!" Wilbert confirmed.

"Bonus! You smooth tongue devil. You certainly know how to talk Bradley Breedlove's favorite language."

"Mister Carlson is satisfied we can prevail because he also encouraged us to keep up the good work!" Wilbert continued. "So let's get to it. What have you got Bradley?"

"Several things boss Bradley has been a busy boy. First off it was a Yellow Cab that picked Brian up. A driver named…hum let me get this right," Bradley put on his glasses., "named uh Gotin Batawa or something close to that, I got the correct spelling wrote down. He's an African fellah and according to his log sheet for May 17th the night of the murder, about 11:20 pm he picked up a drunk at the Lucky Seven Bar and took him to 1257 Lombard Street, which is Brian Carlson's address. The driver didn't remember the bouncer but did recall that a lady helped the drunk get out of his cab and that they didn't tip him very much. He is a long-time regular driver for Yellow Cab and I got all his information right here. A copy of that log sheet is available from Yellow Cab if we need it."

"Next, I haven't had any success locating the bouncer. Only the bartender and one waitress at the Lucky Seven Bar are still there that was working the night of the murder. The waitress told Bradley Breedlove everything she knew but the bartender knew more than he told. Apparently the bouncer that night was kind of a drifter cause the bartender claims he was only hired occasionally on an as needed cash basis. Said he hadn't seen him for a couple of months. He called him Big Larry but claims he didn't know his last name. The bartender did give me an address and phone number but Big Larry hadn't lived there for sometime. It was a boarding house and the landlady remembered him. He only lived there a few weeks because she threw him out for being an asshole. She thinks his last name started with a J, like Jones or Jenkins or Jennings. As of this report Big Larry has not been located. However, Bradley Breedlove might soon need some of your legal clout to gain access to any surveillance or security camera film from the bar, or any nearby businesses that may have recorded any activity on the night of the murder. I have not located any cameras on or near the Lucky Seven Bar but cameras can be small, and some of the people who own them are not real anxious to reveal their existence...but Bradley Breedlove is still at work on that."

"Finally Bradley Breedlove discovered that Katie McDougal lived with her Aunt, Maureen McDougal. Although Aunt Maureen much preferred not to be bothered she felt bad for her neighbor Brian and allowed Bradley Breedlove into the house. She assured me that she had never given Katie a ride anywhere that she could remember. For the most part Katie lived in her basement apartment which has an outside entrance and was pretty much ignored. On the night in question, Aunt Maureen went to bed early as usual and knew nothing of the night's events."

"Aunt Maureen served refreshments and assisted Bradley Breedlove in gaining access to her telephone records for the night in question. On May 18th at 1:46 in the morning a call was placed from the McDougal residence to (317) 256-0706. Bradley Breedlove tracked that number to a fellah named Douglas Anderson. He was a friend of Katie McDougal and remembered the phone call so Bradley Breedlove paid him a visit. He is a real nice fellah, just like the cab driver, said he would be happy to talk anytime. He prefers to be called Doug and remembered Katie calling and asking him for a ride, saying she needed to do a favor for her neighbor. Doug claims he had just gone to bed but jumped at the chance to spend time with Katie McDougal. So he got dressed and rode his motorcycle over to her house. He gave her a ride to the Lucky Seven and they brought the neighbor's bike home. Afterwards he made plans with Katie to hang out the following evening then went home. Got all his information right here, got all the cab drivers info and let's see…hum that about wraps it up for Bradley Breedlove right now…that's about all I got so far."

"Excellent Bradley!" Wilbert complimented.

"Yes indeed I second that, good work Bradley," Sylvia added.

"Bradley Breedlove, Private I and eye, just like it says on my card Bradley Breedlove Private I, doing an honest days work," Bradley bragged.

"Well this is impressive work Bradley, you have a right to be proud," Sylvia conceded.

"Oh yeah I'm a proud rascal alright, but what about that gun? Were there any prints on it? For some reason that question just keeps bothering Bradley Breedlove."

"I have the crime labs report and the ballistics report on the gun right here," Sylvia responded.

"Let's have it," Wilbert instructed.

"The gun was seized and handled according to procedure and regulations. It was dusted and closely inspected but no whole or partial latent prints could be found anywhere on the weapon," Sylvia announced.

"Bradley Breedlove knew there was shit in the soup! Who in the hell uses their own gun to kill then wipes it clean before putting it back in their holster. Shit in the soup, shit in the soup…yes sir! Bradley Breedlove knows soup and Bradley knows shit, so it is easy for Bradley Breedlove to identify shit in the soup!"

"Bradley you have a very good point and you have put a lot on the table tonight. You have earned your spot on the legal team and I thank you for your good work. I'll touch bases with you tomorrow regarding where we are and what we may need from this point forward. Do you have anything else?" Wilbert asked.

"No sir, I do not but…Bradley Breedlove had hoped the fair Miss Maples might be available for dinner tonight. You see Bradley Breedlove does not have a first lady right now and applications are being accepted.

Accordingly Bradley Breedlove is available to interview over dinner. Not saying that you truly have any real chance but you never know…Bradley Breedlove is a man with an open mind!"

"Bradley you are a really good investigator and a really lousy romantic so just stick to business okay?" Sylvia pleaded.

"Your loss Miss Maples…your loss. Once Bradley Breedlove elevates the chosen female to first lady, the job will be closed and all others, including you, will have missed the opportunity to spend quality time with Bradley Breedlove. But so be it I just can't love them all. Goodnight Wilbert and so long missed opportunity…or rather Miss Maples, Bradley Breedlove is leaving now."

"Goodnight Bradley…" Wilbert chuckled while Sylvia Maples glared and shook her head.

*Chapter five*

**O**ver the following weeks, Wilbert and Sylvia built what they felt was a solid defense based on reasonable doubt. Bradley Breedlove was tasked with finding any surveillance film from the night of the murder near the vicinity of the Lucky Seven Bar or the Newride Body Shop.

While the defense was humming along the prosecution was poised and waiting. They had reached tentative plea bargain deals with both prior attorneys, including the most pre-eminent criminal law firm in the state. They were certain the Robinson Law Firm would be forced to do likewise because this was a closed case. The defendant's own gun was the murder weapon, he had motive and there were witnesses to his threat to kill. The deputy prosecutor assigned to the case was completely uninterested in any so-called new evidence that supported Brian Carlson's innocence. He had a solid case and was certain the defense was only trying to position their client for a more favorable plea bargain.

The prosecutor was determined not to give the defense any hope whatsoever so he waived re-discovery.

Sylvia Maples was absolutely delighted when she phoned Wilbert with the news. "This really gives us a leg up!" she gushed.

"I don't follow?" Wilbert responded.

"By rules of discovery the prosecutor should have subpoenaed a deposition from all of our witnesses."

"So?"

"So? Are you kidding? If they took us seriously and got those depositions they would know what's coming from us in the trial. But they don't expect a trial! They are confident that we will have to plea bargain. So we may have an element of surprise which is very rare in criminal trials."

"Sounds like you are saying we are going to solve the case in court during the trial," Wilbert replied.

"No not solve it…just sow big seeds of reasonable doubt," Sylvia explained.

"What's next?"

"The pretrial conference in a few weeks."

"That is just between lawyers, right?" Wilbert questioned.

"Right. A meeting with the deputy prosecutor to discuss trial issues."

"And we are really looking pretty good you think?" Wilbert inquired.

"Given what we have put together from Brian's alibi and the indifferent attitude of the prosecutor toward us, I think we have a real chance for an upset."

"An upset? If we win it will be an upset?"

"Sure it will! Anytime you beat the prosecution in a capital case it is considered an upset. Additionally the press already convicted Brian Carlson a long time ago, and with the murder rate going up they will be watching this trial with a lot of interest."

"Sheez...no wonder I got sidestepped by the big time boys and old Judge Wyckoff. Should have used my head and saved my money," Wilbert grumbled.

"Judge Wyckoff?" Sylvia questioned. "Do you know the judge?"

"No, I paid him for a legal assessment I was hoping for a written report but instead I got a seat on his patio and my ears beaten off."

"I would love the opportunity to sit at Judge Wyckoff's feet. That man is a true treasure trove of legal knowledge."

"Well you know something Sylvia, I'm really glad to hear you say that!" Wilbert declared. "I paid that old foghorn a grand and all he did was ramble for damn near an hour. I have the tape right here and you are welcome to it with the understanding that it did cost a grand."

"That's definitely something most lawyers would want on their bookshelf. But why should I pay you a grand for a tape when I can talk to the judge for the same amount?" Sylvia chuckled.

"Good point. Too bad he's still alive. Tell you what...I really wasn't looking to sell the thing anyway and I am certainly not going to listen to it again, so you can have it. Just remember me with a nice favor or client someday. Soon that is...someday soon!" Wilbert offered.

"Deal...bless you. I'll have it picked up before the day is over," Sylvia promised then bade Wilbert so long, hung up the phone and focused on the matter in front of her.

Just before joining the deputy prosecutor for the pretrial conference, Wilbert and Sylvia agreed that since Sylvia was familiar with the language and protocol she should do the talking.

Several minutes into the meeting however the deputy prosecutor grew restless. He fully expected the defense to pursue a plea bargain and was anxious to get on with it. "Mister Robinson I see you are the lead defense attorney on this case, may I ask if this is your first capital case?" he inquired.

"Why?" Wilbert responded.

"Because if that is so then I should advise that if you intend to pursue a plea bargain in this…"

"PLEA BARGAIN!" Wilbert roared, "We did not come here seeking a freaking plea bargain! Our client is innocent! We came here to let you know that the best move you can make is to drop all charges immediately. We have done our jobs and uncovered evidence you refused to even look at, so now if you take this to court we will whip your ass."

"None of that changes the fact that your client's gun was the murder weapon. He had motive and stated intention, meaning under the laws of this state he premeditated this murder. We will prove that in court and seek the death penalty unless your side is prepared to make some offer," the deputy prosecutor countered.

"The only thing we have to offer is sufficient warning so that you can avoid a very embarrassing public ass whipping. We are serious and came to fight!" Wilbert advised.

"In that case…I'll see you in court!" the prosecutor responded then gathered his notes.

"That you will!" Wilbert promised.

In spite of his bluster, Wilbert was anxious and nervous during the days leading up to the trial. He did not look forward to the drama and uncertainty of a trial and tried as hard as he could to find his client a way out. He had hoped Bradley Breedlove would produce conclusive video that would result in Brian being released and his bonus promptly paid. But Bradley had come up empty, so Wilbert was still searching for anything that would provide a quick kill.

Little did Wilbert know that Terrance Reynolds, the lead deputy prosecutor on the case was also very anxious and nervous. The prosecutor's office had expected and prepared for a plea bargain on this case, they were not well-prepared for trial. Terrance Reynolds had raised the possibility of dropping the present charges against Brian Carlson, launching a new investigation then re-filing charges rather than risk a not guilty verdict at trial. He was assured by his superiors that they had a rock solid case and he was being bullied by Wilbert Robinson who was a master at intimidation. All of Wilbert's strong talk about new evidence and ass whipping was a bluff. An end-run to see if he could get the charges dropped. Failing that, Wilbert would be forced into a last minute plea deal. Terrence felt bullied by both his superiors and by Wilbert. He also felt pressure to get a conviction from the police brass and the mayor's office. So after some serious thought he decided his boss must be right. Brian Carlson was obviously guilty and the case against him was so strong it would never make it to court. But as the trial approached no last minute deal was sought by the defense.

Wilbert and Sylvia had a long preparatory meeting scheduled on each of the three days leading up to the trial. They were determined to be on top of their game, prepared and ready to do battle. When they met for the first meeting Sylvia was bubbling with enthusiasm, "Judge Wyckoff is a legal genius!" she declared. "I've learned so much just by listening to his tape. His defense philosophy fits right in with what we are already doing but he pulls it all together and puts it into focus. His premise is to keep the defense simple, adopt three or four points and repeat them over and over. Drive your points into the jury's head. I have also gained some very important insights about jury selection which quite frankly had been my weak spot and a big worry. In fact I was going to suggest we bring in jury selection experts but I don't feel we need them now."

"Are you certain? I don't mind the expense," Wilbert responded.

"No...no. I much prefer the advice of Judge Wyckoff," Sylvia assured. "Here let me read you a bit that I transcribed, it is almost shocking. The Judge said and I quote, "Do not get caught up in thinking that a jury of your peers means a juror has to be the same color, gender, age or looks like your client. Be smart! If your client has any assets, use them! For example, if your client has sex appeal, use that to select jurors that might find your client attractive. Jurors are people and people are human; subject to and influenced by their wants and desires. From the defense perspective a jury of your peers is a jury that sees your client favorably. And do not forget when selecting jurors, a smart lawyer will structure questions to unwanted jurors that may cause the prosecution to suspect that juror sees the defense favorably and excuse them. That leaves the prosecution feeling as though they are in charge of the selection process while you get the jury that is most favorable to your client..." unquote. I cannot thank you enough for that tape Wilbert, it is absolutely priceless. I have no idea how you got Judge Wyckoff to open up like that and I most certainly owe you."

"You are welcome and you know I am going to remember that you owe," Wilbert assured with a smile then continued. "But honestly I'm very relieved to hear that we are getting some value from my misadventure. You said he was also helpful to our defense strategy?"

"Exactly. What we have fits nicely into four bullet points of reasonable doubt. We stress our points and downplay everything else. Our whole case is based on those four points and the jury only has to buy one of them to find in our favor," Sylvia advised.

"Okay, point number one?" Wilbert inquired.

"Point number one is the fact that Brian Carlson went home from the Lucky Seven Bar in a cab. The cab driver remembers he was helped from the cab by a lady and we have the drivers log sheet. We also have Brian's medical treatment records. A severely sprained ankle, two broken ribs and a hairline fracture of the jaw bone means he was not in physical shape to ride his motorcycle. Plus we know that in addition to his injuries he was drunk. That is point number one," Sylvia responded.

"And point number two?" Wilbert pressed.

"Well...point number two...is just going to have to wait until I come back from the ladies room," Sylvia admitted then excused herself.

By the conclusion of their third and final preparatory meeting the Brian Carlson Legal Defense Team was practiced, knowledgeable, enthusiastic and ready for battle. They concluded their final preparations early so they would have the opportunity to relax during the evening, then get a good nights rest before reporting to court the next day to begin the trial.

On the first morning of the trial Wilbert entered the administrative office of Superior Court #4 well dressed, feeling confident and giving the appearance of being very much in control. He chatted with the staff while Sylvia Maples completed some necessary paperwork before they entered the courtroom and took their seats.

Terrance Reynolds appeared tired as he entered the courtroom with a look of quiet desperation in his eyes. Terrance was accompanied by his co-counsel, a fellow deputy prosecutor named Scott Bollinger. Scott was older and more experienced than Terrance. He had been added to the case at the last minute to replace a much weaker prosecutor when it finally became apparent that no plea bargain was going to be sought. After the prosecutors greeted Wilbert and Sylvia then seated themselves at their table, Wilbert leaned toward Sylvia and loudly commented, "So that's what lambs look like just before they are slaughtered!" Both prosecutors glared at Wilbert who straightened his tie and pretended to ignore them while Sylvia Maples chuckled in spite of trying to keep a straight face.

A couple of minutes later Brian Carlson was led into the courtroom and seated beside his attorneys while several spectators then the jury pool entered and took seats. Suddenly the bailiff announced, "All rise!"

Judge Neil Toliver entered the courtroom and took his seat behind the bench. "Be seated," the judge ordered then banged his gavel. Judge Toliver was a serious man in his early fifties. He was fair minded and known for running a crisp, efficient court. Wilbert watched with interest as Judge Toliver gaveled the court into session, made his announcements then began the jury selection process. Sylvia Maples was totally absorbed and had never felt better about jury selection. She had spent considerable time listening to Judge Wyckoff's insights and was carefully putting his advice to use.

By late afternoon the last member of the jury was seated and Sylvia was absolutely delighted. Because Brian Carlson was a thirty year-old bachelor from a wealthy family, Sylvia wanted as many young women on the jury as possible. The final jury contained eight women and four men, with one man and one woman alternate. Five of the women on the sitting jury were under age forty and Sylvia Maples was deeply impressed with how effective Judge Wyckoff's suggestions had been. She smiled at Terrence Reynolds and Scott Bollinger knowing that they felt as though they had taken charge and constructed the jury. Judge Toliver issued preliminary instructions to the jury then after noting the time, put the trial into recess until the next morning.

Brian Carlson became emotional when he was led into court on the second day. Sitting in the front row of the spectators section was his mother, sister and one of his brothers. Brian had not expected them but they flew in early that morning and planned to stay for the entire trial. Brian waved, smiled and mouthed words until the bailiff's call to rise.

Judge Toliver called the court to order and began the day by summarizing his preliminary instructions to the jury then called on the State for their opening statement. Terrence Reynolds took the floor and for several minutes in a high pitched voice that at times almost sounded desperate, he laid out the states case. He emphasized the fight, the threat and the murder soon after by Brian's gun. Terrence concluded his remarks by vowing to prove beyond a reasonable doubt that Brian Carlson first premeditated then murdered Charles Grant, aka Bear as an act of cold blooded revenge.

Sylvia Maples took the floor for the defense. She was calm, confident and very much in control as she explained to the jury that Brian and Charles Grant did indeed have a fight. Brian stands about 5'11" and weighs about 160 pounds, while Charles Grant stood 6'4" and weighed 348 pounds so obviously Brian lost the fight. He lost badly and was drunk, meaning he was in no shape to ride his motorcycle and took a cab home. She reminded the jury that the burden of proof is on the prosecution and then promised to show that the police did not investigate this case beyond jumping to conclusions about a very innocent Brian Carlson. When Sylvia Maples finished her opening statement she felt as though she had connected with the jury and was very pleased.

The prosecution began their case by calling David Kipling as their first witness. David was an auto body repairman employed by the Newride Body Shop. He testified that he usually arrived at work early and opened the shop while his boss, Charles Grant, usually closed up at night. On the morning of May 18th, he was surprised to discover the alarm was not on and the front door was not locked when he arrived. When he entered the shop he was horrified to find his boss lying face down on the floor. There was blood under his head and his eyes were wide open but completely empty. So in near panic he called 911 then waited outside the building until the police arrived. Scott Bollinger asked a few questions for clarification then offered the witness for cross-examination.

"Mister Kipling, was it common knowledge around your workplace that your boss, Charles Grant always kept a large sum of cash on his person or near by him?" Sylvia Maples questioned.

"Well...it wasn't no secret. Most folks knew he kept a wad of cash...in his pocket mostly," David Kipling replied.

"And was it also common knowledge that on occasion Charles Grant also had a large quantity of cocaine on or near him?" Sylvia inquired.

"Objection your honor! This goes to..." Scott Bollinger protested.

"Over-ruled!" Judge Toliver snapped. "Please answer the question Mister Kipling."

"Well...I can't really say...cause I never saw the stuff but most everybody around the shop said he did," David Kipling responded.

"Objection! That's hearsay!" Scott Bollinger interrupted.

"The clerk will strike from the record and the jury will disregard the witness last response," Judge Toliver ordered.

"You worked with Mister Grant for several years. Is that right Mister Kipling?" Silvia asked.

"That's correct, pretty close to eight years."

"In all that time did Mister Grant have unpredictable mood swings during the work day?"

"Oh yes ma'am, over the last couple of years he did?"

"Thank you Mister Kipling, no further questions your honor," Sylvia announced and returned to her seat.

The prosecution next called the police officers that responded to the 911 call. The senior officer took the stand and testified to what he observed upon arrival at the Newride Body Shop, and the actions he and his partner took to alert the necessary responders and secure the scene. At the conclusion of the police officer's testimony the defense declined cross-examination. The prosecution called the detectives that investigated the case as their third and fourth witness.

Detective Thomas Winslow took the witness stand and reported that he and his partner, Detective Peggy Jackson, began their investigation at the crime scene. Then acting on information gained from the employees of the Newride Body Shop and the victim's wife, they interviewed the staff of the Lucky Seven Bar. They were informed of the fight between the victim and a man named Brian, and of Brian's threat to kill Charles Grant only a short while before the murder. They gained Brian's complete information from his business card which was among many pinned to a bulletin board just inside the front door of the Lucky Seven Bar. Brian Carlson at that point was the prime suspect for the murder of Charles Grant. The detectives immediately obtained an arrest warrant and a search warrant then with uniformed backup proceeded to 1257 Lombard Street and detained the suspect, Brian Carlson pending the search. As a result of searching Brian Carlson's personal effects, a 9mm pistol was found by Detective Jackson. Mister Carlson was placed under arrest and the weapon was promptly delivered to forensics.

"Were there any unusual circumstances that would warrant additional investigation at this point?" Terrance Reynolds questioned.

"Absolutely not sir! All the evidence pointed directly at our suspect, Brian Carlson," the detective concluded.

On cross-examination, Wilbert asked Detective Winslow if he or his partner made any attempt whatsoever to investigate Brian Carlson's alibi?

"Of course!" Thomas Winslow responded. "My partner was more involved in that phase of the investigation but we found nothing to substantiate his claims and moved forward."

"Did you look in any direction other than Brian Carlson as the perpetrator of this crime?" Wilbert pressed.

"It has been my experience that most homicides are solved within the first 48 hours after the event, and this crime fits that predictable pattern. His gun proved to be the murder weapon and that was enough to limit our investigation to Brian Carlson."

"Before you knew that Brian Carlson's gun was the murder weapon, did you ever consider the possibility of another suspect?" Wilbert questioned.

"We followed the lead we had...and that was Brian Carlson!" Detective Winslow snapped.

"Did you or your partner interview the bouncer that was working at the Lucky Seven Bar that night?" Wilbert demanded.

"We did not!"

"Do you even know the bouncer's name?"

"We do not!"

"Let me get this straight detective. The bouncer was a central participant in the altercation that led to an eventual murder and you did not even interview him or at the very least enter his name in the official report?" Wilbert questioned with indignation.

"The bouncer was not available or considered to be relevant!" Detective Winslow growled.

"Not relevant! The possibility that the bouncer could have taken advantage, or been more involved in this situation never occurred to either you, your partner or your supervisors during your entire investigation?" Wilbert questioned in a despairing tone.

"No sir, he was not our suspect!"

"And you call that good police work?" Wilbert shrieked.

"Objection your honor!" Terrance cried out.

"I certainly have no further questions for this witness your honor!" Wilbert loudly interjected with outrage and disbelief.

Detective Peggy Jackson took the witness stand and testified that she found the weapon while conducting a warranted search. The gun was located inside the right rear saddlebag of the suspect's motorcycle. The detective explained that while wearing latex gloves she removed the gun from what appeared to be a custom made holster within the saddlebag. The weapon was placed into a plastic bag then into an evidence pouch and delivered to the crime lab. Following that she attempted to investigate the suspect's alibi with no success. Scott Bollinger questioned the detective about some technical aspects of the search process then offered the witness for cross-examination.

"Detective Jackson, you testified that you attempted without success to contact Katie McDougal which was the neighbor Brian Carlson claims helped him out that night. Is that not correct?" Sylvia Maples asked.

"That's correct," Detective Jackson replied.

"How many times did you attempt to contact Miss McDougal?" Sylvia inquired.

"I visited her home on the day following the arrest but no one answered the door, so I left my card with instructions for Miss McDougal to call but she never did," Peggy Jackson explained.

"You placed your card on several doors in the neighborhood with similar instructions, is that not correct detective?"

"That's correct."

"Did anyone of those neighbors contact you?"

"No."

"And you made no further attempt to contact Katie McDougal, correct?

"That's correct," the detective admitted.

"Following the arrest did you accompany my client, Brian Carlson to jail for the booking process?"

"Er…no. We followed a patrol wagon which took him to the lock-up at county hospital for treatment," Detective Jackson responded.

"So he wasn't in very good physical shape?" Sylvia questioned.

"He could move around…but no, he wasn't in very good shape," Detective Peggy Jackson agreed.

"Thank you detective, I have nothing further for this witness your honor," Sylvia Maples concluded.

In the early afternoon following a long lunch recess, the prosecution called Corey Gilliam, the bartender of the Lucky Seven Bar to the witness stand. Terrance Reynolds was trying hard to be very methodical as he led Corey through a series of routine questions. Without eyewitnesses to the murder, the bartender and the waitress of the Lucky Seven Bar were the prosecutions only bombshell witnesses, and Terrance needed to milk them for all they were worth. After establishing the fact that Corey Gilliam was a co-owner and full-time bartender that worked long hours, he asked Corey to describe the event between Charles Grant and Brian Carlson on the night of May 17th.

"Well it had been a busy evening because of the race but things had started to slow down when Bear showed up…"

"By saying Bear do you mean the victim, Charles Grant?" Terrance questioned.

"Oh yeah…I mean everybody called him Bear. I don't think most folks even knew his real name," Corey replied.

"Thank you, may we have it noted in the record your honor that any reference to the name Bear is a reference to the deceased victim Charles Grant?" Terrance Reynolds asked the judge.

"Mister Robinson?" Judge Toliver queried.

"No objection your honor," Wilbert responded.

"Let it be so noted, continue Mister Reynolds," Judge Toliver commanded.

"Please continue," Terrence instructed the witness.

"Well like I said," Corey began anew, "we had been pretty busy that day but I remember that Brian had been around for some time shooting pool in the back. It had slowed down by the time Bear came in and was probably an hour or more before the fight started. I don't know what the deal was but Brian came up to the bar where Bear was sitting and they had words. Next thing I know Brian hauls off and knocks the crap out of Bear. They started mixing it up and I was surprised because ole Brian was holding his own with the Bear till Big Larry threw both of them out the back door. I figured it was over and things pretty much got back to normal. Then a few minutes later Brian came back in the front door hollering and cursing. He promised to kill the Bear and accused us of hiding him before Big Larry put him out again. And that was the last I heard of either one of them until the police showed up at the bar the next day."

"Had these two men had disagreements before in your bar?" Terrance questioned.

"No, never...they were both regulars and never had any trouble with anyone," Corey responded.

"And you distinctly heard Brian Carlson promise to kill Charles Grant, aka Bear?"

"Yes sir, absolutely!" Corey confirmed.

"Thank you, Mister Gilliam. I've nothing further for this witness your honor," Terrance concluded.

"Mister Gilliam," Wilbert began during cross-examination, "about what time of the evening would you say the disagreement between the Bear and Brian Carlson began?"

"Must have been about eleven o'clock because the news had just come on the TV," Corey responded.

"When Brian Carlson came back into the bar after the fight, did he say he was going to kill the Bear or did he say the Bear was dead?"

"I can tell you exactly what he said cause he shouted it and scared the crap out of me. I thought he had a gun so I ducked behind the bar. Can I tell you his exact words?" Corey Gilliam asked.

"Please do," Wilbert responded.

"Well...he came in the front door and hollered "BEAR! YOU A DEAD MOTHERFUCKER AND I MEAN IT!" Then he asked where Bear was and accused us of hiding him. Said to tell Bear he was dead...completely dead. Then Big Larry threw him out again."

"Was Big Larry the bar's bouncer?" Wilbert asked.

"Uh...yes sir, you could say that...at least for a short time he was," Corey replied.

"Was Big Larry a full-time employee of the Lucky Seven Bar?" Wilbert questioned.

"Well...no, he was a contract worker you might say. He only worked as needed," Corey explained.

"Did Big Larry come right back into the bar after he put Brian Carlson out for the second time?" Wilbert inquired.

"I believe so, but I was busy and can't swear he did," Corey Gilliam answered.

"Did Big Larry work a complete shift at the bar on the night Bear was killed?"

"No...probably about four hours. We only needed him for the peak hours," Corey responded.

"How soon after the fight did his shift end?"

"We stop paying at midnight...business falls off you know," Corey replied.

"Could Big Larry have left the bar for a short while then returned without much notice?"

"Objection! Speculation!" Terrance Reynolds cried out.

"Sustained! Strike the question," Judge Toliver instructed.

"Where you aware that the Bear frequently carried large sums of cash?" Wilbert asked.

"I've seen him pull out a large bankroll and pay his tab with a large bill from time to time," Corey responded.

"Did he have a large bankroll on the night of his demise?" Wilbert questioned.

"He paid with a large bill."

"Where you aware that the Bear may have carried around large amounts of cocaine?" Wilbert inquired.

"Naw...I don't know nothing about no cocaine...nothing at all," Corey insisted.

"Did you know that Brian Carlson kept a gun in the saddlebag of his motorcycle?"

"I heard about it but I never saw it myself. Lot of the guys that come into the Lucky Seven claim to have all kinds of weapons," Corey explained.

"When was the last time you saw Big Larry that night?" Wilbert questioned.

"Just before closing...I think."

"What time did you close?"

"Two am."

"Have you seen Big Larry since?"

"Oh yeah, he drops in from time to time," Corey responded.

"When was the last time?" Wilbert asked.

"Uh...can't say for sure...been a couple of months maybe?" Corey offered.

"Did you close the bar the night of the murder, Mister Gilliam? Wilbert questioned.

"Yes I sure did."

"Did you notice Brian Carlson's motorcycle still parked in front of your bar as you left?"

"There were a couple of bikes parked in front but there wasn't nothing unusual about that. I don't know if one of them belonged to Brian or not," Corey answered.

"Thank you Mister Gilliam, nothing further your honor," Wilbert concluded then took his seat.

The witnesses were all kept in a small room adjacent to the courtroom. When called to testify they entered the court and went directly to the witness stand, then returned to the small room to be released afterwards. When the prosecution called Tracy White to the stand she entered the courtroom then stopped and stared around for a few moments. She did the same thing before sitting down prompting Judge Toliver to ask that she please be seated.

"Oh I'm sorry your judge sir. It's just that I ain't never been in a real courtroom before and I want to remember as much as I can so I can tell my daughter all about it," Tracy admitted.

"Miss White you and your daughter are welcome to visit the court at any time but..."

"Really?" Tracy interrupted.

"Yes, but now we must attend to the business before us so please be seated," Judge Toliver requested.

Tracy White testified that she had been employed at the Lucky Seven Bar for just over three years as a waitress. She was working on the night of the murder and remembered it because fights and death threats were rare at the Lucky Seven Bar. She reported that she was on the other side of the room when the fight broke out. Because the bouncer handled it so quickly she had just considered it an unwelcome commotion until Brian came back through the front door. Tracy testified that she was very near the front door when Brian returned.

"He looked real bad and was leaning to one side then hollered real loud that the Bear was gonna die. Lots of people ducked under tables and the like but I didn't know what to do, so I just stood there with my heart beating fast. I first thought he had killed the Bear already until he demanded to know where he was hiding. Then he kept promising to kill the Bear until the bouncer put him out."

"You said a lot of people ducked under tables...did you see a gun in Brian Carlson's hand?" Terrence Reynolds asked.

"No...I sure thought he had one but I never saw it," Tracy answered.

"Had these two men, Bear and Brian Carlson, had disagreements or difficulties at any time before the fight?"

"Not that I was aware of," Tracy responded. "In fact they used to drink and shoot pool together but for a short while before that night they kept their distance...at the bar anyway."

"Do you know what caused the distance?" Terrence questioned.

"I most certainly do not cause I most certainly did not ask! It's all lighthearted and simple here darling. I don't get involved in no customers business," Tracy advised.

"Thank you Miss White, no further questions your honor," Terrence Reynolds concluded.

Wilbert Robinson took the floor and paused for a few moments before asking, "Miss White, did you then or do you now know Big Larry, the bouncer at the Lucky Seven Bar on the night of the murder?"

"No sir I didn't, he was a scary sort of fellah so I just kinda stayed away from him," Tracy replied.

"I see...do you remember the exact words Brian Carlson shouted when he re-entered the bar?" Wilbert questioned.

"I'm not sure exactly...I believe he said the Bear is gonna die," Tracy responded.

"Did he say the Bear is dead or the Bear is gonna die?" Wilbert pressed.

"Dead, die…I don't know, it's all sounds pretty much the same to me. And I was too scared to swear I could remember his exact words!" Tracy admitted.

"Do you remember if the bouncer came right back into the bar after putting Brian Carlson out?"

"Now I couldn't tell you cause as soon as that mess was over I went right to the ladies room and composed myself," Tracy recalled.

"At what time did your shift end?"

"Let me see…I worked about an hour and a half overtime because of the race. So it must have been about 12:30 when I left."

"Did you see Big Larry again at any time that night after he put Brian Carlson out of the bar?" Wilbert questioned.

"I can't say that I did…but like I said, I didn't spend much time looking in his direction," Tracy explained.

"Thank you Miss White, nothing further your honor," Wilbert concluded.

After a brief afternoon recess Judge Toliver gaveled the court into session. The prosecution entered a Glock 9mm pistol and several large photographs of the crime scene into evidence then called a crime lab technician named Arnold Watts to the witness stand.

After fielding a few routine questions from Scott Bollinger that established his creditability, Arnold testified that he arrived to find the crime scene properly secured with police tape. The scene was a public business that showed no signs of forced entry or struggle. The only collectable evidence found that could be positively identified as being directly related with the murder was three bullet casings found near the body. Arnold identified the casings in the photographs and identified them as 9x19 Parabellum cartridges commonly used in 9mm pistols.

He went on to explain that the following day Detectives Winslow and Jackson brought a pistol to his lab. The gun had been impounded during the search of a suspect and he was asked to determine if it had any connection to the body shop murder. His investigation revealed the pistol to be a 9mm Glock 19 with five unspent rounds remaining in the magazine. The manufacturer and lot number on the 9x19 Parabellum cartridges found in the gun were identical to the casings found at the crime scene. Ballistics confirmed that a bullet fired from the suspect pistol perfectly matched a bullet removed from the deceased. With one hundred percent certainty the impounded Glock 19 was the weapon used to shoot Charles Grant.

Scott Bollinger stepped to the prosecution table and picked up the gun. He then walked past the jury box slowing waving the gun in the air. "Is it your testimony then Mister Watts based on scientific evidence that this gun...this gun...this 9mm glock pistol that is owned by the defendant, Brian Carlson, is the gun that was one hundred percent responsible for the cold blooded murder of Charles Grant?"

"That's correct sir," the technician responded.

Scott Bollinger shrugged his shoulders, "There are certainly no further questions your honor," he concluded then took his seat feeling certain he had just won the case.

"Mister Watts?" Sylvia Maples began on cross-examination. "Was there any money found on the victim or at the crime scene?"

"Uh…no ma'am we conducted a limited search, meaning just the contents of the victim pockets, his vehicle and the office area of his shop. We did not find any money," Arnold Watts responded.

"No money at all…not even ten dollars?" Sylvia questioned with surprise in her voice.

"That's correct no money at all was found on the victim or at the crime scene," Arnold confirmed.

"Did you find any cocaine or other drugs?" Sylvia asked.

"No ma'am we did not."

"Was the gun dusted for fingerprints when you received it Mister Watts?" Sylvia inquired.

"Yes that was the first step in the investigation of the gun," Arnold explained.

"And were any fingerprints found on the weapon?"

"Er…no ma'am, the weapon came up clean for prints."

"Clean!" Sylvia paused and gave a puzzled look to the jury. "You mean there were no fingerprints of any kind on the gun, not even Brian Carlson's?" she pressed.

"Uh…that's correct."

"Is it unusual for you to receive a gun impounded during a search and for that weapon to be completely free of all fingerprints?" Sylvia questioned.

"Uh…yes that's a bit unusual…"

"Thank you Mister Watts, no further questions your honor," Sylvia concluded and took her seat.

As their final witness the prosecution called, Deputy Coroner Phillip Kennedy. After taking the stand and answering a few routine questions the deputy coroner got straight to the point. He testified that he arrived at the Newride Body Shop and found the owner, Charles Grant, lying face down in a small puddle of blood, on the floor of his shop near the office area. The fact that the victim was laying face down meant he was likely lunging toward his assassin when he was shot. Using several large photographs of the victim that had been introduced into evidence, Phillip Kennedy explained that the victim was shot three times. The first two shots to the victim's front forehead were fired from a distance of approximately three feet while the victim was advancing on the shooter. Speckling or a spray of tiny burn holes on the victim's skin around the bullet wound indicates a gun was fired at very close range. The first two shots to the victim's forehead did not leave speckling marks. The third shot and likely the shot that finished the job left heavy speckling around the bullet wound. The third shot was fired after the victim was down, to the right temple at a distance of approximately four inches. Death was likely instant.

"So you are saying that the first two shots could have been fired out of fear or in self defense, but the third shot, fired only four inches from Charles Grant's temple was fired in cold blood?" Terrence Reynolds questioned in a mildly dramatic fashion.

"The third shot was intended to kill," the deputy corner confirmed.

Terrence Reynolds paused and stared at the jury. "Intended to kill," he repeated then advised the judge he had no further questions.

"Mister Kennedy, did you establish a time of death for Mister Grant?" Sylvia Maples asked on cross-examination.

"While we could not be exact, we did establish an estimated time of death as being between midnight and two am on the morning of May 18th," Phillip Kennedy responded.

"Was a toxicology test performed?"

"Yes, of course."

"Was cocaine present in Mister Grant's body?" Sylvia inquired.

"Ah...yes it was," the deputy coroner responded.

"Thank you Mister Kennedy, nothing further your honor," Sylvia concluded.

Scott Bollinger was growing increasingly concerned as the prosecution's case drew to a close. He had begun the trial with absolutely no respect for Wilbert Robinson or Sylvia Maples. They simply were not in his league. He considered Wilbert to be a loud mouth civil attorney and Sylvia a lightweight, second class criminal lawyer. He had expected to roll right over them but had been made uncomfortable by their aggressive cross examinations and grasp of the details. Scott felt the case was still solid and with a strong closing argument a conviction was certain. But they could not afford to lose any ground so he had to impede the defense if possible.

When Judge Toliver called on the prosecution, Terrence Reynolds stood and announced, "The prosecution rests your honor."

"However!" Scott Bollinger added, "The prosecution at this time also seeks a motion to suppress any evidence or witnesses the defense did not produce during discovery."

Judge Toliver called both legal teams to the bench.

"Am I to understand that you have new evidence to present Mister Robinson?" the judge questioned.

"That's quite a stretch your honor," Wilbert responded. "Please allow my colleague to explain."

"If I may your honor," Sylvia put in, "we are the third legal team for this defendant. The original discovery meetings were held before we became the attorney of record. However, shortly after coming on board I called Mister Reynolds asking to schedule re-discovery and he declined. I was stunned and told him I was turning my recorder on, then again asked to schedule re-discovery, and Mister Reynolds again waived the procedure while expressing no interest in defense evidence. I still have that tape your honor."

"That was during the plea bargaining phase! Well before it became apparent that we were going to trial!" Scott Bollinger protested.

"Mister Reynolds did you waive re-discovery?" Judge Toliver questioned.

"Uh…I set that aside during the plea bargaining phase your honor," Terrence Reynolds admitted.

"Then we have nothing to discuss! Motion denied! Court is in recess until 9:15 tomorrow morning," Judge Toliver concluded then rapped his gavel and left the bench.

# Chapter six

*T*errence Reynolds *was feeling beleaguered* and stressed when he left the courtroom. He had previously considered moving his career out of the prosecutor's office and this case was forcing him toward a decision. He was uncertain of his next career move but was seriously thinking about it because he felt that his superiors had bullied him into taking a capital case to court without being properly prepared. Then they replaced his co-counsel at the last minute with a pushy know-it-all and that was the last straw. Winning this case would allow him to walk away from the prosecutor's office on top, a winner. Otherwise it was going to be a difficult slough regardless of which road he chose. He made his way out of the building and was very annoyed to find Scott Bollinger waiting for him in the parking lot. Scott practically demanded permission to cross-examine Brian Carlson if the defense put him on the witness stand. Terrence chose to delay his decision until after he heard Brian's testimony then settled into his car, bid Scott good evening and drove away.

Wilbert Robinson had never felt better. He walked from the courthouse with a spring in his step and gleam in his eye. Wilbert was impressed with the team he had selected for this case. Bradley had delivered the goods, Lucy as usual was on top of the paperwork and Sylvia Maples had done a masterful job. Now he actually looked forward to another day in court, another day closer to a quarter of a million dollars. Wilbert stopped several feet short of his old sedan, looked it over and smiled. "In just a couple of day's baby you are going to be replaced by a brand new Jaguar!" he chuckled aloud.

After spending almost two hours in his office catching up routine business, Wilbert had dinner, went home and retired early. The following morning he met Sylvia Maples at seven am for breakfast and to prep for their day in court. They reviewed, discussed and refined each point in their prepared defense and closing argument until they were satisfied then arrived in court rested and ready for battle.

Terrence Reynolds and Scott Bollinger appeared agitated and ill at ease when the bailiff called out, "All rise!" Judge Toliver entered, gaveled the court into session and got straight to business, "The court now recognizes the defense, Mister Robinson!"

"Thank you your honor, the defense calls Brian Carlson," Wilbert announced then took his seat.

After Brian was sworn in Sylvia Maples took the floor and began examination by asking Brian his age, address and profession. She then asked him to focus on the night of the murder. "Why were you in a fight with Charles Grant?" she questioned.

"Because he owed me money," Brian replied.

"Why did he owe you money?"

"I painted some cars for him. I freelance and work at a few different shops painting cars or bikes. I had filled in for the regular painter at the Newride Body Shop for four days. Bear agreed to pay two hundred a day, meaning he owed me a total of eight hundred dollars," Brian explained.

"Had you experienced difficulty getting paid before?" Sylvia inquired.

"Well the last couple of times my pay was a day or so late but this was the first time I had to wait more than a week."

"Do you know why your pay was late?"

"Well, yeah…Bear started buying and selling cocaine and wanted me to wait until he made a profit," Brian responded.

"Who started the fight at the Lucky Seven Bar that night?"

"I did…I was hanging out shooting pool and drinking when Bear came in. My money was due several days ago and I had already asked him for it two or three times, so I waited for him to say something to me about it."

"And did he speak to you about the money?" Sylvia asked.

"Naw…he didn't speak to me at all. He looked at me then went to the bar and started drinking and talking to other people. A little while later I heard him bragging to the bartender about becoming master of the key before the night was over."

"What is master of the key?" Sylvia inquired.

"Means he had arranged to buy a kilo of cocaine and I knew that meant he had a lot of cash on him including mine," Brian explained.

"So what did you do?"

"When I got ready to leave I went over and asked when he planned to pay me my money and he got real belligerent...said some ugly stuff..."

"What precisely did Charles Grant say to you at that point?" Sylvia demanded.

"He told me he would pay me whenever he fucking felt like it and I could get the hell out of his face," Brian replied.

"Did you respond?" Sylvia asked.

"I hauled off and punched him in the mouth," Brian admitted.

"What happened after you punched him?"

"Well he fought back and we both got threw out the back door of the bar into the alley. I figured the fight was over you know, and started walking toward the front where my bike was parked when Bear totally blindsided me with a sucker punch and I went down. Soon as I hit the ground he started stomping and kicking me, messed me up pretty bad before he stopped and went around front. It took a while but I got to my feet and went around front then back into the bar. I was mad as hell and I wanted Bear to know he was dead and I meant it!" Brian explained.

"You threatened to kill him?" Sylvia asked.

"No! I said he was dead, that means his ass is dead to me. Even if he did pay me my money and apologize I still would not work for him, bail him out when he or one of his guys has screwed up a paint job or even speak to him. There is nothing to forgive or forget, because in my world he no longer exists; his ass is dead to me!"

"Did you go back into that bar seeking revenge?" Sylvia questioned.

"No ma'am I wasn't seeking revenge because I started the fight. But Bear didn't have to do what he did so I wanted him to know I was through with him. I went back inside because I thought Bear had. When I didn't see him I figured he was hiding some place but that bouncer dude pushed me out of the bar. My ankle was really messed up and my jaw and side hurt like hell, so I was in no shape to stand my ground. I wanted to ride my bike home but the bouncer drug me down the street a short distance then threw me into a cab. I was hurting and drunk so I gave the driver my address and let him take me home," Brian responded.

"What happened when you arrived at home?" Sylvia asked.

"Well when I got home, Katie, uh that's my neighbor from across the street...well, least she was anyway..."

"What do you mean by at least she was?" Sylvia interrupted.

"Uh...she was killed. A car hit her motorcycle about two weeks after my arrest," Brian explained. "Uh...she came and helped me get in the house. Then she patched me up some and fixed me a couple of drinks. After awhile she went down to the Lucky Seven and got my bike, then she gave me some sleeping pills and that's about all I remember. The next day the cops showed up and arrested me for murder," Brian concluded.

"Did the police take you directly to jail?" Sylvia questioned.

"Well…no not really. They took me to the hospital jail cause I was still hurting," Brian responded.

Sylvia entered Brian Carlson's treatment records into evidence. The records revealed a bruised eye, a hairline fracture to the right jawbone, two fractured and bruised ribs and a severely sprained right ankle.

"Brian, did you kill the Bear, Charles Grant?" Sylvia asked.

"No ma'am I did not!" Brian firmly responded.

"Thank you, no further questions your honor," Sylvia concluded and took her seat.

"After you left the bar that night about what time did you arrive at home Mister Carlson?" Scott Bollinger asked on cross-examination.

"Uh it was about eleven when I started to leave the bar just before the fight broke out…after that I'm not real clear on time," Brian responded.

"You are not clear on time because you were mad! Bear owed you money and you just lost a fight! You left that bar, rode your motorcycle to the Newride Body Shop and settled the score! You got your revenge by shooting Charles Grant, not once but three times…didn't you Mister Carlson?" Scott Bollinger demanded.

"No I did not," Brian responded.

Scott Bollinger picked up the Glock pistol, "Is this your gun Mister Carlson?" he inquired.

"I'd have to see it up close to be sure," Brian replied.

Scott Bollinger allowed Brian to inspect the gun without letting go of it, "Well?" he demanded.

"Uh…yeah, I scratched a backwards B on it right there, yeah it's mine," Brian confirmed.

"Have you used it much?" Scott inquired.

"Yeah…some…target shooting out in the country mostly," Brian answered.

"Do you have a license to carry this weapon?"

"Uh…no sir, I've never had no license or nothing," Brian admitted.

"Did you have this gun with you when you went back into the bar?" Scott asked.

"No sir," Brian replied.

"Of course you didn't because you had already killed Charles Grant before you went back into the bar…isn't that the real truth?" Scott Bollinger prodded.

"No it is not," Brian insisted.

"Why did you wipe your fingerprints off of your own gun?" Scott demanded.

"I didn't."

"After the fight, you got on your motorcycle, followed Charles Grant to the Newride Body Shop where you shot him dead in an act of cold blooded revenge. Then you rode your bike back to the Lucky Seven Bar, wiped your fingerprints off of your own gun then went inside and made a scene to establish an alibi…tell the truth Mister Carlson…isn't that exactly what happened?" Scott Bollinger boomed.

"No it is not!" Brian responded.

"You were mad weren't you?" Scott demanded.

"Objection! This is badgering the witness your honor," Wilbert protested.

"Overruled, the witness may answer the question," Judge Toliver responded.

"Yes sir I was mad," Brian responded.

"You were drunk and got stomped by a man that owed you money didn't you?"

"Yes sir."

"You had a score to settle...didn't you Brian Carlson?"

"No sir, I was drunk and did lose a fight I started, but I didn't have any score to settle because I was through with Bear as a person," Brian explained.

"You were through with him after you settled the score by putting three bullets in his head, isn't that the real truth Brian Carlson?"

"No sir!"

"You plotted your revenge..."

"Objection! Badgering the witness your honor," Wilbert interrupted.

"Sustained...please limit your cross to questions Mister Bollinger," Judge Toliver responded.

"Did you arrive at the Newride Body Shop still in the heat of battle Mister Carlson?" Scott inquired.

"I didn't go to the Newride, I went home," Brian replied.

"Did you, Brian Carlson, reach into your saddlebag and take out your Glock 19 9mm pistol before you went inside the Newride Body Shop?" Scott asked.

"I did not go to the Newride," Brian repeated.

"The coroner testified that Charles Grant was shot while moving toward the assassin, meaning you feared another beating didn't you?"

"I wasn't there."

"Oh you were there alright; you shot Charles Grant to death out of fear and loathing, then got back on your bike and plotted your alibi on the ride back to the Lucky Seven Bar. Now that is the whole truth isn't it Brian Carlson, is that not the real truth?"

"No it is not!" Brian firmly responded.

"Your honor?" Wilbert interrupted again.

"No further questions your honor," Scott announced while shaking his head as if in disbelief.

The defense calls Gatan Batawa," Wilbert announced. Then as soon as the witness was sworn in he asked, "What is your occupation sir?"

"I am a taxicab driver sir", Gatan responded.

"Mister Batawa I have a Yellow Cab Company log sheet for May 17th, with your name and cab number on it; it this your log sheet sir?" Wilbert asked.

Gatan studied the document then confirmed that it was his log sheet. After entering the log sheet into evidence Wilbert continued. "Mister Batawa did you pick up a passenger at the Lucky Seven Bar around eleven pm on the night of May 17th?"

"No sir, I picked up a passenger at post 34, which is about a third of the block past the Lucky Seven Bar," Gatan corrected.

"That would be entry number sixteen on your log sheet?" Wilbert questioned.

"That's correct!"

"What is post 34?" Wilbert inquired.

"A post is a specific location where taxicabs go to wait for another run. There are several all around the city and the first cab on any post gets the first run off that specific post," Gatan explained.

"Was the run from the Lucky Seven Bar a radio run?"

"No sir...someone came from behind and knocked on the window of the cab. I unlocked the doors and a fellow got in very quickly."

"Did you notice if there was more than one person or did someone help the passenger get in the cab?" Wilbert questioned.

"Someone seemed to push the fellow into my cab then slammed the door," Gatan responded. "I asked the fellow for an address and he gave to me, then I ask for twenty dollar and he gave so I drove him to the address."

"What happened when you got to his house?" Wilbert questioned.

"He seemed to have trouble getting out of the cab until a lady came from across the street and helped him," Gatan replied.

"Did you get a close enough look to identify that passenger if you saw him again?" Wilbert asked.

"Uh...no sir, I did not see him very well. He laid on the seat and moaned while I drove," Gatan responded.

"Did you get a good enough look to say if he was a really big guy or a little small guy?" Wilbert pressed.

"Uh...he was about normal size. It was dark outside but I remember him leaning against the lady and he was just a normal size guy," Gatan explained.

"Ah...normal size, average height...average weight, similar to the defendant, Brian Carlson, is that what you mean by normal sir?"

"That's correct."

"Your log shows you picked up the fare at post 34 at 11:18pm then discharged the customer at 1297

Lombard Street at 11:29pm. Are those times correct Mister Batawa?" Wilbert questioned.

"Yes sir, they are correct," Gatan replied.

"Thank you sir, nothing further your honor," Wilbert concluded.

"Mister Batawa," Terrence Reynolds began on cross-examination, "isn't it fairly common for you and your fellow taxicab drivers to routinely pick-up drunks from the Lucky Seven and other bars throughout the night?"

"No sir, most drunks do not leave until the bars close," Gatan responded.

"Do you get flagged down by people very often?"

"No sir, most are radio calls…that is why I sit on the post with my doors locked," Gatan explained.

"Once the passenger in question was out of your cab did you actually see him go into the house?" Terrence questioned.

"No sir, I noted the time then drove away," Gatan responded.

"Isn't it true sir that when you and your fellow cab drivers get busy you may catch up on your paperwork once business slows down?" Terrence asked.

"Uh…I do not think I understand the question?" Gatan replied.

"Isn't it a common practice for you to fill in several runs at one time on your log sheets. Meaning the pick-up and drop-off times might be just a little off here and there?" Terrence persisted.

"No, I am good driver, long time driver. My paperwork is correct, my car is clean, there are no complaints against me, nothing is made up…all addresses and time is correct...I am good driver..." Gatan responded.

"Thank you sir, nothing further thank you. Nothing further your honor," Terrence announced and took his seat.

Maureen McDougal was not a happy woman when she learned she was being summoned to court to testify during Brian Carlson's murder trial. She was an introverted widow in her mid-fifties that worked long hours as the office manager for a medical practice. When off duty Maureen kept to herself, reading and tending her garden. On the night when Bradley Breedlove rang her doorbell Maureen was feeling lonely and badly in need of male company. She invited him in, cooperated with his investigation, provided refreshments then lost herself to his flirtatious charm. It was a one time affair for which Maureen was grateful and did not expect to repeat until Bradley re-appeared shortly before her summons to court.

When the defense called Maureen McDougal to the witness stand she entered the court searching the many faces for Bradley Breedlove. When she spotted him sitting in the front row of the spectator section directly behind the defense table Maureen smiled and took the stand. She testified that Katie McDougal was her 28 year-old niece who lived in an apartment in her basement on the day of the murder. The basement has an outside entrance and she rarely saw Katie. On the night in question she had retired early and knew nothing of Katie's actions. She informed the court that Katie was killed in a horrible accident, then verified that a telephone record shown to her by Wilbert Robinson was indeed hers. Wilbert entered the telephone record into evidence then closed his examination of the witness. The prosecution had no questions so the witness was excused. To her surprise Maureen was slightly disappointed when the judge excused her. She had just gotten settled in and wasn't really ready to leave. But on the other hand she was happy it was over and left the court hoping that Bradley Breedlove would soon find another reason to pay her a visit.

Next the defense called their final witness, Douglas Anderson, to the stand.

"Mister Anderson," Sylvia Maples began.

"Uh…pardon me ma'am but could you call me Doug. That Mister Anderson stuff makes me think you are talking to my dad."

"Very well then Doug, this telephone record that has been entered into evidence shows that at 1:46 am on the morning of May 18, a call was placed from the McDougal residence to (317) 256-0706, is that your phone number Mist…Doug," Sylvia asked.

"Yes ma'am that's my number," Doug responded.

"Did you receive that call?" Sylvia questioned.

"Yes ma'am."

"And who was the call from?"

"Uh…it was from a friend of mine named Katie McDougal," Doug replied.

"Did Katie call to chat or did she call for a specific reason?" Sylvia probed.

"She wanted me to give her a ride so she could do a favor for her neighbor," Doug explained.

"And did you?"

"Oh yes ma'am, I got right up, put on some clothes and rode straight over to her house."

"What happened when you arrived at Katie McDougal's house?" Sylvia asked.

"Uh…she was waiting on the porch, we talked for a few minutes then she got on the back of my bike and we rode down to the Lucky Seven Bar to get her neighbor's bike."

"Do you remember about what time it was when the two of you arrived at the Lucky Seven?" Sylvia inquired.

"Naw…not really but it was closed and there was just the one bike sitting out front," Doug responded.

"Did you just drop Katie at the bar or did you ride back with her?"

"Well she asked me to ride her neighbor's bike cause it's a big ole Harley Hawg and I don't think Katie had rode a bike that big before. I know she was kinda scared of it so I let her ride mine. I got a little 650 it's more like what she's used to."

"So you rode Brian Carlson's Harley from the Lucky Seven Bar back to his house. Is that correct Doug?"

"Yes ma'am I rode it back and parked it in the drive up close to the house."

"Did you happen to look in the saddlebags while you were in possession of the bike?"

"No ma'am."

"Did you see Brian Carlson?"

"No ma'am."

"Do you know Brian Carlson?"

"No ma'am."

"So this was all for Katie?" Sylvia asked.

"Yes ma'am."

"What happened after you parked the bike"?

"I talked to Katie for a while then went home."

"How long would you say it took you to leave your house and ride to Katie's house after receiving that phone call?" Sylvia inquired.

"Musta took about ten minutes to get ready and it's about a 12 minute ride so about twenty minutes or so," Doug surmised.

That would put you at Katie McDougal's house at around 2:10 and you indicated earlier that the two of you talked for a few minutes. How long did it take for you to reach the Lucky Seven Bar after you left Katie's house?" Sylvia questioned.

"Um...probably about twenty minutes," Doug responded.

Sylvia paused then examined the taxicab log, "Doug, it only took the cab eleven minutes to travel from the Lucky Seven Bar to Brian Carlson's address which is directly across the street from the McDougal's residence. Are you certain it took you over twenty minutes to travel the same distance on a motorcycle?" she questioned.

"Uh...yes ma'am. I mean uh...I was really into Katie and cruising with her on my bike was totally cool...so I kinda took the long way," Doug admitted.

"I see..." Sylvia smiled then continued. "When you left the bar did the two of you ride directly back to Katie's house?"

"Yes ma'am."

"Then if you first arrived at Katie's house at about 2:10, talked for give or take five minutes, then traveled for twenty minutes, would you say that put you at the Lucky Seven Bar at around 2:35am?" Sylvia questioned.

"Uh...let's see...it was a little after three when I got home so I would say yeah, that's about right."

"Thank you Doug, no further questions your honor," Sylvia concluded.

Judge Toliver called upon the prosecution for cross-examination and once again they declined, feeling that this was an after-the-fact witness that was of no value to the case. Judge Toliver then called upon the defense.

"The defense rests your honor," Wilbert proudly announced, then gave a satisfied nod to his co-counsel and took his seat.

# Chapter seven

*J*udge *Neil Toliver was very pleased* with the pace and progress of this trial. There had been few points of order, clashes over the law or deviations from an orderly process. After the defense rested, he gaveled the court into recess for lunch and left the bench thinking the trial would be completely resolved before the day was over. In fact, the tropical breezes from a distant island on which he owned a condominium was calling the judge. Following this case his schedule was clear for just over a week and he planned to spend that time on the island. He had hoped this trial would be of short duration but one never knows so he had not confirmed plans. This trial however was moving along slightly ahead of schedule, so during lunch Judge Toliver allowed his wife to book a late morning flight the very next day.

Following lunch, Wilbert Robinson and Sylvia Maples returned to the courtroom feeling refreshed and upbeat. Wilbert was pleasantly surprised to see Nathan Carlson as he briefly greeted the Carlson family before taking his seat. While trying to review his notes Wilbert became distracted when he noticed the spectator section of the room filling up. He found it odd to see Jeffery Logan among some of the high powered attorneys now occupying many seats.

Wilbert had no knowledge of the fact that word had quickly spread throughout the local legal community that a royal battle was taking place in Judge Toliver's court. The battle was between the elite from the prosecutor's office and two small-time, no-name lawyers. While many lawyers were aware of Wilbert's reputation as a civil lawyer none expected that either he or Sylvia Maples truly had any real chance against the best prosecutors. Yet, the no-name's had held their own and bets were now being placed on the outcome.

Sylvia Maples was very pleased with the large sophisticated audience while Terrence Reynolds returned from lunch appearing tired and seemed not to notice. Scott Bollinger noticed the crowd immediately and seemed somewhat embarrassed as he made his way to the prosecution table. The air hung heavy with anticipation of the closing arguments when the bailiff called out, "All rise."

Upon returning to the bench and gaveling court into session, Judge Toliver noted that there was no rebuttal evidence from either side then advised the jury that they would now hear closing arguments. The state with the burden of proof goes first and last. "Mister Reynolds, you may begin," he instructed.

Terrence Reynolds took the floor and thanked the judge. Then for more than twenty minutes he reviewed and summarized the prosecution's case against Brian Carlson. He held up the gun, frequently pointed to the large photos of the crime scene, raised his voice and smacked his fist into his palm in an effort to drive home his points. Finally, Terrence held up the large close-up photo of Charles Grant's head. "Ladies and gentlemen, this was a man, a husband, a father and a business owner and he was murdered in cold blood. The shot that killed this man was fired from only four inches away. Only four inches…that was intentional, that was revenge, meant to kill, meant to satisfy a score. That bullet was fired by this gun…and this gun was in the hands of its owner Brian Carlson. It's all here. There is nothing complicated about it. Brian Carlson is guilty of the murder of Charles Grant. The police did their job and arrested him. I have done my job in prosecuting him and now, as a juror it is your responsibility to finish the job and find Brian Carlson guilty of premeditated murder in the first degree. Thank you ladies and gentlemen and thank you your honor."

"The court will now recognize the defense, Mister Robinson," Judge Toliver announced.

Wilbert straightened his tie then took the floor. "Your honor, ladies and gentlemen of the jury, to find Brian Carlson guilty of murder you must be certain beyond a reasonable doubt. If you believe the injuries, the broken jaw, two broken ribs and the severely sprained ankle that this man sustained in that fight prevented him from riding his motorcycle, then that is reasonable doubt and you cannot convict. If you believe Brian Carlson went home in a cab that night just as the cab driver testified then that is reasonable doubt and you cannot convict. If you believe someone else at that bar knew that Charles Grant was in possession of a large sum of money and bragging about making a large drug buy...and that same someone also knew there was an unaccounted for gun in Brian Carlson's saddlebags, then that is reasonable doubt and you cannot convict. And...what happened to the money? Everyone agrees that Charles Grant had a large sum of money in his possession that night...but what happened to it? No money or drugs were found in Charles Grant's pockets or at the crime scene. There were no drugs and only one hundred forty two dollars and eighty three cents found in Brian Carlson's possession at the time of his arrest, and Brian's bank account held less than one thousand dollars with no recent deposits...so what happened to the money? The prosecution has not accounted for that large sum of missing money, meaning that missing money creates reasonable doubt and you cannot convict."

"Ladies and gentlemen Brian Carlson did not kill Charles Grant. The police department has admitted under oath that they did not even investigate this case. They focused on Brian and Brian alone. Where is the bouncer at the Lucky Seven Bar that night? Why wasn't he interviewed? Why didn't he testify? Why don't the police even know his name? And where are the witnesses to the murder itself? Are there any video cameras near the Lucky Seven Bar or Newride Body Shop that might contain pertinent information? The gun was wiped clean of fingerprints, that's very unusual and would not benefit Brian, so who wiped the gun clean? We don't know the answer to any of these questions because the police did not bother to ask! They took the lazy way out without even once considering an alternative suspect. If you believe this was a poor investigation then that is reasonable doubt and you cannot convict. The fight in that bar started around eleven and Brian Carlson entered Gatan Batawa's cab at eleven eighteen. Now…if you believe Brian Carlson did not have time to get thrown out of the bar, then ride to the Newride Body Shop, kill a man, then ride back to the Lucky Seven and get thown out for a second time before climbing into a cab down the street all in just eighteen minutes, then that is reasonable doubt and you cannot convict."

"Ladies and gentlemen the burden of proof is on the prosecution. Brian Carlson did not have to testify here today but he wanted to. Brian wanted to tell the honest truth and clear his name. Yes he had a fight. Yes he was very angry. Yes he had too much to drink and yes the gun was his. But no…he did not use it! AND…the prosecution has not proven that he did. Brian went home in a cab. Unfortunately and without knowing it by leaving in a cab Brian set himself up as the fall guy. He left behind a three hour window of opportunity for someone to remove, use and then put that gun back into his saddlebag. That is exactly what happened! That is why the gun was wiped clean of fingerprints. If you believe it is possible that a killer still walks among us then that is reasonable doubt and you cannot convict."

"Reasonable doubt…the injuries my client suffered creates reasonable doubt. The limited time frame creates reasonable doubt. The cab ride home, the missing money and the sloppy police investigation all create reasonable doubt and you cannot convict this man if you have any reasonable doubt whatsoever."

"Finally ladies and gentlemen, I must remind you that convicting a man of first degree murder is a very serious and sobering business. You must be certain beyond a reasonable doubt for a very real reason. If you are not certain beyond a reasonable doubt then you face the awful possibility of condemning an innocent life to death or imprisonment. And even worse is the fact that the tragedy continues because the real killer remains free to kill again and again. Brian Carlson is an innocent man and I beg you to understand that every shred of evidence the prosecution has offered is cloaked and covered with reasonable doubt. In the United States of America sloppy police work and circumstantial evidence must never be enough to cost a human being their life or liberty. I challenge you as responsible citizens to recognize and honor the principle that justice cannot be served in the face of reasonable doubt and find this innocent man, Brian Carlson, not guilty! Thank you ladies and gentlemen and thank you your honor," Wilbert concluded then took his seat.

"Mister Reynolds," Judge Toliver responded.

"If I may your honor?" Scott Bollinger inquired.

"Proceed," Judge Toliver allowed.

"Ladies and gentleman let me assure you that there is no doubt that Charles Grant is dead. There is no doubt that Brian Carlson had a fight with Charles Grant. There is no doubt that Brian Carlson threatened to kill Charles Grant and there is no doubt that Brian Carlson's gun did just that. Could he ride his motorcycle with his injuries? You bet he could, adrenaline fueled by anger and alcohol easily overcomes pain or limited mobility. But Brian Carlson didn't even have to ride his motorcycle. He likely put the gun in his pocket before he got thrown out of the bar and took the cab home. Then he had nearly three hours to get his revenge and stage his alibi. Brian could have borrowed a car or had someone drive him. He did the job then wiped his fingerprints off the gun when he put it back into his saddlebag after his bike was delivered home. We don't know exactly what route he traveled to kill Charles Grant because he won't tell us. But we do know Brian Carlson fought with Charles Grant, had a score to settle with Charles Grant, threatened to kill Charles Grant and Brian Carlson's gun fired the fatal bullet four inches from Charles Grant's face. Throw out all that talk about cabs and helpful neighbors and let's talk about murder...cold blooded first degree murder. Motive, weapon, threat and opportunity all came together and resulted in the planned cold blooded murder of Charles Grant by the defendant Brian Carlson. Ladies and gentlemen you are smart people, you understand there is no doubt that is what the facts show. And there can be no doubt that yes ladies and gentlemen, the police in fact did their job and arrested the right suspect. There can be no doubt that we the prosecution have done our job in prosecuting this suspect on behalf of the state and there can be do doubt that it is now your responsibility as citizens of this state to find Brian Carlson guilty of murder in the first degree. He is guilty and guilty beyond a reasonable doubt! That is the truth and that must be your finding! Thank you...and thank you your honor," Scott concluded.

Judge Toliver thanked both legal teams then read his instructions to the jury. He warned, advised, instructed and defined their responsibilities then ordered the bailiff to sequester the jury for deliberations. After the jury left the courtroom, Judge Toliver advised that court would be in recess until the jury has reached a verdict.

Court will be called back into session exactly thirty minutes after the court clerk notifies both legal teams that a verdict is in. With that said Judge Toliver left the bench and the courtroom began to clear very quickly. Sylvia Maples assured the Carlson family that they could retire to their hotel suite and still return to the court in time for the verdict, while Wilbert collected various papers and notes.

The time was 2:55pm and there was nothing to do but wait so Wilbert and Sylvia decided to wait at Wilbert's office since it was close by. Sylvia had an assistant deliver some routine work from her office and for over two hours both lawyers caught up on various unrelated work. Lucy stood by, just as she had during the trial, producing needed documents, manning the phone, keeping the coffee fresh and the schedule under control. She was on alert for the call from the clerk's office which allowed both Wilbert and Sylvia to relax and concentrate. As six o'clock approached Lucy ordered dinner and when the food arrived both lawyers put away their work to eat and relax for the remainder of their wait.

"I think we did good...yep...real good," Sylvia smiled.

"I'll have to admit it was quite an experience," Wilbert admitted.

"So what do you think? Criminal law starting to grow on you?" Sylvia asked.

"Not a chance, I like money...not drama!" Wilbert responded to Sylvia's amusement. "Do you have any idea how much longer before this is over? It has already been over three hours," he complained.

"One never knows with a jury. From my experience most juries are usually done in three or four hours. If it goes a lot longer that usually means the jury is split and one or more of them are going to have to be converted," Sylvia explained.

"Well if only one or two of them are holding things up can't the judge just replace that juror with one of the alternates that agrees with everybody else?" Wilbert questioned.

"Wilbert Robinson you know better than that!" Sylvia lectured. "It would be highly irregular for any judge to stick his nose into the jury room...I think you are fishing for some crooked possibilities."

"And I think you might be getting to know me a little too well! So what do you think? We got anybody to work with on this thing?"

"We have already used up everything we had to work with on this case in court Mister Robinson and I think we done a darn good job. We don't need a fix, this we will win on our own," Sylvia insisted.

"I'm sure you are right...but I'll keep my fishing poles baited just in case," Wilbert replied.

As the evening turned into night Lucy sat and repeatedly slapped her knee while laughing at the show on television while Sylvia dozed and Wilbert read. When 10:00pm approached Lucy announced that she was a night-owl and would remain on alert while all others slept. Wilbert didn't argue, he went straight to his couch, made himself comfortable and quickly fell asleep. Sylvia assured Lucy that she would only take short naps and would occasionally check in just to see if Lucy might need a nap, but Sylvia also fell into sound sleep. Lucy was unbothered; she continued to watch television for another three hours before she too dozed off. The ringing phone at 5:06am startled all three of them awake. The verdict was in; court would be called into session at 5:40am. Lucy sprung into action quickly calling everyone on her notify list while Wilbert and Sylvia freshened up then headed for the courthouse.

As he made his way down the hall then into the clerk's office and on into the courtroom, Wilbert was amazed at the number of people that were waiting for the verdict. Some of them looked as though they had not left the building and Wilbert wondered who they were. The early morning hour felt very odd to Wilbert as he watched the court reassemble. After the familiar call to rise from the bailiff, Wilbert watched with interest when the jury was led back into the courtroom. He stood with confidence and gave his client a reassuring pat on the back when Judge Toliver asked the defendant to rise. Judge Toliver then asked the foreman of the jury to rise and state her name. A slender brunette in her early forties rose from her seat and identified herself as Susan Warren.

"Miss Warren has this jury reached a verdict?" Judge Toliver asked.

"No sir. We are deadlocked ten to two. Ten not guilty, two guilty," Susan reported.

"And am I to understand that this jury does not feel it is possible to reach unanimity?" the judge questioned.

"That is correct your honor. Even if you put us back in there for six months I don't believe it would change a thing and as I already reported sir, it was starting to get real ugly in there. The two guilty voters have dug their heels in and the not guilty voters aren't budging either so I really feel ten to two is the best this group can do," Susan responded.

"Very well, thank you Miss Warren. Ladies and gentlemen of the jury on behalf of the State of Indiana I thank you for your service. You are now excused. Bailiff please remove the jury," Judge Toliver instructed.

Once the jury had left the courtroom Judge Toliver continued. "On the basis of a hung jury, I hereby declare, in the case of the State of Indiana verses Brian Carlson, a mistrial. I will schedule a hearing to establish another trial date on December 8th at 9am. The defendant shall remain in the custody of the sheriff's department and with no other business pending this court stands adjourned!"

A stunned silence fell over the courtroom and lingered until well after Judge Toliver left the room. No one seemed to know what to do until Terrence Reynolds stepped forward and offered his hand to Wilbert, "You put up one hell of a fight counselor," he complimented.

"As did you sir!" Wilbert replied while shaking Terrence's hand. "But I do wish one of us had won," he added.

Terrence smiled and offered his hand to Sylvia Maples while Scott Bollinger enthusiastically grabbed Wilbert's hand. "Counselor, you have turned my opinion of you completely around and you now have my respect. In fact you could have a future in the prosecutor's office if you would like to consider it," Scott offered with a glowing smile.

"I'm very flattered counselor, I really am," Wilbert responded, "but I am not prepared to consider any career moves at the moment."

"Of course not, but we will be in touch," Scott assured then offered his hand and a big grin to Sylvia Maples.

After sharing a brief conversation with his son, Nathan Carlson met privately with Wilbert Robinson for several minutes. Following that meeting Nathan collected his family, left the building and flew home to New York.

Wilbert advised Lucy that in order to decompress and recuperate he was taking the next two days off. He instructed her to schedule a meeting with the Brian Carlson Legal Defense Team to discuss the outcome and future of this case immediately following his time off. Wilbert then had a brief discussion with Sylvia Maples before he bid her farewell and slowly made his way out of the building. Wilbert was deep in thought as he attempted to cross the street and was startled when a big silver Mercedes whooshed by just before he stepped off the curb.

Judge Toliver was driving the car and the judge was in a big hurry. The long jury deliberations had thrown a wrench into his plans and he was desperately trying to make up loss time so he could catch his flight to the island. Ordinarily Judge Toliver considered long jury deliberation as due process and would have insisted that the jury continue to try for a unanimous verdict but time had become a personal issue. He was first notified at 10:26pm, then at 1:51am and again at 3:38am that the jury felt it was hopelessly deadlocked. Each time he instructed them to keep deliberating but was again notified of the same result at 4:57am. On this occasion for Judge Toliver time had run out. He needed to clear this case and get moving on his personal agenda. He interpreted the jury foreman's statement that ugly words were now being used in the jury room as verbal abuse with the potential to escalate and used that as grounds for declaring a mistrial. The judge used those grounds because he knew they were very unlikely to be scrutinized or challenged. He smiled as he eased the Mercedes onto the freeway; there was very little traffic so he would make good time driving home. His wife was waiting with their luggage so now it was clear sailing. They would catch their flight and be on the island before sunset.

Three days later Lucy was keeping a careful eye on her boss as she made fresh coffee and prepared for the Brian Carlson Legal Defense Team meeting. Wilbert Robinson had returned from his two days off in high spirits. He had a spring in his step and acted as though he was on top of the world. Upon arriving at the office he announced that from this day forward the Robinson Law Firm was going to become a lot more selective about the cases it accepts and the office hours are going to be reduced to thirty per week. At first Lucy didn't believe her ears and decided she would believe those things when she saw them. But sure enough before the day was over Wilbert had declined to take two rather small cases and had the hours of operation re-lettered on the office door.

By 3:30 that afternoon, Lucy, Bradley Breedlove and Sylvia Maples had assembled in Wilbert's office for the scheduled meeting.

"Good afternoon and thank you for being here," Wilbert began. "We have been on quite a journey together and as you probably suspect it is not over yet. I have a letter from our client they would like me to share with you. Quote...*To the Brian Carlson Legal Defense Team. Thank you for your exemplary work and outstanding efforts on behalf of our son Brian. We are indeed very pleased and satisfied with your representation and do consider it a success. In any other field of competition a score of ten to two represents a resounding lopsided victory and we feel it also should have in our son's case. Nonetheless, because of our respect for and deep faith in each member of the Brian Carlson Legal Defense Team we are eager to retain your services. We have absolute confidence in the ability of this team to achieve victory and stand ready with any and all needed resources and support for your next engagement in this battle. Again thank each of you for your skillful efforts. You have given this family hope and we are now confident of your ultimate success. With sincere regards, Nathan and Marguerite Carlson.* Unquote. Now, having read that letter I must ask each of you individually if you are willing to remain on the team," Wilbert explained. "Lucy...how about you?"

"You couldn't beat me off the team with a stick," Lucy giggled.

"Hum...okay, Bradley?"

"All in! All in! You know Bradley Breedlove don't let go! I'm in...all in!"

"Sylvia?" Wilbert asked while still smiling at Bradley's remarks.

"How about I just ditto Bradley," Sylvia offered then broke out laughing causing the others in the room to join in.

"Okay folks," Wilbert called out while regaining his composure, "the Carlson family is anything but cheap, they have seen fit to refresh our retainers and/or provide a bonus. This is not reward money. This money is advance payment for the hard work we are going to put in before and after we go back to trial. Lucy," Wilbert handed her an envelope which she promptly tore open.

"My Lord what is this for?" Lucy questioned as she stared at a personal check from the Carlson family. The check was made payable to her for the amount of ten thousand dollars.

"It's your bonus for being a member of the Brian Carlson Legal Defense Team," Wilbert reminded her.

"Oh I just love those Carlson people...they got a whole lot of class," Lucy responded through a wide grin.

"Bradley, this is a bonus and will not affect your billing in any way. What this does is insure that you will be willing to put this case at the front of your agenda until it is resolved. Are you good with that?" Wilbert asked.

Bradley took the envelope, looked inside at his check for ten thousand dollars then raised both his arms over his head and looked at the ceiling. "Me and you baby!" he cried out. "Yes sir, you and me!" He put his arms down and looked at Wilbert, "All in boss...Bradley is all the way in...no doubt...you call Bradley comes running...all in, all in!"

Wilbert handed Sylvia her check, it was another retainer check for twenty five thousand dollars. "I hope that is satisfactory. It is my understanding that this is a refresher and our win bonus remains the same," he explained.

"I have no complaints," Sylvia responded. "How soon do we get back to work?"

"Right now!" Wilbert responded.

By the time the meeting adjourned everyone had a to-do list. The new trial date had not been established but the Brian Carlson Legal Defense Team wanted to get off to a running start. It was agreed that Bradley should track down the bouncer from the Lucky Seven Bar and again attempt to locate any video evidence. Bradley was also assigned to locate any customers that were present at the Lucky Seven the night of the murder and to time out the drive from the Lucky Seven Bar to the Newride Body Shop. Among many other things Wilbert and Sylvia agreed to seek a medical expert to testify regarding Brian's ability to ride a motorcycle while injured and to recruit jury selection experts.

The Brian Carlson Legal Defense Team had progressed from having no chance whatsoever to getting within two votes of winning it all the first time out. They had fought to a draw and were now confident, well paid, poised and determined to seize complete and total victory in the second battle. Their growth was measurable and they were indeed becoming a formidable legal team.

# Chapter eight

*Terrence Reynolds had been pleasantly* surprised by the hung jury and mistrial. He felt he had lost this case as soon as Wilbert Robinson finished his closing argument. The longer the jury stayed in deliberation the more convinced Terrence became that all was lost. He had begun to map out a new career path for himself and was fully prepared for the worst when the mistrial was announced. As much as he was pleased, Terrence was more surprised by his gut level feeling of misgiving. For a brief moment he wondered if he truly believed Brian Carlson was guilty.

Scott Bollinger became absolutely terrified of losing the case even before Wilbert concluded his closing argument. Scott was deeply impressed by Wilbert Robinson and Sylvia Maples. They had dug up fresh evidence, established a creditable defense, fought like hell and crafted a brilliant closing argument. It was a lot to overcome and he had tried his best but did not think he had done enough. He could not bear even the suggestion that a loss was very possible and spent most of the time waiting for the verdict pacing around-and-around his office. Scott was both shocked and greatly relieved by the mistrial. He knew he had dodged a bullet and left the courthouse in the company of a newspaper reporter, attempting to spin the mistrial into a perceived win for the prosecution.

The following day Terrence Reynolds returned to his office and workload. He put the hearing for the Carlson case on his calendar and smiled. He now felt vindicated for his initial hesitation to take the case to trial. His superiors had been pushy and arrogant, insisting on having their way and it nearly cost them a conviction. They persuaded him that even without proper preparation he would easily crush any opposition in a short march to victory...and they were wrong.

Now he could take his time and properly investigate the case then build a solid prosecution. Terrence leaned back in his chair and advised himself that this case had taught him two very strong lessons. Number one, not every seemingly open and shut case will be plea bargained, and number two, never ever waive discovery. After double checking all the necessary paperwork to re-file charges against Brian Carlson, Terrence set the case file aside; he was in no hurry to re-try this case. He was hopeful that Wilbert Robinson would agree to a new trial date several months down the road. Terrence wanted to take a break from the case for a while then come back to it fresh, start a new investigation and build a solid new case.

His hopes were dashed however when Wilbert demanded a speedy trial during the hearing and a trial date of February 23rd was established. And the deputy prosecutor's hope again suffered injury when his investigators reported no new information. His demands that they look in new directions was met with their insistence that there were no leads to follow. Scott Bollinger was not concerned. He had suggested they simply wait for discovery and see what the Robinson team turned up. That was not good enough for Terrence. He was still searching for that missing piece of evidence that would slam the door on this case when a junior deputy prosecutor named Julia Patterson asked for a minute of his time.

Julia was working on a drug case and her suspect was trying to buy down his charges. A small time drug dealer named Arthur Richardson, aka Artie, had been arrested while trying to sell a kilo of cocaine to an undercover police officer. Artie had first offered the information on his drug supplier in exchange for a lesser charge but the police already had that information. So Artie confessed that he had witnessed a murder and would finger the killer in exchange for a lesser charge. Julia wanted to talk to Terrence because Artie claimed to have witnessed the murder of Charles Grant.

"Have you grilled him?" Terrence asked.

"No sir. I thought I would see if you were even interested first. This guy is not real creditable and I'm not leaning toward making a deal," Julia explained.

"Well let's at least hear what he has to say," Terrence suggested. "Put him in an interview room."

Artie entered the interview room with a suspicious look on his face. In spite of being 36 years old, Artie was short, thin, had small boyish features and was scared to death of going to prison. He settled into a chair and fidgeted nervously until the prosecutors entered the room.

"So you witnessed the murder of Charles Grant?" Terrence asked without taking a seat.

"Uh…yes sir, I shore did!" Artie confirmed.

"Okay…tell me about it! Right from the start, including why you happened to be a witness," Terrence ordered taking a chair directly across from Artie.

"Well…okay. I mean we are working on a deal here right?" Artie questioned.

"If you got something to sell, I have a lot of capital to buy with and that is as good as it is going to get for you! So what is it going to be Artie? Have you got some legitimate information or not?" Terrence demanded.

"Hey you know something? I can dig that man…so here is the straight up truth," Artie responded. "Bear or I mean Charles Grant was an old friend and a customer of mine. But he was still a new customer, meaning I had only sold to him a couple of times. Now I don't usually take no chances, especially with new customers so I always get to the meet point early and scope things out. Now on the night he got took out, I was supposed to meet Bear at his place, the Newride Body Shop at midnight. He had ordered up a key and was paying cash. I got there around 11:15pm and parked my car across the street, got out and walked to each side of the building and checked out which windows I could see through. I noticed the back was all fenced off and thought the place seemed pretty secure, so I got back in my car, scrunched down in the seat and watched. About 11:35, give or take a couple of minutes Bear roared up.

He got off his bike and seemed to be limping a bit as he entered the shop. I stayed right where I was cause my appointment was for midnight and I don't like surprises."

"About 11:50 I saw another bike roll up. Only this dude cut his engine and lights then let the bike silently roll into the lot. I knew some shit was up when the dude stepped off the bike and pulled a ski mask down over his face. He pulled a gun from his belt then stepped through the front door of the shop. I jumped out of the car and raced to the side of the building and looked through the window just in time to see Bear rush out of the office toward the dude. The dude shot him twice and Bear fell flat on his face. Then the dude looked around real wild like for a minute or two before he leaned down and shot Bear again real close. He went through Bear's pockets then stood up and looked around again. After that he went into the office. He took the money that was on the desk and put it into his pocket, and then he checked out all the desk and file drawers before he hurried back past Bear and stood beside the front door. It seemed like he stood there forever smoking cigarettes and watching through the door. At first I couldn't figure this dude out until it dawned on me that the lousy murdering bastard was waiting for me. Apparently that miserable son-of-a-bitch planned to hit both of us, me and Bear. He had Bears money but he sure as hell wasn't going to get my drugs even if he waited ten days. Finally he got tired of waiting I guess. He pulled his ski mask off and threw it in the back of an old Ford Bear had been tinkering with, kicked the door open and marched across the lot to his bike then rode off."

"You said he took off his ski mask and threw it into the back of an old Ford?" Terrance questioned.

"Yeah, yeah right...Bear had an old piece of junk Ford; it's just a frame and couple of fenders but its real old. Bear claimed he was restoring it...but hell it's been sitting in the same place right inside the front door for years. The dude took off the ski mask like he was mad or really pissed off and threw it; kinda like in disgust or something...you know what I mean? I saw the thing go inside that old Ford."

"What color was the ski mask?" Julia Patterson asked.

"It was dark blue or black with red circles around the eyes," Artie responded.

"Did you see this man well enough to identify him?" Terrence asked.

"Oh hell yeah, I seen him real good...and I've seen him around before too," Artie assured.

"Do you know his name?"

"Naw sir, I don't."

"Okay for now Artie. If your information pans out then you will probably face a simple possession of a small quantity charge. If not then I don't think Miss Patterson here will have much mercy," Terrence concluded.

"Oh well then...if that's the case I'm home free baby...home free! I told you the truth and I can eyeball that dude anytime you serve him up," Artie boasted.

Terrence Reynolds and Julia Patterson returned to Terrence's office deep in thought.

"Artie Richardson knows enough intimate details of the murder to make his story creditable while he himself is anything but," Terrence explained to Julia. "What we need to do here is gain additional evidence before we have Artie attempt to identify our suspect."

"You mean go after the ski mask?" Julia questioned.

"Exactly! get a forensics team out to the Newride Body Shop and see if that old Ford is still there holding the final nail in Brian Carlson's coffin," Terrence ordered with a satisfied gleam in his eye.

The next morning Terrence Reynolds, Julia Patterson and the forensics technician were all smiling as they met in the prosecutor's office. The Newride Body Shop had been taken over by Charles Grant's brother, Thomas Grant. The old Ford had been left where it was, ignored and for the most part unbothered since Charles Grant last worked on it. Amid some clutter on the rear floor pan of the old car the investigators found the ski mask. Upon examination of the mask in the lab several human hairs were found inside it.

"We could get a hair sample from your suspect and test for a match, that would be a good jump shot...but DNA identification would be a slam dunk," the technician advised.

"Isn't that overkill?" Julia Patterson questioned. "We've got an eyewitness and evidence containing the suspect's hair!"

"If you had a hair sample from the suspect could you make a one hundred percent match?" Terrence asked.

"Negative," the technician replied. "Can't even reach one hundred percent with DNA but we can get very, very close."

"Well the truth is I'm facing a giant legal gorilla on the other side of this case so I need every scrap of evidence as precise as possible. How long will that DNA analysis take?" Terrence questioned.

"No more than two weeks if you sign off on the priority forms," the technician advised.

"Don't you want Artie to ID the suspect first?" Julia inquired.

"No ma'am," Terrence responded. "I'm certain that little weasel would finger the Pope if he thought it would keep his ass out of prison. We need Artie's identification as confirmation of existing concrete evidence that will slam the door and close this case. Do you have the priority forms with you?"

"Yes sir, right here," the technician replied with a satisfied smile.

In just over two weeks Terrence Reynolds invited Julia Patterson to a meeting in his office to discuss the findings of the DNA analysis. The technician took great pains to explain that the evidence was handled in strict accordance with the law. First a virgin sample of the original evidence had been separated out and sealed so the defense had the option to obtain an independent analysis. Then once the DNA line was received back in the lab, in the interest of a nonbiased discovery, they compared that line against every line available in their database. The comparison matched one individual already in custody with a ninety-nine percent degree of certainty.

Terrence Reynolds studied the report and mug shot of the suspect for several moments before writing a name on a note pad. "Julia, get a photo of this man, three different police officers and seven inmates at random. Put those eleven photos on a board with this guy and let's see who Artie picks out."

"When Julia Patterson reported that Artie had quickly and without hesitation picked the suspect that matched the DNA, Terrence Reynolds, Scott Bollinger and Police Detective Thomas Winslow immediately went to the jail and interviewed the suspect. When confronted with an eyewitness and the DNA evidence from the ski mask, the man broke down and asked for his lawyer so he could enter a plea. Terrence Reynolds went immediately back to his office and made several phone calls, the first of which was to Wilbert Robinson.

As soon as he concluded his conversation with Terrence Reynolds, Wilbert immediately called Nathan Carlson then Sylvia Maples. Following that he rushed out of his office, ordering Lucy to cancel the remainder of his appointments for the day. Late the next morning Wilbert called Lucy with instructions to cancel his appointments for the remainder of the week, and to schedule an emergency meeting of the Brian Carlson Legal Defense team for 3:30 the following afternoon. Lucy protested to no avail then went about the business of canceling appointments and rescheduling meetings while wondering and worrying about what her boss was up to.

When the Brian Carlson Legal Defense Team gathered for their emergency meeting, Bradley and Lucy appeared very serious and concerned. Wilbert began the meeting by thanking everyone for being there then went on to explain that an eyewitness to the murder of Charles Grant had surfaced. "Charles Grant's drug dealer was waiting across the street from the Newride Body Shop when he arrived that night and the drug dealer saw everything. He saw the killer arrive and noted that the killer was wearing a ski mask which he discarded inside the shop after killing Charles Grant. The prosecutor got lucky because after all this time the ski mask was still there in the shop within a pile of debris. The crime lab found human hair inside the mask from which they took a DNA sample and matched it to the same man that the drug dealer picked from a group of twelve men. That man has now pleaded guilty to the murder of Charles Grant and entered into plea bargain negotiations with the prosecutor. Ladies and Gentlemen that man's name is Lawrence Harvey Jacobson, aka Big Larry!" The room erupted in cheers while Wilbert beamed with pleasure.

"That's right folks, at 5:39pm two days ago, our client; Brian Carlson walked from the Marion County Jail a free man!" Again the room erupted in cheers and again Wilbert beamed. "Miss Maples and I picked Brian up from the jail and took him to his house on Lombard Street where he packed two suit cases then briefly chatted with a few neighbors. Following that Miss Maples and I drove Brian to the executive terminal of the airport where he was reunited with his family in a noisy, joyous celebration before they all flew back to New York. The Carlson family asked me to delay this meeting so they could have the time and opportunity to write the following letter. In fact I have two letters to read but first I want you to know that the Carlson family has sent each of you a bottle of Dom Perignon. It is chilled and this is probably a good time to pop the corks."

After the champagne began flowing Wilbert returned to his remarks. "Now the first letter I have is one I am certain each of you will find very special. Quote...*Dear Mister Wilbert Robinson, Miss Sylvia Maples, Mister Bradley Breedlove and Miss Lucy Wilcox, I want all of you to know that I have always been a rebel. Throughout my whole life I've been determined to go my own way and have my own way. I didn't need nobody and I didn't help nobody either. Once I got into trouble and was sitting in jail day after day I realized that this time there was nothing I could do to help myself. Then to make things worse, the people that were supposed to be helping me were all trying to get me to plead guilty to a crime I didn't commit and sign my freedom away. I had about given up and figured I had this coming for being such a rebel...I had never really given life a fair chance and now it had come back and bit me in the ass. I was scared and didn't know what was going to happen when Mister Wilbert Robinson and Miss Sylvia Maples showed up. You guys listened to me, you believed me then you and your team went to work...for me. I will never forget how proud and excited I felt when you guys stood up in court and fought like hell for me. I have no doubt whatsoever that I would not be a free man without your efforts and there are no words that can truly express my gratitude or how I really feel. I do want you to know that my team, the Brian Carlson Legal Defense Team, gave me more than just freedom. You gave me hope, a new outlook and a new chance at life...this time as my father's son. Thank you Wilbert, Sylvia, Bradley and Lucy. I don't love many people but I truly love and will always remember my special legal team. You have earned my highest regards and deepest respect, thanks. Brian*...unquote."

After finishing the letter, Wilbert took a break. He sipped champagne and listened to the comments regarding Brian's letter. After Bradley returned from the men's room Wilbert called the meeting back to order.

"Before I continue I should let you know that each of you will receive a copy of both of these letters. Okay the final letter is from the Carlson family, quote...*To the Brian Carlson Legal Defense Team. First please know that each of you and one guest are invited as guests of honor to the welcome home party for our son Brian. The party will be held at our home on Long Island, New York at 7:00pm, January 16th. Transportation from your home to ours and all expenses will be provided. Please RSVP prior to midnight this date*...unquote. Can we get this RSVP done right now so Lucy can respond following this meeting? Lucy how about you? You up for the party?" Wilbert questioned.

"I'm not sure just how this is gonna work...you mean we got to go to New York?"

"A limousine will pick up you and your guest at your house. It will take you to the airport where the Carlson family jet will fly all of us to New York. Waiting limos will take us to and from the Carlson estate and the same jet will fly us back," Wilbert explained.

"I gotcha and I'll be ready and waiting for that limo," Lucy promised.

"Bradley? Think you can make the party?" Wilbert asked.

"In New York, hob-knobbing with old money...Bradley Breedlove...on the scene...all the devils in hell couldn't keep Bradley Breedlove off the plane. Bradley got big time hob-knobbing coming up...oh yeah oh yeah!"

"I'll take that as a yes, Sylvia?" Wilbert responded.

"I would be delighted to accept," Sylvia Maples replied.

"Great, we are all on board; Lucy will make certain you have printed details. Okay, back to the letter.

Quote…*The family very much looks forward to receiving you in our home and thanking each of you personally for your outstanding and successful efforts. As a family we are quite aware that we have received far more than we paid for from Brian's legal team. We received excellent legal service that gained our son his freedom and we received a second chance to share life with our son. The legal services we will gladly pay for but the second chance granted to us has no price…it is priceless. To comport our sincere gratitude to you, Will, Sylvia, Bradley and Lucy we have exercised the liberty of scrapping our settlement agreement with you and replaced it with what this family feels is but a token of our appreciation that we hope you will find meaningful. One million dollars has been taken from the Carlson family treasury and divided as follows: one half for the leader of the team, one fourth for the co-counsel, one eighth for the detective and one eighth for the administrator. The checks are enclosed with this communication and once again please accept our sincere and heartfelt thank you! We very much look forward to personally greeting each of you at the party. With great respect and best regards, Nathan and Marguerite Carlson*…unquote," Wilbert concluded.

Because his check was so much larger than the other team members Wilbert felt an obligation to know if they felt satisfied with their share. So, just as he had with the bonus checks, he distributed these checks one at a time. "Lucy as the most hardworking yet understated member of the team I am happy to recognize you first. Here is your envelope and let me know if you are satisfied with it," Wilbert instructed.

"Well I wasn't expecting nothing so I ain't rejecting nothing," Lucy chuckled as she opened the envelope. "Good lord in heaven! Is this for real?" Lucy questioned in true shocked surprise. "Oh my word...I ain't never seen this much money..."

"So I'll take it that you are satisfied with the settlement?" Wilbert asked.

"I would really hate to see somebody try and take it away from me," Lucy responded as she stared at the cashier's check for one hundred twenty-five thousand dollars.

"Fine," Wilbert replied. "Bradley your envelope and of course let me know if you find it satisfactory."

"Jumping Jehoshaphat! Bradley Breedlove is all that and a bag of chips! On a well earned cruise...way out in the ocean...uh-huh. That's where you will find Bradley Breedlove uh-huh. But don't come looking cause Bradley Breedlove won't be working...ah naw. Bradley is gonna slow down now and let the ladies enjoy his company."

"I'll take it you are satisfied with your settlement?" Wilbert questioned.

"Satisfied?" Bradley shrieked as he held tightly to his cashiers check for one hundred and twenty-five thousand dollars. "You called me in and made this possible, so you are the first man in my life that I ever wanted to kiss...Bradley Breedlove is happier than a pig in slop!"

Wilbert chuckled and shook his head. "Sylvia, thank you! I could not have climbed this mountain without you. This is not exactly what we agreed on but I think you will find it acceptable...if not just say so. He handed Sylvia her envelope then sat back to watch her reaction.

Sylvia looked at her check for two hundred and fifty thousand dollars and smiled. "You know just a few months ago I would not have believed any of this but right now I agree with Bradley. You are one man I would like to kiss Mister Little Man."

"Okay...moving right along. That pretty much adjourns our meeting folks and as much as I really hate to say it, this has been our last meeting as a legal team, at least for right now anyway. So in conclusion I have a personal comment to share. I cannot think of one single soul in my entire life that has meant more to me as a person and as a professional attorney than the people in this room. Please accept my sincere and heartfelt thank you to each of you for your hard work, long hours, your outstanding contributions to the team and to our ultimate success...Thank you!" Wilbert concluded.

After the champagne had been consumed, Wilbert bade farewell to Bradley, then Sylvia and finally Lucy before he locked the door to his office, rode the elevator to the first floor and walked out the front door of the building.

Wilbert Robinson took a deep breath, looked around, straightened his tie then smiled. He was an attorney...a successful attorney and his brand new Jaguar sat waiting for him at the curb.

# CHANDLER  HALL

*From university prince…to backwoods king*

# Chapter one

*Just before the sun came up*, word arrived that the Federals were getting mighty close and would probably over-run the manor long before noon. Throwing aside all previous plans, the keepsake furniture, a few trunks and nine boxes of family treasures were quickly loaded aboard two wagons then spirited away for safekeeping amongst three trusted families whose homes had hidden cellars or other highly secure storage.

\*\*\*\*\*

One hundred and eighty two years later, Jerry Chandler was taking the slow route to earning his masters degree at Indiana University and very much enjoying the pace. It had taken Jerry six years to obtain his undergraduate degree and so far, by taking time off for foreign travel and making clever changes to his program, he had stretched his pursuit of a masters to nearly four. He was confident he could easily push a doctorate program to six years and did not care to speculate beyond that. Jerry wore designer clothes, had a platinum credit card, lived in a large luxury apartment near campus and drove a very expensive sports car. He was comfortable, secure and lazy because his parents paid all of his bills and would continue to do so as long as he was in pursuit of a degree.

Over time however Jerry's parents, Norman and Marie Chandler, begin to realize that their only child had become a professional student. While they could easily afford many times over what they spent on Jerry, they did not want him to become a spoiled bum and became determined to find a way to end his dependence.

On a brisk late winter morning quite without any warning, a letter from a law firm that represented a major home developer appeared in their mailbox. The letter addressed a proposition regarding some property the Chandlers owned. After some discussion, Norman and Marie decided to use the property and proposition as a means to put Jerry completely on his own. Three weeks later with the proper paperwork completed, they drove to Indiana University in Bloomington. Their son was actually on campus in the library studying his favorite subject when they tracked him down with what they considered urgent news.

Jerry was startled and not especially happy to see his parents unexpectedly. He squirmed in his chair as they explained the reason for their visit.

"A few years back after your grandma died," Norman explained, "no one was left living on the old family estate down in Ketchan, Tennessee except your cousin Thelma. Then after a couple of years she moved in with her children. Since it has stood empty but the neighbors, Tom and Esther Cunningham, look after the place. My sisters wanted to sell. But since your mother and I thought it might make a nice retirement property for us, we bought out my sisters and own the estate free and clear. Well about two years ago, while you were lounging about in Europe Jerry, your mom and I spent a few days at the country estate. We had intended to stay two weeks but it didn't take very long for us to realize that we were city people. That's a little strange for me because I grew up on that estate...well between boarding schools anyway. But nonetheless your mother and I have determined that we have no foreseeable need for the estate and since it was surely to be part of your inheritance, we see no reason not to give it to you now. Especially now! I say especially now because the nearby town is expanding. New sub-divisions are spreading out, meaning those eighty-two acres are suddenly worth quite a bit more than just a few years ago. There is already a substantial offer on the table and I'm certain it can be negotiated upward."

"And don't think for a minute you have to sell," Marie put in. "There has been a Chandler on that estate for over two hundred years and you know that Chandler Hall has long been eligible for historic designation. Why with all the development down there that place would make a perfect restaurant or Bed and Breakfast. Why you could even create a living history museum of sorts if you so choose Jerry dear. Or better yet you could live the life of a country gentlemen landowner and take up residence there yourself. I'd like that, why you could own horses and even lecture at the nearby college."

Jerry stared in silence as his father took the conversation back over. "Now here's the deal son, the property is already in your name and if you want to take advantage of the financial gains offered by this developer, your time is limited to about ninety days. Either way you should go down there and assess things.

"This property is your future, what you do with it matters big time Jerry my boy. Your mother and I checked with the registrar on our way in and happily discovered that you already have enough credits for graduation. At present you are enrolled in only two classes and both are electives. So at the end of this semester Jerry, you graduate...isn't that wonderful! You graduate and the money stops. After this semester that property you just inherited must finance your future. You may wish to sell only part of it, all of it or none."

"Either way if you wish to pursue a PhD your mother and I will pay the actual tuition expense only for the prescribed time of the program and not a day beyond. All other expenses of life and education you must pay from your own labor or with proceeds from your estate."

"This is all final and you have no say in the matter. The property is now yours. We will not be renewing your apartment lease here in Bloomington. Your credit card will expire at the end of June and I suggest you promptly get about your business. The Cunningham's have the keys to the estate and are expecting you so just give them a call. You will find their number and other important information in this packet. Now of course your mother and I would love to stay and chat but we have many things to do yet before our flight to Hawaii. We are still looking for a retirement place and well you just never know. Keep us up-to-date on your decisions. I know you will make your mother and I very proud...so long pal, see you at graduation!" Norman concluded as he stood and prepared to leave.

"Bye Jerry dear...do your absolute best with the place. Chandler Hall is very special and let us hear from you more often!" his mother instructed while parting.

Wearing a fake smile Jerry hugged then bid his parents farewell but poor Jerry was completely stunned. After they left he sat perfectly still for several minutes feeling as though he badly wanted to cry, even wail out loud. *How dare his parents just waltz in and totally destroy his complete world in mere seconds? How dare they check with the registrar then declare him a member of this years graduating class? It was all just completely unbelievable and the thought...just the thought of his precious credit card being canceled made his heart stop beating. And, if all of that wasn't traumatic enough, what could possibly make his parents think that he had any desire whatsoever to own his grandparent's old southern barn that is buried somewhere in brambles and sticks of Tennessee?* "We're both castoffs damnit!" Jerry growled. "Off they fly to Hawaii...having shit on two birds with only one drop. They cut me loose and they cut the old southern dump loose...two for one...hell I'm going to get drunk...I mean really, really drunk!"

## Chapter two

*J*erry exhaled a deep sigh as he steered his car off the main highway and onto Stony Creek Pike. "Why do southern people call a road a Pike? And just what the hell is a Pike anyway?" he grumbled as he headed toward Ketchan, Tennessee. Along the way Jerry noticed a fairly new manufacturing plant of some sort, a few recently constructed industrial parks and several home sub-divisions, some newly built. There was construction in progress as Jerry passed through Ketchan and he chuckled with the thought that the twenty-first century was coming to the backwoods after all. The construction ended and only a couple of home sub-divisions appeared as he followed Stony Creek Pike away from Ketchan and towards Chandler Hall. He passed wooded areas, farm land and a large tract of land being prepared for a housing sub-division. Then he rounded a bend in the road and felt his pulse rate quicken as Stony Creek Pike suddenly became very familiar. Only a short distance ahead was the creek and just beyond that was the lane leading to Chandler Hall. Jerry's throat became very dry. He was a teenager on his last visit here and remembered the place well, or at least he thought he did.

When he turned his car onto the lane Jerry noted with little surprise that it was still unpaved gravel. In spite of that however, the lane was shaded by dense trees and wound to the right before it reached the clearing that revealed the large and expansive grounds of Chandler Hall. Off in the distance set the mansion, a two-story white structure with green shutters. The building had a big chimney on each end with an upper and lower porch across the front supported by large columns. The lane split with one arm leading to several small buildings set back some distance away, while the other arm curved right up to the front of the mansion then on in a wide circle back to the entry lane.

Jerry noticed a pickup truck parked in front of the mansion then he saw Tom and Esther Cunningham on the porch waving. For a brief moment Jerry paused with a flashback of his grandma and grandpa waving from the porch. He felt uncertain when he stepped from his car but the Cunningham's were jolly, middle-aged, well-fed country folk who could not have been nicer or more helpful. They gave him a brief tour of the immediate grounds surrounding the mansion then showed Jerry the basics of the house.

While Jerry happily stuffed himself with Esther's chicken, biscuits and lemonade, Tom explained his position on the real estate development going on.

"My place butts right up against yourn to the west and north a bit, been thataway for generations and well…me and Esther would just assume keep it thataway. Now I know your pa said the place here is yourn now, and you just might be entertaining the idee of selling and that's your shore nuff right. But if'n you do take a notion to sell, I'm askin you to let me and Esther have first crack at whatever your selling. I purely despise them developer bastards. They row people up like corn stalks and make a stinking fortune fouling up the land with idiots in clap board houses. Well…hell! Now I done got all worked up…but all I'm ah saying is if'n you take a notion to sell, me and Esther got a dollar or two, and as your neighbor I'd shore like to count on you giving me and Esther first crack…course we would much rather you stay and bring the place back to life. Hell I can get you all the help you need and…"

"TOM!" Esther shouted. "Tom…you old darling…let the boy eat and settle in. We will have plenty of time to talk later." The Cunningham's each gave Jerry a big hug then hopped into their pickup truck and disappeared down the lane. Jerry was really glad they had been there to greet him and now he was glad to see them leave.

For a long period of time Jerry stood on the large front porch and studied the house. *It seemed so much larger when I was a kid;* he thought then opened the front door and walked into the grand foyer. *Some mansion…this is just a four-bedroom house…hell there are bigger houses on frat row back at school. Why in fact there are probably bigger houses down the street in one of those subdivisions.*

The house was basically a large rectangle with the grand foyer, large winding stairway and back hall in the middle. On the right side of the stairway on the first floor was a large parlor leading to an equally large dining room with a kitchen behind. On the other side of the stairway was a large sitting room. Behind that was his grandpa's library and behind that a storeroom. Upstairs were two very large bedrooms on each side of the grand hall and a doorway leading to the outside porch. The house had been remodeled only to the extent that the wall that separated the small kitchen house behind the main dwelling had been removed, creating space for a modern kitchen. Electricity, two bathrooms upstairs and two half-bathrooms downstairs had also been added. In spite of its age Chandler Hall was still impressive. It stood straight and erect showing little signs of age or wear. The quality of the home spoke loudly through the strong oak floors, large stone fireplaces, polished mahogany doors, mahogany crown molding and woodwork in every room and many dazzling chandeliers made of the finest crystal of the time. Because the home had always been in the family, several pieces of original furniture were still in use and most of the replacement pieces were now very old but still elegant and very usable. The floor length windows were adorned with heavy draperies and thick hand-hooked rugs were scattered about in different rooms.

On the grounds of Chandler Hall stood five usable buildings, closest to the house and the most recently constructed was a four-car garage. A short distance beyond was a barn, a stable, an antique blacksmith shop and a smokehouse. Approximately 100 yards past the smokehouse were several really old buildings and shacks badly in need of demolition. The remainder of the estate was comprised of pasture land, a corral, three ponds, farm land, wooded areas and a couple of gently rising hills. The legal boundaries of Chandler Hall measured 82.4 acres and the market value of the estate could easily make Jerry wealthy but not rich.

Jerry stood in the grand foyer and studied the old grandfather clock. That same clock had fascinated him as a kid because his grandpa had told him that clock had been here all his life too...and the damn clock was still here and still working. He stared up at the large crystal chandelier hanging from high above then slowly walked from room to room. Jerry was very aware of the fact that except for his car and clothes he had never really owned anything. At this point he really wasn't sure he wanted to own anything. But...he did not want to be responsible for a stagnant pile of money that was sure to keep shrinking either.

Feeling as though his butt was sitting squarely on the horns of a huge dilemma, Jerry decided to just hang out at Chandler Hall for a few days without any thoughts of the decisions he needed to make. *Maybe...just maybe I will get a vibe or something by hanging around and getting a feel for the place,* he thought as he retrieved his stash of marijuana from his car then helped himself to some very old brandy from the liquor cabinet.

After trying out every couch and chair in the parlor then the sitting room, Jerry went upstairs and spent nearly an hour trying to decide which bedroom was larger or the master bedroom in which he should sleep.

# Chapter three

*T*he next morning Jerry had cereal and fruit for breakfast then wandered outside the house to the buildings beyond. He walked into the stable and considered the possibility that he could easily own and breed horses. But he could not think of any real use for horses except for racing or show and of course those big dumb work horses that pull fancy carriages along busy city streets. *Doesn't matter why you breed them,* Jerry thought, *the only reason to have them is because you love them. Hum...the last time I came close to a horse it was right here in this stable and that horse scared the crap out of me. I never did really like horses and still don't! And I really didn't like helping Smitty muck out the stalls.*

Smitty was an old black man that worked for Jerry's grandfather, although the two men could more accurately have been described as best friends. Jerry did not understand it but his grandpa and Smitty took great pride in sharing and drinking from the same bottle. As a kid during his summers at Chandler Hall, Jerry often spent the day with Smitty. Sometimes working, sometimes fishing and sometimes making music and dancing in a barn down the road with other folk, who also should have been working. Smitty and Jerry's grandpa were about the same age and for the first few years of his life Jerry felt as though he had two wonderful grandpa's, one white and one black. He remembered the horror of coming to Chandler Hall for his grandpa's funeral only to discover that Smitty had died over a year before and no one had even told him. "To hell with horses!" Jerry muttered on his way out of the stable.

The blacksmith shop was completely confusing to Jerry. He had no idea why it was kept in near original condition. Having little appreciation for antiquity, he quickly moved on to inspect the barn only to find it full of old farm tools and implements. Finally Jerry found an all terrain vehicle in the garage and used it to spend the remainder of the day exploring the vast grounds of Chandler Hall.

He started in the wooded areas with the attitude that everything, including the trees, bushes, insects and dirt belonged to him. So he took his time and closely inspected anything he found of interest. When he emerged from the woods Jerry crossed an overgrown pasture then closely examined the old corral. Unimpressed, he set off at high speed across a broad meadow then up to the top of the steepest hill. Feeling like a kid, Jerry dashed down one hill and up the other several times. Finally he stepped off the vehicle, stretched out his arms and screamed at the top of his lungs. He laughed, fell to the ground and rolled over and over to the bottom of the hill, laughing all the way. After lying in the grass for nearly an hour Jerry made his way back up the hill to the all terrain vehicle and drove back to the garage just as darkness began to approach.

Following a hearty dinner prepared by a temporary housekeeper the Cunningham's had provided; Jerry sat on the large front porch and looked at the many vivid stars in the dark sky while assessing his day. At times he had felt like an idiot, at other times he felt like a rich land baron. He had closely inspected a lot of the ground he now owned and had a lot of fun doing so.

During his inspection he had fantasized about many things and possibilities, including going all out and becoming a big time farmer or rancher. Maybe growing grapes and making wine or putting in a large fish farm or better yet a golf course or family fun park. Maybe a nudist colony or a private spring break facility…perhaps a freaky retreat for college students. The housekeeper interrupted Jerry's thoughts; she had tidied up and was leaving for the night. Once assured she would return the next day, Jerry bid the housekeeper farewell. He then decided to take a nice hot bath, watch a movie and call it a night.

The following day Jerry slept late and was absolutely delighted when the housekeeper showed up right on time at ten o'clock. She quickly prepared a delicious country breakfast for Jerry and made a large pot of coffee. Next she put his dinner, which she brought already prepared, and several snacks into the refrigerator.

While Jerry devoured his breakfast, the housekeeper made his bed and tidied his bathroom. She returned to the kitchen planning to leave for the day but when she saw that Jerry had eaten all of her freshly made biscuits, she was delighted and made even happier when he asked if she would make more. Jerry reminded the housekeeper of her grandsons so she first made a large tray of biscuits then she made a large tray of cookies that filled the kitchen with a wonderful aroma. She made a fresh pot of coffee then assured Jerry that she would be back at the same time tomorrow, or if for some reason he needed help before then her number was in the speed dial. She was singing as she made her way out while Jerry was once again feasting on biscuits and sausage gravy.

After breakfast Jerry was stuffed and decided to spend the day indoors. For close to an hour he sat on the upstairs porch in one of the oversized cane back rocking chairs sipping the good hot coffee and nibbling from the tray of delicious and still warm cookies. He had all but decided to take a nap when he changed his mind and headed for his grandpa's library. As a child the library had always been off limits. Not just to him but to everyone, even grandma. No one dared go into grandpa's library unless he invited you in. The few times Jerry did get inside the library were brief and he really didn't remember much about it. *Funny,* he thought, *I've been through the entire house and covered most of the grounds and outbuildings but still I have not been in this room. Well grandpa...it's my room now...this room and all its secrets are now all mine!*

Jerry threw open the heavy French style doors and stood perfectly still. The room appeared untouched from the last time he saw his grandpa sitting at that very same roll top desk that is still in the same spot. The walls were lined with bookshelves and crammed with books, journals, diaries, scrapbooks and various later generational media like tapes and disc. On a small circular table sat the old world globe that he loved as a kid. His grandpa would spin the globe then tell him a tall tale about whatever place the globe stopped on.

With his coffee and cookies close by Jerry settled in the big overstuffed chair behind his grandpa's desk and began skimming through some of the journals and record books on a nearby shelf. At first he was just curious but quickly got drawn into the details of past dramas and events, many of which were spelled out in very salty detail within the pages of the diaries. After a couple of hours, Jerry took a break from reading and went for a brisk walk around the grounds before heading for his new found favorite spot on the upstairs porch. From this spot he could survey much of the grounds while getting high and pretending to be George Washington or some big famous landowner.

When the munchies set in, Jerry took the snack tray from the refrigerator and returned to the library. He figured out that the journals and record books containing the history of Chandler Hall lined nearly one whole wall and were stored chronologically. The oldest books were at the top so Jerry decided to amuse himself with a little history. Once he had retrieved several older journals and sat down at his grandpa's desk Jerry was shocked. The documents were over two hundred years old. *Why a smuck like me shouldn't even be handling this kind of stuff,* he thought. *I mean those historical society type people outta be dealing with this...hey wait a minute, I think I saw some white gloves in a chest upstairs.* Jerry hurried to the chest and retrieved the gloves, pleased that he had earlier discovered them and now had the good sense to use them.

"Now let me see..." he mumbled as he scanned the ancient journal. After skimming through four journals, Jerry took a large flat book from the top shelf and discovered what looked like the architectural plans for the Chandler Hall. He was quite amused and took considerable time studying the plans before he nearly jumped out of his chair. Chandler Hall had a basement or more accurately a cellar as described in the plans. There was a trap door in the dining room leading to it and Jerry was now excited.

He hurried to the dining room. A large thick carpet covered most of the floor and the large dining table was sitting squarely on the area of the floor containing the trap door to the cellar. Although he could have easily called for help, Jerry suspected the cellar held hidden treasure and he was not going share it or the news of it with anyone. So for nearly half an hour Jerry struggled and grunted and pushed. The antique table was made from oak, cut from the nearby woods and it seated fourteen.

Jerry was exhausted and had to briefly rest after finally moving the table far enough to roll back the rug. After doing so, he discovered the two slots in the floor that allowed you to slide your hand between the boards and lift up the trap door. Now very excited, Jerry made a fast trip to the garage, grabbed two halogen lights then returned to the dining room. He slid his hands into the slots and pulled but nothing happened. He tried over and over but the door, if it was a door, wouldn't budge. Jerry returned to the garage and looked around for something to help open the door then thought about Smitty. He chuckled while grabbing a pry bar and block of wood. Many times he had heard Smitty say, "Ain't no pint in pussyfootin round boy, hit it right da furst time and dere won't be no need fur a second." Jerry returned to the dining room, properly positioned the wood block then used the pry bar to quickly pop open the trap door.

# Chapter four

*J*erry's heart was beating fast when he sat the trap door aside revealing a crude set of narrow steps. He lowered the light into the cellar then gingerly proceeded down the steps. The cellar was a square room about six foot wide and six foot across. It probably measured seven feet deep and the walls and floor were dirt. The large rough hewn support beams of the dining room floor ran across the ceiling of the cellar, which except for two very old wooden barrels was completely empty.

Jerry looked slowly around with growing disappointment. "It has got to be a criminal offense to have a hidden cellar with nothing of value stashed in it," he grumbled while inspecting the barrels.

Both barrels were empty but the lid from the second barrel scraped some dirt from the wall as Jerry set the lid on the floor. Inadvertently Jerry again hit the wall with the lid of the barrel as he put it back in place and more dirt fell from the wall. For a brief second Jerry started to panic and rush for the steps but paused and realized that the cellar was not collapsing around him.

He poked and prodded at the spot in the wall and more dirt fell. Soon he recognized a piece of wood buried in the wall and used the pry bar to quickly knock away the dirt that covered a wooden rectangular panel about three feet wide and around two feet high. At first Jerry thought the panel was a trap door but as he tried to pry it open he discovered the panel had sides and was indeed a box. In fact there were two wooden boxes, one stacked on top of the other.

After several minutes of digging, prying and struggle, the wall released the heavy boxes which Jerry nearly dropped as he lowered them to the floor. Jerry was sweating, breathing hard and dirty when he pried the lid from the boxes. Inside each box a note lay atop several items wrapped in rags. The first box contained several heavy pieces of a complete formal silver serving set. The second box held some assorted silver pieces, a small cherry wood chest containing a complete set of silver dining utensils, along with several pewter dishes and cups. Jerry was not impressed. He closely inspected the boxes then re-examined the hole in the wall looking for something more but found nothing. Not satisfied Jerry went to the kitchen and got the longest knife he could find. When he returned to the cellar he slid the knife into the wall in several places hoping to strike another box.

When no more boxes or treasure could be found Jerry placed the lids back on top of the boxes then left them lying on the floor. He collected his tools and the lights then made his way out of the cellar, taking the note from the first box with him. Just before placing the trap door back into place Jerry stuck the light back into the opening and took another look at the boxes. He noticed the words "Chandler Hall" scratched on the lids, probably with a knife. *I should drag those boxes up here and inspect them real close,* he thought. *Naw...what's the point! A bunch of old silver isn't worth much.* Without another thought Jerry put the trap door back in place then once again struggled mightily to get the table back into place. He really hadn't discovered much but the cellar was still his secret. Dead tired and hungry Jerry ate his dinner took a quick shower then went straight to bed and quickly fell sound asleep.

Early the next morning Jerry sat at his grandpa's desk and examined the note he found inside the box in the cellar. *"One of nine cases trusted to three of the most respected and upstandin families of Tennessee. Delivered from Matthews Manor fer safekeepin til such time as the strife of war has ended. All cases oughta be stored in the most secure places of hidin as all hold the Matthews family treasure. I pray it be God's will that all shall be well and back to normal soon. Amen*
*Joshua Matthews"*

"Hum...now I wonder who is Joshua Matthews?" Jerry thought aloud, "And I wonder if more than just two cases came here? Hum...just what war is this guy talking about? The Civil War maybe...hum. Well I got the records so let's just see what I can find out." Jerry dived head first into his research, he paused only to greet the housekeeper, eat and take a call from the Cunningham's.

By early evening he had discovered that Joshua Matthews was the owner of Matthews Manor which had been a breeding plantation. And while such plantations were favorite places to visit for many local landowners, they were prime targets for raids by union forces during the civil war. Such was the fate of Matthews Manor. It was occupied for a short while then burned to the ground and its slaves set free by union troops. But not before Joshua Matthews and his son Clay sent their most valuable treasures to others for safekeeping. A short time later Joshua Matthews was killed fighting in a battle against the union troops over a nearby bridge. His son Clay was captured as a confederate solider and imprisoned until the war ended.

When Clay returned home he went looking for his family's treasure. He claimed that among other things, he and his father sent four wooden cases to High Gate, the plantation and home of Carter Armstrong and his large family. Two of those cases contained over sixty pounds of gold. Unfortunately for Clay, High Gate had also been burned to the ground and the gold was never found. Clay accused the union troops of taking the gold but they quickly produced the records of their raid on High Gate. There were many items of value but no gold coins, bars or jewelry was on their list. Clay sent word to Chandler Hall that he was coming to claim his possessions held there but died in the backroom of a tavern under suspicious circumstances before he made the trip. No other mention of the Matthews family, the missing gold or the treasure at Chandler Hall could be found.

"Wow!" Jerry exclaimed. "Over sixty pounds of missing gold. Dumb son-of-a-bitch should have sent his gold to Chandler Hall. Wonder what happened to it? Seems strange that it just disappeared. Oh well it doesn't help me at the moment, all I got is a lousy silver service."

Jerry ate his dinner then decided to spend the next day touring the county. He got up early and spent the entire morning cruising many of the back roads and lanes of the county. He stopped at home for breakfast then continued to cruise until about an hour past noon when he arrived in Ketchan. For the remainder of that afternoon, Jerry talked with bankers, the chamber of commerce, developers and business people in Ketchan and both neighboring towns. He had dinner with the Cunningham's then drove back to Chandler Hall cursing his father for pulling the plug on his ideal life. "Thanks a lot dad," he grumbled while parking his car in the garage. "Once I was the prince of Indiana University, now I am the king of Hickville! I much prefer to be the prince, thank you very much!" He made his way to the house, stood on the porch and looked around. "Man when it gets dark in the country hell it is really dark," he muttered then went inside. After a few phone calls to old friends Jerry went up to his bedroom and called it a night.

Following a restless night, Jerry struggled out of bed and took a shower. He dressed then stepped out on the upstairs porch just as the housekeeper came down the lane. Jerry watched as she stepped from her car surprised that she was not alone. A much younger woman stepped from the other side of the car and accompanied the housekeeper to the door. Jerry hurried back inside and down the stairs. The young woman appeared to be rather attractive and that peaked Jerry's interest. At the bottom of the steps he regained his composure, telling himself that after several days in the country, a young female mule would probably seem attractive at first blush. So he tried to appear cool and unconcerned as he entered the kitchen.

The young lady's name was Peggy Simpson and she was the twenty-three year old granddaughter of the housekeeper. Upon her arrival, Peggy had no idea that Jerry was a young bachelor or that her grandmother and the Cunningham's were trying to play matchmaker. Peggy came along because her grandmother had asked her to make her special pecan pancakes, while her grandmother fried sliced potatoes, eggs and bacon.

Jerry found Peggy to be very attractive and her pecan pancakes were a serious piece of heaven. Peggy was pleased when Jerry complimented her looks, but she was thrilled when he sincerely complimented her cooking while eating all of her pancakes. They chatted easily and seemed to enjoy each other's company but both were more than a little suspicious of the other. Jerry was cautious about getting too cozy with the hired help, while Peggy now suspected her grandmother was trying to set her up with a college egghead that probably couldn't tie his shoe without directions. After the housekeeper completed her chores the two women left and Jerry returned to his favorite spot on the second floor porch.

The time had come for some serious decision making so Jerry rolled a nice big joint and settled back into his favorite rocker. He looked out over the grounds and thought about his apartment back in Bloomington. *Hum…my lease expires in a couple of months and unless I renew it I don't have a place to live. Well there is no point in renewing, I'm certainly not going to pay for it and I know mom and dad won't. I don't think they will let me move back into their house either, not since they have given me this one. So all that means I got no place to live. I could sell this place and pay my rent in Bloomington, but then I would be trying to manage a shrinking pile of money and that is not my idea of a good time. Hum...looks as though I gotta make something work here. I need something that pays all the bills without much if any effort from me. Something that pays all the expenses of this place and the rent on another, like my apartment in Bloomington. Well...all my research so far points to one thing. One big thing is missing in this county even though these hicks don't seem to know it. What's missing is a golf course and country club; nowhere in this whole county and most of the next is there a golf course. I don't care for golf but it is a staple of American business life and every community large and small needs a golf course. Chandler Hall Golf and Country Club could fill that void and bring some sophistication to some of these hillbillies. With nice big annual dues, various fees and limited snotty membership rolls, money will be spilling out of every drawer and I won't have to lift a finger.* Jerry paused and smoked his joint. *The only problem with this plan was financing,* he thought. *It cost money to lay out a golf course and build a clubhouse. There was no way he was parting with the mansion so a new clubhouse had to be built far away from his private residence. Hum...yes this mansion was now his private residence and he was certainly not going to consider a mortgage on the property. Nor was he about to ask his mom and dad for financing. So his only option seemed to be selling a few acres for construction money.* But, Jerry did not want to part with even one acre. "Chandler Hall used to spread over 300 acres!" he grumbled. "But by the time I took ownership the place has been sold down to a measly 82. And I will just be damned if I ever give up or mortgage even one of those." For the remainder of the afternoon, Jerry ambled around the property trying to make sense of his dilemma.

After dinner he went to his grandpa's library and sat behind the roll top desk. "If I had that missing gold I'd be good to go," Jerry chuckled then sat upright, scratched his head and stared at the diary that told the story of the Matthews gold. *I can find out what happened to that gold,* he thought. *It might even be possible to claim it, if it is truly unaccounted for.* Jerry got up and paced about. It could be done. He could find out what happened to the gold…but it was expensive and risky…yet it could be done.

At first he decided to sleep on the decision then quickly decided that he had little to lose and everything to gain, so Jerry made some very precise notes from the diaries. He called the Cunningham's and told them he would be gone for a few days then charged up the stairs and on to his bedroom. He hurried into bed anxious to get a good night's sleep and an early start for Bloomington the next day.

# Chapter five

*T*he next afternoon, Jerry arrived in Bloomington, Indiana. He had been gone nearly a week but drove straight past his apartment and went directly to the mathematical science lab.

Professor Winfred Gilstead was surprised and happy to see his former student. "What brings you back to lab Jerry? Need a refresher in quantum mechanics?" he questioned with a smile.

"No sir," Jerry responded in a serious tone. "I need to use the benefits of them."

"You don't mean a trip do you?"

"I do!"

"Oh my...my, my! If it were most others I would say no and that would be the end of it!" Professor Gilstead sighed. "But you Jerry...you and a very few others really know just how this process works. I know you are very aware of the grave risks so what can I say? Your reasons must be of extreme importance."

"You know I would never take this chance professor if this mission was not of critical importance, and if I didn't think I could pull it off."

"Yes I'm sure Jerry...but you do remember your visit can only be for observation...you cannot..."

"Professor I have spent the last three years of my life in postgraduate study on this very subject. I have studied and experimented with you and several other professors. This is probably the only subject I truly love studying and now that it is necessary to put my studies to use I know I can do this...I must do this. I can pull it off and I won't screw it up."

"Okay Jerry okay...that I cannot argue with," the professor sighed. "Do you have the parameters?"

Jerry handed the professor his notes.

"My gosh 182 years? That's a long time back! And this timeframe really pushes against the maximum allowable. It is going to take at least three full days to write this formula...and no, you cannot help. You already know that you cannot participate in writing your own formula."

"I'm good. I'm good with all of that and ready to go for it. I'll just hang out until you call," Jerry responded.

"The distance back and this timeframe is really going to drive the cost pretty high...are you certain you need that long Jerry?"

"Need every minute sir, absolutely!"

"Well it is going to be damned expensive, just keep that in mind."

"Hey come on professor, I'm a Chandler, you know I'm good for it," Jerry grinned.

"Tell that to the hound dogs in the bursar's office after you get the bill. Right now you have dumped a very large project on my desk and I need to get to work so farewell Jerry. I will call when the formula is complete."

Over the next five days Jerry fell back into his old routine, almost as though he had never been to Chandler Hall. He made up for lost time with two old girlfriends, visited his hangouts and entertained his friends, sleeping late and partying hard. Jerry was twenty-eight years old and because of his age, expensive clothes, sports car and luxury apartment, he found it rather easy to impress then seduce undergraduate women, particularly sophomores and juniors. He was busy after another such conquest when he received a message to report to Professor Gilstead.

"Your formula has been completed Jerry and I hope to God Almighty that you know what you are doing. You are set to triparticalize tomorrow morning at precisely ten hundred hours GMT and reparticalize exactly 50 hours later. This is your last chance to change your mind and if not, review your parameters and timeframes. Then I suggest you get as much rest as possible. You are going to need it for this experience. Any questions?"

Jerry had no questions; he was excited and jumping for joy but careful not to appear so in front of Professor Gilstead. He reviewed and approved his final parameters, coordinates and timeframes, signed the releases and the financial responsibility form then agreed to be in the lab for prep the next morning at eight hundred hours. He expressed his thanks to Professor Gilstead and left the building still fighting to restrain his exuberance.

Jerry had promised the girl he was pursing that he would meet back up with her at a coffee house near his apartment, but went to the gym instead and briefly worked out to get his excitement under control. Following that he grabbed a take-out sandwich on his way home, took a long hot shower, a sleeping pill and went to bed well before nine o'clock.

It was a little after six am when Jerry awoke excited and feeling great. He went for a quick jog, had cereal for breakfast then drove the long way to the science lab. He smiled as he guided his car across campus with a serious and confident attitude. He was finally going to enter the world he had studied and imagined for many years.

Although still very much in its infancy and posing considerable risk, time travel is now possible. A good understanding of molecularzation and of worm holes, made by the bending of time across the universe, has allowed for passage backwards in time with designated return to the launch station. This delicate procedure requires precisely calculated formulas to access and control a process using light-speed-acceleration of sub-atomic human particles through specific worm holes, and many successful trips have been logged. Travel into the future however, is made much more difficult by parallel universes and the paradoxes of advancing rhythms. Jerry had been trying to solve one of the more difficult aspects of future travel and never once thought he would ever consider a trip into the past. But now he had reason. His mission was booked and his ship was waiting. In little more than a couple of hours he would leave the present world and enter the past.

Professor Gilstead was nervous and worried. "You know you absolutely cannot do anything whatsoever that could possibly change human history?"

"I know," Jerry replied.

"And I'm certain you also know you will not come back if you do. There have been accidents in the past. We cannot remember them because if someone goes back in time and alters human history they lose their place in history. All trace of them and their memory is forever erased from time. I don't want to lose you or your memory Jerry, so you must promise you will be very careful. Observe but do not alter human history."

"I promise I will return professor," Jerry assured. "I have almost solved one of the parallel universe problems and I have to return so I can complete my research and take the trip I really want to take, which is to the future."

"Good luck my boy I will be right here waiting for your return."

"So long professor, see you on Thursday," Jerry responded with a big smile then stepped inside the transporter. The machine was a slender floor to ceiling metal enclosure about four feet square. Inside there was a white circle on the floor and a corresponding circle on the low ceiling. On the front wall was a twenty inch video screen and on the side wall a sliding compartment.

Jerry placed his hand flat against the video screen and it flashed to life. First it displayed the current time, date and temperature. Next the screen flashed "Welcome Jerry Chandler. Please confirm your destination." After Jerry pressed the confirm button below his displayed destination the screen commanded him to remove and store all items of covering. The side compartment slid open and Jerry removed all his clothes, socks, shoes, underwear, watch and ring. Only bare naked skin could be transported. Jerry's personal items would stay locked inside the compartment and would never leave the lab. Only Jerry was headed back to the past. Once he arrived in the past he would be invisible to the human eye as long as he remained naked. If he put on clothes people could see the clothes but not him.

Completely naked, Jerry tapped the "Instruction Complete Box" on the screen and the side compartment slid shut. The screen then advised Jerry to position himself in the center of the white circle on the floor and stand perfectly still with his arms at his sides. Almost as soon as he had done so, a soft red light begin flashing on the screen and grew brighter until suddenly a bright ring of intense white light filled the circle in the ceiling above Jerry. The bright ring of white light slowly descended downward completely encircling Jerry's body and continued down until it reached the white circle in the floor then all went black.

Jerry had no idea how long the darkness lasted before the soft red light again started to flash on the screen. As before, the red light grew brighter until the bright ring of white light suddenly filled the circle in the floor. Slowly the light rose upwards, again encircling Jerry's body then stopped when it reached the white circle in the ceiling. The white ring of light snapped off, but the bright red light continued to flash on the screen for several minutes.

Finally the red light dissolved to green then grew faint and was replaced with a bright flashing message:

## DESTINATION ACHIEVED
Matthews Manor, Gibson County, Tennessee, USA
### Tuesday April 12, 1864
1242 GMT
71 degrees Fahrenheit
## OUTBOUND MISSION COMPLETE
*(System shut down in 31 seconds)*
When the screen went blank and the interior lights came on Jerry took a deep breath then pushed the exit button and the door snapped open.

# Chapter six

*J*erry *stepped from the transporter* and found himself standing in the front yard of Matthews Manor. He glanced back at the transporter and saw only a large tree. Jerry rubbed his eyes and stared hard at the tree before he saw his handprint glowing at about eye level in the bark of the tree. He relaxed and smiled. His handprint was the door handle to the transporter and his ticket to safety. No matter what, he now needed only to return to this tree and place his hand on his handprint to re-enter the transporter. And if necessary immediately return to 2046, the year from which he had just left.

Feeling confident, Jerry stood with his hands on his hips and looked around. Matthews Manor had none of the charm or sophistication of Chandler Hall. A short dirt lane led from the passing road to a flat faced two-story house without any porch and badly in need of paint. A short distance past the house was a small shack with a big chimney and past that appeared to be many more shacks and buildings. Jerry was quickly reminded that he was barefoot by the pebbles and hard grass underfoot. For a moment he panicked because he was naked then remembered that he was also invisible and relaxed.

He gingerly made his way up the lane to the front door of the house. The door was open so he stepped inside and walked from room to room. He saw no one on the first floor except for a middle-aged black woman sitting in a rocking chair near the back door and an old black man in the dining room. Jerry crept close and stared hard. The silver service the old man was polishing looked exactly like the silver he had found at Chandler Hall. *Makes sense,* Jerry thought, *now I know I am really onto something.* Pleased with his discovery, Jerry continued his tour. The Matthews house did not qualify to be called a mansion as far as he was concerned. It had a small foyer, only one parlor, a straight staircase and the four bedrooms were small by his standard. Most of the furnishings were rather simple and coarse and nothing about the house spoke of any quality. Having seen no one upstairs, Jerry walked through the back hall and right past the lady sitting in the chair.

As he stood on the rather shabby back porch and looked out, a truly foul odor hit his nostrils and he soon discovered that when the wind blows in the wrong direction the hogs made themselves known. The pens were more than two hundred yards away and next to the hogs were the chickens; in fact chickens were everywhere. Jerry had never seen so many chickens in his life. He stepped from the porch and walked down the back lane of Matthews Manor.

The little shack with the big chimney was the kitchen. The wonderful aromas coming from the shack drew Jerry like a magnet. He stepped inside and was surprised by how small the shack was. A large older black woman and a younger much smaller woman were cooking and talking.

"...and dat's da las time fa dat!" the younger woman concluded with a howl.

"Frum de talk ah heah goin round, mayhap it de las time fer da hole bunch," the older woman replied.

"You reckin dat's tru?"

"Ah stuffed sum vittles in Big Junior's gullet aftern he made his livery tuh Massa Josh and he tol me Mistah Lincoln's boys was awinning da fight and it won't be long fo freedom comes."

"Lawd I sho hope he aright..."

Jerry was hungry and focused on the food the women were cooking then placing on a large table against the wall. He knew once he ate the food it could no longer be seen, so he grabbed a piece of chicken and stepped outside. He quickly ate it before anyone could report seeing a piece of chicken vanishing before their eyes. He repeated this procedure with many different food items until he satisfied his stomach and decided to continue his tour, leaving the cooks confused about the food they noticed was missing from their table.

Next to the kitchen was a long rectangular building. It set two steps up off the ground and was overflowing with kids, babies and nursing women. Jerry hurried away to the next shack a little further down the lane. He thought it odd that the shack had a wooden crossbar on the door. He would later learn the crossbar was used to lock the slaves in at night and was used on all slave quarters throughout Matthews Manor. He would also learn the difference between a shack and a building was the floor. A building had a wooden floor while the floor of a shack was dirt. This shack contained a makeshift table, two old buckets for stools and the worst beds imaginable. They amounted to nothing more than several rags and animal skins piled on top of a lot of sticks. There were several bed piles in various places around the room. At another building he watched women make clothes, some cutting fabric, others sewing. Nearby two men seemed to be making shoes, while another seemed to be doing nothing more than watching the others work.

There was a lot of banging and clanging coming from the blacksmith shop so Jerry changed directions and wandered out toward the barn. A short distance beyond the barn he was shocked to find a whipping post. He closely inspected the chains and metal cuffs used to restrain people and shuddered. He walked toward the other side of the barn and could not believe his eyes. Stocks…old fashion medieval stocks…and in use no less. A completely nude young black woman was bent over in the stocks. The bottom log of the stock was only about three feet high, meaning an adult had to bend at the waist to place their neck and forearms on the log. The top log locked them in place, leaving the victim completely defenseless. Jerry closely inspected the lady; she had a nice body with a big smooth firm behind. *She can't see me,* Jerry thought as his manhood began to rise. *Even if I was visible she still couldn't see me…and she is naked so I'm sure she is expecting it. What am I NUTS? That could change history and I would be stuck here forever! Nice try baby but I'll pass. Damn she looks like a sweet rocking piece…sure is tempting but not worth being stuck here for! No…no thanks.*

Jerry decided to finish his tour and was approaching the lane when several men came in his direction. He paused and listened as they passed by headed for the stocks. From their conversation Jerry learned that the older white gentleman was Joshua Matthews, owner of the plantation. The middle age man was Oliver Mullins, the overseer for Matthews Manor. A middle-aged black man in fancy clothes was called Domo and the rest of the black men where slaves under his command. Apparently Joshua Matthews intended to teach the woman in the stocks a lesson. He snarled at her.

"Nah you in dese here blocks cause you wants ta scuffle an carrys on. Dis whut ah wench gits fer strugglin. You ah wench…you was maid by the lawd almighty to be covered by a man and gits knocked. So ain't natchal fer you ta be doin all dat scufflin. And you shoulda done throwed least one sucker by nah. Parently white man seed ain't good nuff, nar don't git far nuff up in ya fer you ta throws me a sucker."

The overseer dropped his pants and produced his manhood.

"Go head Mistah Mullins plant ya seed in dis wench. Soon as he done Domo, you push his seed further on up in dere, an leave yur own. Den have da rest of dem boys do da same. Ah bets you throws me a sucker after dis ya uppity wench. Ah gots six big peckers pumpin ya full o seed an if you don't throws me a sucker, ah'm gonna keep em pumpin in you till ya do…even if'n ah has ta puts you in dese blocks everytime…ya hears me wench."

The woman said nothing until Domo entered her then she cried out in obvious pleasure and continued to do so until the last slave slid from her.

Jerry was stunned; he sat and watched the whole thing with wide eyes. The first two men to enter the woman lifted the top log from the stock then helped her into a nearby shack.

"Domo!" Joshua Matthews called.

"Yassah."

"Lock two fresh youn bucks wid big peckers in dere wit dat wench, an make right sho you tells em ta keep dey peckers in her da rest of da nite. An if'n she gives em any troubles or starts ascufflin, put her ass back in da blocks an ah'll make sho every swingin pecker on dis heah plantation slides up in her fo da day is thru. You heah me?"

"Yassah!" Domo confirmed.

"You heah whut ah done said gal?" Joshua shouted at the shack.

"Yassah massa," came a weak reply.

Jerry had seen enough and started back to his tree to relax for a while. *Wait a minute,* he thought, *there isn't even room to sit down in the transporter and I need to rest and chill for a while.* He abruptly changed course, went into the house and made himself comfortable on a large couch in the parlor.

As the day drew to a close Jerry was very concerned. He expected the raid by federal troops would come tomorrow but none of the preparations he expected where being done. Joshua Matthews had supper with his overseer and three other white men. Following the meal the men retired to the parlor, which as Jerry would soon learn was Domo's domain.

After serving brandy and then lighting each gentlemen's cigar, Domo took a seat at the harpsichord and played two selections with such skill and beauty that he brought his audience to their feet in applause several times. Jerry was surprised to discover that Domo was a naturally gifted musician and producer of erotic shows. Over the years Domo's talents had paid rich rewards many, many times over for his Master and his master's son, Clay. Domo's third selection was up-tempo and brief. He stopped in mid-song then loudly clapped his hands over his head. The door swung open and a slave girl in fancy clothes entered the room. The door closed, the music resumed and the girl performed a provocative strip dance until she was completely nude and writhing to the rhythm of the music in the center of the floor. Domo stopped playing and the girl hurried over then stood perfectly still beside the harpsichord. Domo again loudly clapped his hands and another girl wearing a different style costume entered the room then stripped in a very teasing fashion while dancing to the sassy music.

Domo increased the fury and tempo of the music as the third girl entered the room. She undressed quickly, a gifted dancer who obviously preferred to be naked and moving her over-heated, well-formed body seductively to the beat of the heady music. Finally as the music slowed, a tall beautiful light-skinned mulatto dressed in only a shear gown entered. Not an eye blinked as she slowly twirled around and the sheer fabric swirled about making her appear to be a nude illusion. She stopped in the center of the room and suddenly the gown fell away revealing her stunning female form. Firm supple young breast accented by her thin waist, tight round butt and smooth flat stomach that ended with the soft thin brown hairs that guarded her most private flesh. The slave girl stepped away from the gown, placed her hands on her hips and slowly started doing a bump and grind routine, which only increased the temperature of an already overheated room.

Once again Domo punched up the music and the other three girls joined the mulatto in an intensely seductive erotic dance. Jerry was excited and breathing hard when the music stopped. His manhood throbbed and he wanted in on the action but knew he had no chance. He watched, holding his swollen manhood in his hand as Domo passed around a bowl from which each gentleman took a slip of paper. The women stood in a straight line before the harpsichord as each of the gentlemen unfolded his paper and read out the number written on it. The first number read out was number three and the third girl in line immediately went and sat on the lap of the gentleman with that number. The second number called was number one and so on until each gentleman had a girl in his lap.

Domo put out all the lights, allowing the fireplace to cast a flickering glow over the room. He then sat down at the harpsichord and played soft mood music while the wenches of Matthews Manor pleasured their master's guest. Jerry couldn't take anymore so he stepped out into the yard and relieved his aching manhood where the evidence of his act would not be detected.

Finally full of food and drink, and empty of seed, the men made their way out. A short time later the overseer reported that all the slaves were locked down and said goodnight. Joshua Matthews nodded then retreated to his sleeping chambers to be pleasured by his special bed-wench. Jerry returned to the parlor with the intention of sleeping on the couch. But neither the room nor the couch smelled especially fresh after playing host to an after supper orgy, so Jerry went upstairs, found an unused bed and went right to sleep.

# Chapter seven

*T*he *shrill, flat off-key notes* of a distant bugle startled Jerry awake. At first he was dazed and confused because he did not recognize his surroundings. As he gathered himself he glanced at a clock on a chest. It was six am. Jerry stretched then chuckled with the thought that even though he was invisible he still had to use it. The outhouse proved to be the most disgusting place Jerry had ever experienced in his entire life and he vowed to never open that door again. He would use it out in the woods from now on. "Son-a-bitch," Jerry mumbled as he walked across the yard toward the back lane, "and I thought Boy Scout Camp was rough!"

He stepped upon the back porch and watched the overseer unlock several shacks and buildings. The overseer blew his bugle inside the door of one building and a couple of shacks. Apparently some needed a little extra help waking up. From one building came only young men and from another only young women. A few scattered older men and women emerged from various other shacks while no one came from the big nursery building. The smell of bacon frying led Jerry back to the kitchen and he got his breakfast the same way he got his lunch and supper the day before. This time the cooks were too busy to notice the missing food so Jerry made off with a cup of coffee and a dessert pastry to finish off his meal.

A big unhitched wagon sat outside the blacksmith's shop so Jerry climbed aboard and settled back to watch the plantation began another day. People seemed to move about mechanically, going about their daily routines. Jerry was puzzled, he fully expected federal troops would raid this place today yet there was no sense of urgency in the air at all. Joshua Matthews walked down the lane right past the wagon where Jerry was sitting and into the blacksmith shop. He talked briefly with the muscular black man inside then walked out, paused and looked hard at the wagon. Jerry was beginning to wonder if Joshua had spotted him when the plantation owner reached out and shook several spokes in the large rear wheel. Satisfied Joshua started back up the lane then stopped to talk with Oliver Mullins before the two of them disappeared into the house.

Jerry was surprised to see the young woman who had been in the stocks come walking down the lane. She held her head high; her gait was quick and strong. Apparently she was unharmed and unbroken. Jerry was confused because the woman was smiling. He did not know that Domo had quickly followed the orders he was given. Domo did not approve of the stocks, nor did he approve of his master's handling of the girl. He made certain that he and his slaves had highly aroused themselves by hand so the time they spent within the unfortunate girl was brief.

Domo knew that Oliver Mullins would only notice
that two men and the one girl came out after he unlocked
the shack in the morning, so he quickly picked two
particular male slaves then locked them in the shack with
her. The first slave Domo chose was a young man called
Tom who worked hard most days. His main interest was
eating and sleeping. The second slave chosen was a
grown man called Ben. Ben was big, aggressive and no
friend of Domos. But, Ben and the girl in the shack were
sweethearts. Romance among slaves was forbidden on
the plantation but Domo knew the secrets. He had
witnessed many of their attempts to share brief stolen
moments of affection. He had tremendous respect for
love and for lovers, so Domo done the young woman a
big favor. He also gained a new friend by arranging for
Ben and his sweetheart to spend the whole night together
while Tom happily snored away.

Jerry watched as the young woman briefly
stopped at the kitchen. Then, all while eating from the
food in one hand; she collected a large basket of clothes
from the nursery, balanced it on her head then joined up
with three other women. They headed to the nearby
creek to wash clothes, talking and laughing about Oliver
Mullins and his lack of sexual prowess.

Just as Jerry started to climb out of the wagon a
little black boy came down the lane like a flash and
streaked into the blacksmith shop. The big black man
walked out and looked down the lane just as a sleek
chestnut mare thundered off the main road, up the lane
and just past the house. Clay Matthews, dressed as a
confederate solider leapt from the horse almost before it
stopped. He threw the reins to Domo then rushed into

the house. Jerry jumped from the wagon and ran to the house. He hurried inside then rushed to Joshua's office.

"They already across the north fork and unless we can cut em down in Bradford Valley ain't nuthin gonna keep em from overtakin the place", Clay exclaimed while gasping for breath.

"How stout are our troops?" Oliver Mullins asked.

"They ain't stout atall, most of em are just farm boys...kinda like me. Ain't none of us got no soldier learnin or nuthin but we fight like hell. Course that ain't quite been enough gainst these Federal fellers so far."

"Clay, git Willie and Big Jim, hitch up da small wagon den go dig up da gold. Bring it back tuh da workshop inside da barn. Mister Mullins, see to it dat ah has da planks ta make a dozen or more large storage cases and git Domo in heah!" Josuha ordered.

Suddenly the urgency Jerry had expected was in the air and he was excited because he had finally heard mention of the gold. He watched with growing anticipation because he fully expected the raid today. Over the next few hours nine large heavy boxes were constructed but Clay Matthews rode out to rejoin his regiment shortly after delivering the gold.

Joshua Matthews ordered the slaves about as he placed his valuables and a handwritten note inside each box. Many things he ordered them to wrap two or three times. Jerry watched closely as Joshua carefully stacked gold bars in one case until it was half filled. He pushed a false bottom into the box until it snapped into a grove in each end of the box then he hammered the ends tight. On top of the false bottom Joshua tightly packed several heavily wrapped pieces of fine china and crystal candlesticks until the box was completely full. He hammered the lid shut and repeated the process with a second box, except Joshua ran out of gold bars before the box was half full. He placed two big heavy burlap bags on top of the gold and pushed the false bottom into place then stuffed the box as he had the other.

When the last box was hammered shut Joshua wiped his brow then took out his pocket knife and scratched the destination on each box. On three boxes he scratched "Hargrove Acres"; he scratched "High Gate" on four boxes and "Chandler Hall" on two. It was early evening and no one had eaten since Clay had first arrived so Joshua decided to take a break for supper. Jerry silently agreed and followed closely hoping to snag one more good meal without getting busted.

While Joshua headed for the dining room, Jerry headed for the kitchen. He had tried to feast off of the sideboard in the back hall of the house but found it much easier to hide and eat in the kitchen. Almost as soon as he swallowed the second slice of ham that he removed from a serving tray, Jerry had an idea and decided to hurry back to the barn. Just as he stepped out of the kitchen, the same little black boy that had ran down the lane earlier in the day suddenly darted out of a nearby shack. He ran across the lane, slipped in some mud and fell. In the fall he momentarily wedged his foot under the side of the kitchen, almost right in front of Jerry.

"Cum back heah...you lil bastid" Oliver Mullins called out. He hurried out of the shack, saw the boy down and swung his leg back to kick. His boot was aimed precisely at the head of the child who cringed with wide frighten eyes. Just as Oliver's leg swung forward

Jerry instinctively stuck his leg out, causing Oliver to trip and loose balance. He ran a few awkward steps down the lane to regain his balance and by the time he turned around the boy was long gone. "Cum heah you lil black bastid! Ah'm gonna wrang yo skinny lil neck! Whare you at boy?"

Jerry chuckled and left Oliver Mullins scratching his head over what just happened. He hurried back to the workshop area of the barn. It had been a cloudy day and it was getting dark so it was hard to see real close. In spite of that Jerry located two boxes with "Chandler Hall" scratched on them and pried the lids loose. He wasn't exactly sure which boxes held the gold but he knew it was headed to High Gate, so he identified two boxes with "High Gate" scratched on them and pried those lids loose then quickly switched the lids and hammered them shut. Just as Jerry was leaving the barn Oliver Mullins stepped through the door.

"Whose makin all dat ruckus? Jacob...dat you? Ah knows it is...cum on out of dere boy!"

Jerry side-stepped Oliver then hurried back to the kitchen.

Following supper Jerry watched as Joshua supervised while four slaves covered the boxes with a mountain of hay. Then for several minutes Joshua paced up and down the lane before returning to the house and pacing around the parlor then his office. Jerry was also anxious. He was scheduled to leave the very next day and the raid had not yet happened. *The whole reason for this trip is to watch and see what happens to the gold so I need this raid to happen and fast,* Jerry thought as he watched Joshua Matthews pace and fret.

After spending some time behind his desk, Joshua nodded when Oliver Mullins reported all the slaves were locked down for the night, except for little Jacob who was no doubt hiding somewhere. He nodded again when Oliver asked permission to take a particular wench to his cabin for the night. "Enjoy yurself Oliver. Take two wenches tuh bed if'n it'll make yuh happy…mayhap it'll be da last happy you knows fur a spell. Night!" Joshua climbed the stairs to his bed chamber worried and anxious about his future while Jerry stretched out on the couch with identical concerns for his.

At first Jerry found it difficult to sleep, *the raid should have happened today,* he thought, *could my timeframe be wrong or did I buy into a made-up story. Wait, maybe the raid comes during the night…that makes sense.* For a while he wandered around the house. Had a big slice of a cake he discovered on the sideboard in the back hall then stood out on the back porch for nearly thirty minutes. Finally Jerry returned to the couch and drifted off to sleep.

# Chapter eight

*T*he *big clock over the fireplace* said 5:38 a.m. when Clay galloped his mare at full speed up the lane then rushed into the house and up to his father's bedroom. Jerry followed close on Clay's heels then stood just inside Joshua's bedroom door and listened to Clay's report.

"I'm sorry Pa...ah truly is. We fought them sumbitches hard as we knowed how but hell Pa...there's just too dang many of em. And...the way they moved across Bradford Valley yesterday, I know they will be riding down on us before noon."

"How many fightin troops you brang wit ya?" Joshua asked as he climbed out of bed.

"Didn't bring none Pa...a lot got kilt and they took some prisoner and the ones left are mostly all farm boys. New recruits that went back home to protect the family homestead, like me. We on the retreat right now but we gonna reform in about a week and set up an ambush at Wilson's pass."

"So we gots no troops tu defend da place, jist you, me and Mister Mullins. Hell, dat ain't warth spit...but ah's suspected it might come ta dis so ah done warked out a plan. Git Domo in heah."

"Hey Pa, don't forget bout the slaves, we got plenty rifles and I suspect with their help we could put up one hell of a fight. I could get to teachin em how to shoot and everythin right away. Whatcha think Pa?"

"Ah thanks ah gots da dumbest damn son in Tennahsee. If'n you thanks fer one minit dat ah slave is gonna fight ta stay ah slave, you is ah cumplete imbecile. You gos an gives a rifle tu one o dese nigras an dey will shoot you wit it. You git Domo in heah, den git down ta da barn an make sho da big wagon an da buckboard is hitched up...nah git."

Jerry listened as Joshua instructed Domo to first summon Mister Mullins to his office. Then order the cooks to cook everything in the kitchen and put the food on the sideboard first, then on the dining room table when the sideboard became full. He then instructed Domo to bring several strong young slaves to remove his treasured French armoire from his bedroom and take it to be loaded onto the big wagon.

Jerry was getting frustrated with the pace of things, *come on guys get a move on. I got a jet to catch!* He thought then decided to hunt down the food that was sending out wonderful aromas. He leisurely ate from the growing supply of delicious food on the sideboard while several young men slowly lowered the heavy armoire down the stairs. It had taken nearly an hour to get this far because Joshua was totally in the way, hissing and panicking at every bump or misstep. Jerry stepped outside to pass gas and noticed that a steady rain had begun to fall. He walked across the lane and on to the barn where he watched Oliver Mullins supervise the uncovering of the boxes that were just covered up yesterday.

Clay drove a team of horses pulling the big wagon up the lane and stopped beside the house. Domo followed with a team pulling the buckboard. After the armoire was securely loaded, Joshua ordered Clay to tie his mare to the back of the wagon so he could leave everything at Hargrove Acres, hop on the mare and rush straight back here. Oliver Mullins was assigned to drive the buckboard and make deliveries to High Gate and Chandler Hall then return to Matthews Manor as fast as possible. There seemed to be a growing sense that the Federals would wait out the rain before making any raid so the men stopped to eat and discuss plans for close to an hour.

When a passing rider told Domo that federal troops were on the Carlton plantation, which was less than eight miles away, the mood at Matthews Manor immediately changed to panic. The remaining pieces of furniture were hastily loaded onto the big wagon while the harpsichord wrapped in a lot of blankets and several trunks were loaded onto the buckboard. Clay drove the wagon to the barn followed by Oliver Mullins with the buckboard.

Under Joshua's direction, the wooden cases marked "Hargrove Acres" were quickly loaded, or more accurately thrown on back of the big wagon, the remaining cases were thrown onto the buckboard. The wagon barely stopped at the barn before Clay headed the team down the lane with Oliver Mullins following. Jerry ran down the lane and climbed aboard on back of the buckboard. The loads were shaky but Clay and Oliver set their horses to full gallop when they turned onto the main road.

Jerry hung on, trying to find a comfortable spot while being pelted by the rain. He was very aware that his time was running out and he would soon need to get back to his transporter but he had to see this out as far as he could. With four horses pulling the big wagon while only two were pulling the buckboard, Clay quickly left Oliver behind. After about two miles the road became bumpy but neither Clay nor Oliver slowed their horses. Both remained at full gallop and the ride became really wild for Jerry. A sharp incline took the road on a hard turn as it rose over a narrow ridge then plunged into a valley. When the big wagon hit the hard bump in the curve it tipped slightly and swerved but kept right on going. When the buckboard started into the turn and hit the hard bump it sent Jerry flying off into the weeds, while two wooden cases slid off and bounced into the thickets then plunged into the gulley.

Jerry was dazed. He sat up and watched the harpsichord bounce from the buckboard and disappear into the thickets. The big wagon was long gone and the buckboard kept right on going at high speed. Jerry jumped up and took off running after the buckboard. He ran for nearly a quarter of a mile before he realized he had no chance of catching a buckboard he could not even see anymore. Dejected and angry Jerry turned around and slowly began to walk back to Matthews Manor. As he came back to the sharp curve in the road he tried his best to identify the spot where he saw the wooden cases and harpsichord bounce off the buckboard but it was useless. There was a large rise on one side of this narrow road and a sharp drop into a gulley on the other side. Everything but him bounced off the buckboard on the gulley side and disappeared into the thickets and brambles, or down into the gulley below. "Oh well," Jerry sighed, "I don't even know which boxes those were and it's not like I could have taken them back with me so I better get a move on and get back to my tree."

As he jogged down the road, Jerry was relieved when the rain slowed to drizzle. He reached the smoother section of road and knew he was nearing Matthews Manor but was really starting to sweat the time. He picked up his pace now desperate to get to his tree. He had to be in the transporter by or before his mission launch time of twelve noon. If he was not present the transporter would return to base empty with no recorded data. Meaning his mission never existed. Jerry began to wonder if Professor Gilstead could write a formula that would send an empty transporter to fetch him or anyone who missed their launch. Could it be done using only a DNA sample? He thought of several related questions then smiled to himself thinking that perhaps he had discovered a whole new challenge on which a doctorial thesis could be based. Suddenly, almost without realizing it he arrived back at Matthews Manor... and was shocked.

Federal union army troops were everywhere, some moved around, some remained on horseback while others stood talking to various people. Jerry stood at the edge of the lane and looked for a few moments then went straight to his tree. He looked hard but could not find his handprint so he stepped away and looked around for the right tree. He looked but knew this was the right tree so he again closely examined it but no handprint could be found. Jerry's heart began to beat fast as he quickly made his way to the house. The big clock over the fireplace said 11:18 and Jerry was confused. He went outside and looked around and spotted a pocket watch hanging with a lot of other stuff from the jacket of a soldier so he walked over and glanced at the time. *11:20, this doesn't make sense,* Jerry thought. *Something has gone wrong.* As he started back to his tree, Jerry noticed several slaves searching about and calling the name Jacob. He looked down the lane and saw a black lady sitting on a stoop crying. Two union soldiers stood close apparently talking to her.

Suddenly Jerry stopped in his tracks as a paralyzing chill ran down his back. The little black boy named Jacob was missing, that's why so many are searching and calling his name. But Jerry knew the boy was not missing, the boy had run away. He ran away yesterday after his encounter with Oliver Mullins. In fact Mullins reported him missing to Joshua Matthews last night. Jerry walked back to the tree and looked but his handprint was not there. *Of course not! Son-of-a-bitch!* he thought. Jerry knew that it was because of him that the child ran away. *If I had let Mullins kick him, the damn kid would be here. Injured but here. BUT! Since he is not here on the day these slaves are being emancipated that changes human history and it is my fucking fault. Man this totally sucks. I am freakin stuck in this shitty place and time for helping a kid. Aw man…this is just so wrong. Sure I knew the rules and I took the chance by coming here…but come on man…hey wait a minute, as soon as my launch time passes I will lose invisibility and my ass is completely naked.*

For several moments Jerry pondered his situation and kept an eye on his tree, just in case. He thought about going into the house and finding some clothes, likely something of Clays would probably fit. The problem was if he waited to become visible before leaving the house he would have some fancy explaining to do to Joshua Matthews and the Federal troops. If he left the house before he became visible they would probably shoot because they would only see moving clothes. Finally he decided the woods across the main road offered the best cover for a strange naked man. Perhaps after dark he could sneak out and find some clothes.

Dejected and feeling as low as one can get, Jerry got to his feet, took one last long look at his tree then slowly walked to the end of the lane. He stopped at the edge of the road and looked back. My *timeframe was off by one day. I got here a day too soon*, he thought. *But I don't think it would have mattered anyway. Just wasn't my gamble to win.* Jerry started to cross the road and hide in the forest but waited for a rider coming down the road. A union solider galloped into view and approached with a sure even gate. The solider slowed then turned his horse into the lane of Matthews Manor riding right past Jerry who watched with little interest then broke out in a wide grin. Sitting snuggly on the back of the horse, holding tightly to the solider was little Jacob. For the first time in his life Jerry truly wanted to kiss a little black boy. He rushed back to his tree and found his handprint brightly glowing with the words "Mission Launch in 12 minutes" flashing within the handprint. Jerry took a quick last look around then placed his hand in his handprint and slipped inside the transporter.

# Chapter nine

RETURN TO OUTBOUND LAUNCH STATION ACHIEVED: TOTAL MISSION COMPLETE! System shut down in 31 seconds. Please claim and replace your coverings.

As the screen went blank the side compartment snapped open and the interior lights came on. Jerry took a deep breath then slowly struggled to put his clothes on. He was totally exhausted and needed to be helped from the transporter. A pleased and relieved Professor Gilstead was prepared and waiting. He had two assistants immediately take Jerry home along with a sufficient quantity of concentrated liquid nutrients. It was expected and well-documented that time travel, particularly the particalization process and light-speed-acceleration physically depleted the human body and it requires several days of complete rest to fully recover.

Jerry slept for nearly eighteen straight hours his first day back and spent most of the next four days in bed. With lots of undisturbed rest and by consuming mostly the liquid nutrients, in about five days Jerry started to feel like his old self and went for his mission debriefing with Professor Gilstead and his staff.

At the beginning of the debriefing, Jerry casually entered his credit card numbers on the invoice of charges without even looking at the bill. He then launched into an exciting conversation with his professor that would last for most of the next three days.

The many variations and possibilities of the science and of his time-travel experience fueled Jerry's imagination and renewed his professor's passion and enthusiasm for discovery. Jerry posed the question of possible rescue missions meaning reparticalization of previously transported DNA on a separate inbound mission. Professor Gilstead was intrigued and highly impressed with the question. He advised Jerry that if he could develop even a rough basic formula that could suggest the creditable possibility of such a mission, that would qualify him for the prestigious Roxwell Fellowship. The Roxwell by itself would more than generously pay all the expenses of his doctorate program, but more importantly it would lead to many other lucrative fellowships. Then make him much sought out for professorships, lectures and speaking engagements.

Jerry Chandler was walking on air. He had never been happier in his life. He quickly decided that the most important thing to come from his trip to the past was this possible discovery of a theory that was his ticket to the future. As far as Chandler Hall was concerned it could sit in moth balls. He had just been on a time trip to try and discover what happened to some missing gold. The trip was unsuccessful because his timeframe had been slightly off so he ran out of time before he could solve the mystery. But it didn't matter because that wasn't who he really was anyway. The Roxwell Fellowship was a much better deal without all the hassle. Jerry considered the trip a great success because he loved science and exploration. Now he had a date with destiny. Thanks to the time trip he now had a real viable challenge to break down the barriers to safe and routine time travel. He now saw himself as a budding scientific genius with no desire to return to the country so he did not give Chandler Hall another thought. Jerry spent day after day in the library, studying the theories and sub-calculations that might provide his breakthrough.

A notification from the Bursar's office that the charge for his time travel expenses exceeded his credit card limit and had been denied irritated Jerry. He frowned at the notification then entered his fathers address in the "Bill To" section and returned the invoice still without looking at the amount. A few days later he was notified that his father had also refused the invoice and now the Bursar was demanding immediate and complete payment for his time travel expense. Jerry was outraged; he was engaged in serious research and refused to be bothered by mundane ordinary financial details. He threw the notification away.

Though he did not need them to graduate, Jerry regularly attended his two elective classes and was preparing for the final exams when he was notified that because of his unpaid lab expenses he would not be allowed to participate in commencement exercises or ceremonies. Jerry chuckled, *Fair enough,* he thought, *my parents saw me graduate from boarding school, prep school and undergraduate, they can live without seeing me walk across another stage. I had no plans for any phony celebrations anyway.* He went back to his studies without any further thoughts about commencement.

Late into the following week Jerry hurried to the science lab to discuss an exciting possible equation with Professor Gilstead. To occupy himself while waiting for the professor to finish giving a lecture, Jerry read the many different postings on the bulletin board. He became instantly angry when he discovered his name on a list of students who were not allowed to take final exams or receive degrees because of various infractions. Jerry's infraction was failure to pay lab fees.

Outraged and boiling mad Jerry stormed into the Bursar's office and demanded to know how dare they hold his Masters Degree hostage? He was met by an aggressive Bursar that demanded to know how dare Jerry try and steal nearly one hundred and forty thousand dollars from the university. It was an ugly confrontation that sent Jerry storming out madder than when he stormed in.

Back in his apartment he paced and fumed aloud. "I don't have time for this shit! I got serious research to do that can lead to a prestigious fellowship and these assholes are whining about a few measly dollars. They don't even need the damn money. Hell they run experimental travel missions all the time and nobody gets a personal bill for those. This is bullshit and I don't need bullshit…but I do need my degree and hey I've earned it already so they are just bluffing. They gotta award me my degree. Maybe not in public but who cares. I'll sue if I don't get it and in the meantime I'm going to ignore the bullshit and concentrate on my research. In fact since I'm not going to be allowed to take finals, I'll have more time and that's just what I need."

Over the weekend Jerry took a break from his intense studies and caught up on partying. He had intended to party for only two days but he liked his company and got swept up in feeling good so the party stretched to four days. Jerry was fighting off a hangover and trying to get back into his research the day following the party when he received notification that his apartment lease would expire at the end of the upcoming month. The lease which had existed for five years was self renewing but the prior payment arrangements had been cancelled. Now the management company needed for Jerry to enter and confirm new payment information.

Now Jerry's head really started to hurt. "Son-of-a-bitch!" he snarled into the air. "First this ungrateful school starts freakin with me and now my damn landlord. Hey come on...let's just settle down folks, I'm right on the verge of greatness and my fellowships will easily pay you greedy little moneygrubbers. To hell with this nonsense! I'll deal with this lease and the school on my schedule." He took a shower then went out and had a large satisfying meal.

Since he was no longer attending classes, other than making an occasional visit to the Mathematics Science Lab to chat with the professors, the library had become the only building on campus that Jerry utilized. Everything he needed for his research was there so he spent many hours of each day happily using the resources of his favorite place.

Six days after getting the notice of his expiring apartment lease, Jerry was dealt a crippling blow. When he arrived at the library on this day he was informed that his student ID card was no longer valid and that he should report to student administration to have his card renewed or reissued. Until then he was no longer permitted access to the library.

He didn't even bother, he knew the school administration was now holding his student ID hostage for their measly little lab fees. *First no commencement,* he thought, *and then no finals in classes I really wanted to ace. Then the threat of no degree awarded, then the landlord starts crying for money and now I can't even use the library. Well you know what? Enough is enough, fuck these games. I am Jerry Chandler! I do not have to tolerate crap. I have my own personal country estate with my own private library and that's exactly where I'm going to finish my groundbreaking research. Then some Ivy League University will kiss my ass and demand my degree from this place.*

Jerry studied his calendar closely. He had a few weeks left before his credit card expired. *For charges under 140 grand,* he thought with a chuckle. *Now was the correct time to move shop anyway.* With that decided Jerry spent the next five days saying his goodbyes and partying, until a moving company emptied his Bloomington apartment then delivered his belongings to Chandler Hall.

# Chapter ten

*U*pon *Jerry's arrival* back at Chandler Hall the Cunningham's were again waving from the porch and the housekeeper had filled his refrigerator with delicious food. Much to his surprise Chandler Hall felt warm and reassuring...like an old friend...like coming home...in fact it was home. Jerry immediately felt comfortable and his mood brightened considerably. He briefly explained the importance of his research to the Cunningham's then spent little time socializing after the movers arrived.

He quickly changed the library from his grandpa's domain into Jerry's research lab then plunged right into his work as soon as his virtual communicator was installed. Over the next two weeks Jerry emerged from his lab only to eat and sleep. He worked late into the night and the housekeeper and the Cunningham's were becoming concerned. On two occasions Peggy Simpson accompanied her grandmother to Chandler Hall and made her pecan pancakes. Jerry wolfed down the pancakes with much gratitude and heavy compliments but immediately returned to his research.

Peggy was miffed because Jerry had not seemed to even notice her. He paid close attention to her food but she had been invisible. Later that day the Cunningham's and her grandmother agreed that Jerry needed to get out of that lab and get some sun. They also agreed that Peggy probably had the best chance of making him do that. Peggy wasn't so sure, Jerry was a math nerd and she was anything but.

The next day she again made her pecan pancakes for Jerry then invited him for a walk around the grounds of Chandler Hall. Jerry gobbled up the pancakes with enthusiasm but declined the walk and returned to his lab. Angry at his rejection Peggy went home. In just over an hour she returned to Chandler Hall and barged right into Jerry's lab. Jerry was outraged until Peggy explained that she had baked him some marijuana brownies.

"WHAT!" he howled. "Hum...let me try one of those. DAMN! That's good...let me try another. Amazing...just as good as the first! Maybe better. Let me try another just to make sure these really are that good!" His initial outrage quickly turned to delight as he happily consumed most of the brownies then joined Peggy for a brisk walk.

Jerry found the walk and Peggy to be refreshing. The grounds of Chandler Hall were lush and green this time of the year adding to the feel of exclusive affluence and Peggy was an uncomplicated, honest person that he was starting to like. His mental production seemed to have improved measurably following that walk and Jerry was impressed. Several times over the following three weeks he invited Peggy for a walk while frequently requesting more pancakes, brownies and any other food items she was willing to make.

On one of their walks Jerry was surprised to learn the housekeeper was really not a housekeeper at all. Although she had told Jerry to call her "Aunt Ginny," the lady's name was Virginia Simpson and she was the wife of Harlan Simpson. Together the Simpsons owned and farmed over 260 acres of land and raised six children. On their 21st birthday each child was given twenty-one acres. Some moved away but no one was allowed to sell their land. All of the usable land, except for an acre here or there for homes, was being farmed by two of the sons. The profits were split proportionately among all of the family. Peggy was the daughter of one of the sons. Her grandfather, Harlan, still found plenty to do around the farm but her grandmother, Virginia, now had an empty nest. When she learned from the Cunningham's that they were seeking a part-time housekeeper to cook for Jerry, she jumped at the opportunity and insisted on looking after Jerry and still will not accept any pay. Jerry was speechless and now saw the housekeeper and Peggy in a whole new light.

Several days later, Peggy climbed aboard an inflatable chair and floated around the swimming pool in her backyard. She was a little anxious and trying to sort out her future. More than a year had passed since her graduation from Tennessee State with her bachelor's degree. Originally she had planned to go on to law school, but as she progressed through college her interest in law had dwindled. On the other hand, interest in her minor, business administration, had grown considerably. Now she was considering the possibility that a Masters

Degree in Business Administration might be more satisfying than a law degree. She dare not discuss it with her parents because her mother would insist she do both, while her dad would continue to preach that she should stay home and run the farm office. The thought of running her own business was exhilarating but the family farm was not the kind of business she had in mind.

Peggy also wanted a serious relationship but none of the local boys were of the slightest interest. She had no intention of becoming the wife of a farmer or a country hick. She was intrigued by Jerry Chandler because he was different from the locals but ambivalent about a relationship because she considered him a nerd.

Peggy was examining the curriculum of an Ivy League graduate school when her grandmother called full of concern about Jerry. He had not eaten his breakfast. He looked as though he had not slept all night and he sat at the table and just stared at his food. She could not get him to eat or say anything that made any sense so she wanted Peggy to check on him.

This babysitting business was growing old and that's exactly what Peggy planned to tell Jerry. But when she arrived at Chandler Hall and saw his condition, then could not really make any sense of what he muttered, she took a marijuana joint from her pocket and lit it. Jerry immediately responded, taking and smoking the joint while Peggy cooked him a fresh breakfast.

When he finished eating Jerry looked at Peggy as though he was going to cry. "I have completed my research," he announced in a low wavering tone. "I have absolutely finished and triple checked the data. I have created a new formulaic paradigm that positively and completely proves my hypothesis is totally not possible with the current level of existing technology. Peggy...I have just spent months creating positive proof that I was wrong. No one gets recognition for proving what cannot happen. All this work and research has been a big funky waste of time."

"That's a real shame...no wonder you are hurting. I know you gave it your all...but it's not the end of the world is it?" Peggy asked with an encouraging smile.

"Well...it very likely could be...for me anyway. Shit don't look too good right now," Jerry responded.

"Want to talk some?"

"You got any more weed?"

"Yeah, a lot."

"Let's go to the upstairs porch and sit for a while," Jerry suggested.

After settling into his favorite rocker and smoking another joint while sizing up Peggy, Jerry looked out over the grounds of Chandler Hall and sighed. He took his time and carefully explained to Peggy just what his research would have meant had it been successful and just how heartbreaking it had been to discover concrete proof to the opposite. It was painful, to say the least, to be the one that destroys and discredits your own hypothesis. Now all the wealth, prestige and opportunity that would have come with such a breakthrough have vanished like snow in July. Leaving him only the dreary realities of Chandler Hall to deal with.

Peggy understood and greatly sympathized with Jerry's research disaster. She honestly felt that since he had the ability to factually disprove a legitimate hypothetical theory that clearly demonstrates he is a master of advanced scientific research. And, that fact should not be taken lightly. She had never been great at math or science and admitted that she was even a little jealous of his analytical mind. She did not understand however why owning Chandler Hall should present him with dreary realities.

Jerry explained that while he was involved in research his father dumped the burden of utilities, insurance, taxes and upkeep of Chandler Hall on him beginning at the start of the coming year. In addition, Indiana University put the thumbscrews on his dad for some unpaid fees and his dad told them to get it from him or put a lien on Chandler Hall. The fellowship would have paid all this but now without any hope of a fellowship, he had no way to pay the bills or make Chandler Hall pay for itself. Sure he could sell or lease a few acres to pay bills but that only limited the options for making the place profitable.

Peggy lit a new joint and paced around the porch. She was curious about Jerry's options for making Chandler Hall profitable, then was shocked and very intrigued when he suggested a golf course. He went on to explain that according to his research there was no golf course in the county and he had various statistics that showed the profitability of courses in rural areas.

Additionally, by owning and operating a golf course there were no problems that plagued farmers like animal health, crop production or weather. The difficulty he faced with this proposition was, since his initial research, he had discovered that he barely owned enough land for a golf course. To really pull it off he needed to buy and convert ten to twenty acres of rough looking land that borders his to the north.

Peggy was impressed and delighted. Her family owned the land Jerry described. In fact, the Simpson family owned over thirty acres of rocky scruff land that borders Chandler Hall. They would happily sell that land to Jerry but not the developers. But that all meant nothing if Jerry could not afford to buy it.

"Doesn't make sense to sell land so you can buy land," Jerry commented.

"No, sure doesn't," Peggy agreed. "But you could rent out some pasture or farm land and use that money to buy."

"Yeah, but then my land would be tied up for the duration of the lease...hum well it is something to think about. Selling any acreage might be a problem if there is a lien being filed by the university and leasing may be a way to raise funds and without sweating it. Regardless I sure as hell gotta find some kind of way to pay expenses but I will be damned if I will go work a lousy job just to support Chandler Hall."

"Can I ask you something that is totally none of my business?" Peggy asked.

Jerry chuckled, "Those are the best kind, fire away."

"Why do you owe the university such a lump sum? I thought all student loans were repaid over time."

"I don't owe them for a student loan...I owe them for what they call lab fees. What that really means is I took a trip back into time and they want me to pay for it."

Peggy scooted to the edge of her chair with wide intrigued eyes filled with awe and admiration. "You took a time trip? That is totally cool...I was a freshman at Tennessee State when the first successful trip was made...where did you go? Tell me about it?"

Jerry smiled as he looked deep into Peggy's eyes. He had not seen that kind of enthusiasm for his exploits from anyone. He liked her...she was cool. "I'll have to get my debriefing notes to tell you what happened on the trip," he explained.

"You don't remember?" Peggy questioned.

"No. You see one of the phenomena or tradeoffs of time travel is loss of memory of the experience. You cannot permanently retain a memory that was not generated in present life," Jerry explained. "That's the reason for an extensive debriefing as soon as you recover. The farther you get from the experience the less you can remember. I pushed things with a long trip that required a longer recovery period. In fact, it takes at least two hours of recovery for every one hour of actual mission time. I was gone for over two days and took five days to recover. That put me at some distance from the trip before I was debriefed, so I did not remember every detail. Typically after about one week the total memory is gone forever. Except for a brief temporary flashback that can be prompted by something familiar to the experience, like a stretch of country road or a barn or something. But it's all cool most of the story is written down. I'll get my debriefing notes while you whip us up a drink or snack."

# Chapter eleven

$A$s *Jerry no longer considered* the hidden cellar under the dining room to be significant, he told Peggy the entire story beginning with the discovery of the cellar. When Jerry finished his story Peggy was glowing with excitement and enthusiasm.

"Wow!" she exclaimed. "You know you probably saved little Jacob's life."

"No, I'm sure I didn't. If he was meant to die then I would not have made it back. He was meant to be alive and on that plantation when I left," Jerry advised.

"I had no idea the risks of travel were so great," Peggy gushed.

"That's precisely why my hypothesis was so worth investigating. If it had worked out it would have made time travel much safer," Jerry sighed.

"You didn't mention anything about the gold on your trip."

"Yeah I know. I was very careful to not make any reference to the gold or give any official reasons for my trip," Jerry confided.

"Why?"

"I would instantly lose all respect of the scientific community and especially my professors if they knew I used the resources of the science lab and advanced quantum mechanics to go on a treasure hunt."

"Oh…I see!"

"I did attempt to make some personal notes following my debriefing but that was more than a week after my return so I didn't remember or write much. In fact here is my exact entry; *The trip was unsuccessful because of a faulty timeframe that did not allow sufficient time to complete my investigation. Disposition of search item unknown!* I wasn't too concerned or disappointed because I was really excited by the possibility of a new research theory and I never gave the gold another thought…until now."

"Have you been back to the cellar since you returned?" Peggy questioned.

"No, for what?"

"Well to bring the silver serving up for one thing," Peggy suggested. "And maybe take another look around while you are down there."

"Why should I waste my time with some old silver?"

"It may be worth enough to pay your fancy lab fees," Peggy chuckled.

"You're joking right?"

"No! Old silver is valuable Jerry. And if it was made in Europe by a well-known silversmith of the period it could be worth even more."

"Really?"

"Really!"

"Feel like joining me on an adventure underneath the dining room," Jerry asked with a broad smile.

With Peggy's help Jerry found it much easier to move the heavy dining table. He rolled up the carpet and popped open the trap door. With halogen lights in hand he made his way down the narrow steps, set the lights on the floor of the cellar then extended his hand to Peggy.

Jerry looked around in disbelief because the big wooden boxes were nowhere to be found. He frowned then scratched his head. Was it possible someone had actually discovered this cellar and ripped off the silver while he was gone? *Come on*, he thought, *that's nuts.* He glanced at the wall and was stunned, there was no hole. "Wait a minute, wait just a freakin minute! What the hell is going on?" Jerry demanded.

Peggy looked totally confused and was beginning to suspect Jerry was just high and spinning a tall tale.

Jerry took his pry bar and poked the wall where the hole had been. As before dirt fell from the wall. Jerry poked harder, more dirt fell and soon he saw a piece of the familiar wooden panel. He worked furiously for a few minutes until he had uncovered first one panel, then the second, one stacked on top of the other.

Peggy was completely amazed. *Who on earth would think of digging a hole into the side of a dirt wall to hide something,* she thought.

Knowing the panels were really boxes, Jerry worked furiously at freeing them and was sweating when he and Peggy lowered the boxes from the wall to the floor. Jerry took his time examining the cases while Peggy stared with wide excited eyes.

The words "Chandler Hall" was scratched onto the lid of both boxes. "Well it looks like Mister Mullins was successful making his delivery after all," Jerry mumbled following a sudden flashback of being thrown from the back of the buckboard that Oliver Mullins was driving. He pried the lids loose and set them aside, revealing a note in each box and several rags. It didn't take long to discover the rags held fine china and crystal candlesticks, a find that thrilled Peggy to her very core.

Suddenly and very much to Peggy's surprise, Jerry had another flashback and remembered seeing Joshua Matthews pack the boxes. Jerry also remembered that he had switched the lids on two of the boxes and roughly began emptying both boxes.

"Hey, hey take it easy, this stuff is really valuable and precious," Peggy protested.

"Get it oulta the way, quick! Get that stuff out of here?" Jerry insisted then used the pry bar to beat on the ends of both boxes as soon as they were empty. Peggy didn't quite know what to think. She guarded the new found treasures from Jerry's assault and was completely stunned when Jerry reached into one box and pried the false bottom loose. He did the same with the second box then removed the false bottom, revealing two heavy old burlap bags. When Jerry attempted to pick up one of the bags over a hundred gold coins broke free and spilled into the box on top of the second bag and several gold bars. Jerry removed the false bottom from the first box then stepped back to admire the soft glowing reflection the stacks of gold bars cast across the pretty features of Peggy's beaming face.

"I did it...I claimed the gold! I did it...and didn't even know it! In fact, I would never have known it without you Peggy."

"How did you do that?" Peggy quizzed in disbelief.

"I switched the lids on these boxes! You see Peggy, before I went back in time these two boxes were lying at the bottom of that gully lost forever. I switched lids meaning two different boxes are now lying in that gully and the gold was delivered to Chandler Hall then buried in this wall. I did it! I really did it! And you made me know I DID IT! I've never been so excited and horny in my entire life," Jerry admitted, his heart pounding and eyes sparkling. "I'm horny but for more than just sex Peggy. I can't explain. It's...belief...it's knowing...it's...I really want you...I think I..."

Nervous, excited and breathing hard, Peggy was probably the only person on the planet that truly understood what Jerry meant. She felt exactly the same and pressed her lips to his, inflaming their intense passions and freeing the electricity they shared to meld the two of them into one.

It was there on the floor of that dank cellar of Chandler Hall in the intense grip of achievement, discovery and meaningful new love, that Jerry Chandler and Peggy Simpson unleashed all of their pent-up passion, needs and desire on each other. They became inseparable in that dank little cellar and in just a little over two weeks following that night they were married.

With 62.46 pounds of gold, that was worth slightly more than two million dollars, Jerry and his new bride set about building the Chandler Empire. First they refurbished Chandler Hall Mansion, adding a large sunroom and paving the entry lane with concrete. While redoing their house, Peggy traded her twenty-one acres of fertile family farmland for the thirty-six acres of scruff land that bordered Chandler Hall.   After clearing the scruff land, Jerry and Peggy hired an experienced professional marine biologist then quickly developed Chandler Hall Commercial Fisheries to take advantage of a wholesale supply shortage. It was a wise move. The shortage of fresh fish was profound so Jerry and Peggy developed eight separate fish farms spread over four acres. They promoted the biologist to general manager of the fisheries and then allowed him to earn a small percentage of ownership by using his good management skills to operate efficiently and produce large quarterly profits.

With a solid income stream in place Jerry and Peggy moved on with their dream. Late in the spring during their third year of marriage after many months of preparation, the happy young couple proudly opened the instantly successful Chandler Hall Golf and Country Club. And, in late fall of the same year Chandler Hall Tennis Club opened. It was built to appease the many golf widows created by the golf course. But, the tennis club held wide appeal and was expanded twice during its first year of operation.

Delighted and totally amazed by their success, Jerry and Peggy took time off to travel. They first visited Jerry's parents in Hawaii then traveled on to Europe and various parts of the Middle East before returning home. Impressed by the spas of Europe the couple soon opened Chandler Hall Indoor Sports and Spa to a limited membership.  This facility featured batting cages, a firing range, archery, basketball, handball, a swimming pool with a high diving board, a lap track and workout room with many spas and whirlpool baths scattered about. It was intended to be a semi-private facility but just like the Tennis Club, the popularity and demand for use forced Jerry and Peggy to expand the facility then make it available to the general public.

In just a very few years Jerry and Peggy had built a very successful empire using a sports theme. It was a proven winner in a growing, sports starved county and had made the young couple rich beyond their wildest dreams. They had never been happier or more in love and were lounging about in their plush offices planning a new facility for indoor go-cart and midget car racing when Tom and Esther Cunningham called full of excitement and invited them to dinner the following evening.

When they arrived the Cunningham's were anxiously waiting. Tom explained that he and Esther had purchased a large tract of land that included a deep gulley just below the bend on Oleo Road. The land wasn't good for much and was an eyesore that offended them so their plan was to clear most of the land, develop a religious/nature retreat and donate it to their church. The exciting news was that while the land and gulley was being cleared the work crews found a pre-civil war era harpsichord and several pieces of a precious antique silver serving set, including a small chest containing antique silver dining utensils. The silver had been cleaned, polished and was going to be used tonight at dinner. Meanwhile the harpsichord had been restored and a professional musician from their church was going to play it for the first time since it was lost. The Cunningham's were bursting with excitement while Jerry was in shock.  He stared at the antique silver with the certain knowledge that he had seen it before. Jerry then turned his attention to the harpsichord and the erotic flashbacks of its last performance over 187 years ago in the parlor of Matthews Manor, only two nights before the Union Army raid.

www.ingramcontent.com/pod-product-compliance
Lightning Source LLC
Chambersburg PA
CBHW072307020726
47501CB00002B/421